P is for Pluto

P is for Pluto

Jackie Kingon

GUARDBRIDGE BOOKS
ST ANDREWS, SCOTLAND

Published by Guardbridge Books,
St Andrews, Fife, United Kingdom.

http://guardbridgebooks.co.uk

P IS FOR PLUTO

This is a work of fiction. All characters and events portrayed in this book are fictitious, and any resemblance to real people or events is purely coincidental.

ISBN: 978-1-911486-43-5

To Al and Michael with love.
To Roseanne Clausen, my oldest friend.
To Sheilah Lewis, the inspiration for Molly.

1

ATTENTION EPICUREAN GASTRONAUTS and all lovers of good food! In case you missed the press release from Carbon Copies Media, Molly's Bistro, my five-galaxy rated restaurant has been chosen by Interplanetary Foods to open a branch on Pluto. Yes, Pluto! The planet that put the image of the Disney dog in the middle of its red and blue flag rather than—as many would have preferred—an image of Miss Pluto. Pluto, the planet with an inferiority complex because it was downgraded to dwarf planet by the spoilers who have never been there.

For those of you whose mouth waters hearing the words Molly's Bistro, it's in New Chicago, the capitol of Mars, at the base of Olympic Mons—the inspiration for my soaring delectable Olympic Mons soufflé.

I sit in a corner of Molly's dining room under its vaulted stained-glass ceiling with my chef and head waiter discussing if "golden calf" should be a daily or weekend special. Waiters cover tables with light blue tablecloths, fold napkins, and set places in anticipation of the dinner crowd.

Suddenly, my palm signals a call. It's Toronto Kim, who Interplanetary Foods hired to be the manager of Molly's Pluto. I wave at my staff, who knows how anxious I am to get this call, put a finger to my lips, mouth the word "Pluto," and go to my office.

I slide behind my desk and press "Extra Light Communication". Interplanetary Foods gave me a subscription because without it, communication from Pluto to Mars will take about four and a half hours, getting an answer near nine hours later. Then I press "Accept". Life-sized pixels of Toronto flicker into focus.

"So, Toronto, how's the construction going?" I ask.

"Please call me Tonto, Molly. All my friends do."

"Will do," I say.

Tonto clears his throat. "First, the good news. The architects and interior designers did a great job copying Molly's Bistro. Of course, they all expect to be invited to the opening. You will love it when you see it. But the bad news is we had trouble finding a qualified chef."

"What's the problem?"

"The good ones want to make their own creations, not reproduce recipes from Molly's Bistro. And when we broadened our search, bean counters, egg coddlers, barrel dredgers, and anyone who could boil water applied."

"Are you serious?"

"Molly, this is Pluto! I'm going to give it another week. Otherwise, I have to tell Interplanetary Foods to consider scratching the project."

"Maybe my chef here can find someone. But I'll admit it will be a tough sell getting someone to relocate to Pluto."

"Worth a shot," he says, waving as his image fades.

Then, almost as quickly as sizzling one of my two-inch-thick stem-cell porterhouse steaks on a flaming grill and drizzling it with warm shallot butter, Tonto calls again.

"Guess what just happened?"

"You found a chef."

"Yup. Herb Tarragon, a graduate of Titan Culinary. He's currently a sous chef at Pluto Dogs. Said he didn't mind copying the recipes from Molly's Bistro and says he could learn a lot doing it. In fact, he had been to Mars and ate at Molly's Bistro and considers it an honor to be with a restaurant of such quality. He will need time to study the menu. When he feels confident that he can recreate your menu, we'll try it out by opening as a 'pop-up' restaurant."

"Pop-up restaurant?"

"Means temporary—a limited time. We'll do a three-week run. Of course, it will have a different name in case it doesn't go well. But if it does, we'll tweak some changes, replace the sign with the Molly's Pluto sign, and have a series of pre-opening dinners for the press and reviewers."

"Are you sure this will work?" I ask.

"Trust me. Interplanetary Foods has done this before. Ever hear of Ganymede Gum-balls?"

"No."

"How about Planet Paris?"

"Planet Paris! Everyone's heard of Planet Paris. It's the solar system's top restaurant."

"Well, Ganymede Gum-balls and Planet Paris are one and the same."

***

A month later, Tonto sends me holos of Herb Tarragon working in the kitchen. Even my difficult but brilliant chef, Mario Bugatti, is impressed.

Tonto sets a date for the grand opening. I book reservations on the Mars-Pluto shuttle for my husband Cortland, my twin daughters Becky and Lois, and Becky's husband Burton.

As I add a silver jacket to my travel bag, Tonto calls, his voice a fallen soufflé.

"What happened?" I ask.

"Herb Tarragon died."

"Died? How? When?"

"Pluto police just called me to let me know that they received an anonymous message about a body found at the wholesale food market early this morning. The name Herb Tarragon and information that he worked for Molly's Bistro was in his pocket."

Trying to put one thought in front of another, I say, "The chefs shop early at our wholesale food market too because that's when they have the pick of the best produce. But wasn't he a young man in excellent health?"

"Yes. Or so we thought."

"Have they determined if it was a natural cause?"

"Yes, if you call a knife in his back a natural cause."

2

I DECIDE TO GO TO PLUTO and meet Tonto and see the restaurant. My family, knowing that I solved two crimes in the past, roll their eyes and say that they hope I don't plan to stay and solve this one. Becky shakes her rainbow-colored hair, elbows Lois, and says, "Who wants to go to a restaurant on a rock in the middle of nowhere?" I tell them they know nothing about Pluto. Lois sneers. "If we know nothing, it's probably for a good reason."

My husband, Cortland, a successful music producer who shares their opinion, is relieved to be off the hook and immediately makes other plans.

I ask my beanstalk-tall best friend, Jersey, a Mars native, if she would like to go with me, and she leaps at the chance because last week she had a rare argument with her husband, Trenton, the first human android.

Our friendship goes back to the time I first came to Mars from Earth and Earth's moon, and we were security guards at Mars's Culinary Institute. At the time, we were teased that we were like the ancient cartoon characters Mutt and Jeff because Jersey was tall and thin (and still is), and I was short and fat. I'm still short by standards set by worlds with lower gravity than Earth's where most people grow much taller than those conceived and born on Earth, but I am no longer fat. And I still suffer watching Jersey eat anything and not gain an ounce while I look at lettuce and can gain two.

Jersey sees me and smiles as though she has just eaten a delicious chocolate cream puff. She is intelligent and brave, pretty but not beautiful, and wears brown corduroy slacks and a beige blouse. Her hair is newly washed, gracefully parted, and smells like mowed grass.

We travel on the Mars-Pluto shuttle. It's named the Titanic. Something about that name makes me nervous, but Jersey is sure it was named after Saturn's largest moon, Titan, and can't understand my concerns. Compared to other shuttles like the Mars-Earth and Mars-Venus shuttles that resemble deluxe cruise lines, this shuttle is spartan, cramped, and the food a motivation for the overweight to diet. They do, however, have Sunni and Shia sushi, but to everyone's horror, it's served on the same plate. The tea and coffee, albeit dispensed from overpriced vending machines, is decent.

I try to make Jersey feel better by commenting on her new haircut. But it's a wrong move. She says it's too short and she now looks the way she said she said would never look. She has downloaded several books to her palm and keeps flipping between *What Came first: Space or Time* and *What Came First: Time or Space?*

After days of boredom, broken only by watching rejected films from rejected film festivals, we near Saturn. Everyone is excited and crowds into the clear-domed observation lounge to see the glowing sunlit side of the rings. A sign says that light inside the lounge is dim for better viewing. Jersey says the real reason is because they're cheap. A voice says the rings are as wide as the distance from Earth to its moon but less than a mile thick.

"They looked much better from a distance," I say. "All I see now are moving bands of washed out yellow-brown particles with spaces separating them."

Jersey says, "Reminds me of pictures of a large billboard I saw in an Earth History class of Times Square, New York City, in the twentieth century of a man smoking a cigarette who blew smoke rings on a camel. I even remember the words on the sign: 'I'd walk a mile for a camel.' But animal rights activists said camels were an endangered species because all it took was one straw to break their backs, so they were forced to remove it. Shortly thereafter, people drove their own cars."

"That's very dangerous! I'd rather ride a camel."

Jersey thinks. "Do you think Times Square is an irrational or transcendental number like 'pi-r-square'?"

"Probably both because I studied Earth's customs and celebrations and learned that their New Year's Eve celebration was both irrational and transcendental. But it probably has more to do with quantum theory."

"Yeah, you're right. Everything has something to do with quantum theory. Even the theory is made of quantum." Jersey points. "Look, from this vantage point, the rings now look like an ancient vinyl record circling a yellow gas giant. But I know that they're made mostly of ice and rocks, some small as a grain of sand."

"I wonder what would happen if one of those particles hit us," I say.

Suddenly, as if on cue, we hear a strange sound followed by a rumble. A second later, a siren wails. Red lights blink.

A voice booms, "This is your captain. Our outer hull has been pierced by a fragment from the ring. Nothing to worry about, folks. Our space horoscope says, 'A tall dark person will solve a problem that will impact your life.'"

Jersey's face looks ashen; she clutches a rail in a vice-like grip. "What does that mean?" she asks, her voice pitched high in manic desperation.

A moment later, the captain says, "Aster, a tall, dark person who works on the ship, just plugged the hole with plasteen used to cover small holes on the inside the layers of the hull."

"And if they're large holes?" Jersey shouts toward the ceiling.

"What about large holes?"

Silence.

"Wonder if they consider that a minor detail?" I say.

The captain's voice booms, "No stunt questions. You guys writing an expose on 'interplanetary trams'?"

Everyone glares at us.

Shortly after, the lights blink green, and we hear an all clear signal. Everyone visibly relaxes.

The voice says, "Because no one panicked, extra after dinner mints will be served this evening."

Jersey says, "We never got any after dinner mints."

"They're in the casino. But you have to win them," says another traveler, who turns when she overhears.

I say, "I'm lucky with mints, very lucky if they're chocolate covered. Let's go to the casino later. I bet I can win some." And I do win. Lots of them.

***

We finally approach Pluto. Its reddish-brown sphere fills two thirds of our view. Jersey frowns as she has done for much of this trip, takes a swallow from a Mars Malt, and says, "I never thought Trenton would be so stubborn. When he told me that the first Android convention would be held not far from our home, I assumed I would go with him. But he says it's for androids only."

"He has a point, Jersey."

"It's reverse discrimination. We're married. He should have protested."

"As first human android, he's somewhat of a celebrity. My in-law Elvis became an android."

"Yeah, and he's probably going too."

I sigh.

"You would have thought they would make an exception, but Trenton said it was a private event, and private events can make their own rules as long as they abide by the law." She drains the last drops of beer and looks at the empty glass.

Hoping to change the subject, I say, "Interplanetary Foods decided that the city of Valentine, Pluto's capital, was the best location for my bistro. It's in Tombaugh Regio, a large heart-shaped area the size of Texas in the western part of Sputnik Planum. It's the largest glacier beyond Earth and made of mostly of nitrogen."

"Do you think people there have more sex because the region is shaped like a heart?" Jersey asks.

"Jersey, please."

"Well, they could!"

I continue. "Pluto's surface is varied and porous creating extraterrestrial quicksand."

"So how did they manage to build anything that wouldn't sink?"

I reach for a guidebook in a pocket on the side of the seat open it, flip pages and stop. "Ah, here it is, I remember reading this, 'Pluto's engineers and architects created a series of insulated interlocking platforms that float on Pluto's surface. If one sinks, the other platforms disengage from it to join together, fill in the gap, and continue floating. Then, using the principle that created magnetic levitating trains called Maglev, which uses super conducting magnetic repulsion, they built structures above the platform whose bases were repelled from the platform causing them to float on top of the magnetic platform. When magnets are cooled to extreme temperatures, the magnetic field is dramatically increased.'"

"And Pluto sure is cold. And its light gravity must help keep everything up," Jersey says. "I wonder what Trenton is doing now."

"You could give him a call."

She signals a porter for another beer.

"More beer?" My voice drops to a low, confidential tone.

"You'll have to use the bathroom, and there are none nearby."

"Nope. Upgraded to an android bladder. I only go once every twenty-four hours. You should consider upgrading. No one has been able to find a way to shorten lines for the ladies' room until now."

"I prefer to be the way I was born for as long as I can."

"But you told me you take longevity enhancers so you can live about two hundred years."

"Everyone takes them. They're sold like vitamins over the counter in drug stores."

"Trenton can make it to three hundred and fifty."

"Trenton's an android. Most of his body can be replaced and upgraded."

"Just saying. A time for everything, and everything in time."

I take another brochure from a pouch near my armrest. "Says here that Clyde Tombaugh discovered Pluto in 1930, and it has a two hundred forty-eight-year orbit."

"One birthday every two hundred and forty-eight years. You should double those longevity enhancers, Molly."

"I would if I could." I smile.

Jersey looks at her palm, keys the same two books, and wrinkles her brow.

"If you can't decide between those books, pick something else."

She nods and scrolls through more selections. "Got it," she says. "It's a psychological thriller."

"What's its name?"

"*My Relatives: A Theory* by Albert Einstein."

She looks down, clicks on the first page, takes a deep breath, clicks her palm shut, and slaps her arm on the chair. Her fingers drum a slow beat. "Can't concentrate! I'm calling Trenton."

"That's the sprit. Forgive and forget." I take what's left of the mints I won at the casino last night and offer some to Jersey. "Here, eat a few of these. It'll give you energy. By the way, did you buy Extra Light Communication before we left? Interplanetary Foods gave me a subscription."

Jersey wrinkles her brow and pops a few mints into her mouth. "Thought I didn't need it. Can I call on your palm?"

"No. The code only works for me, and I can only use it if I document that the call is necessary to restaurant business."

Jersey sighs.

"Well, Interplanetary Communications has a deal for unlimited use of Extra Light for two months. It's a thousand solars."

"That's a lot of money."

"Give them a call, Jersey. You can think about it and get it later if you think it necessary."

"Just a minute, they're giving more information. I'll put it on speaker palm."

"Information or a sales pitch?" I ask.

A cheery robotic voice says, "Take advantage of the opportunity for getting Extra Light duty free for a limited time only. You'll regret it if you don't."

"Threat or opportunity?" I say.

Jersey puts her finger to her lips. "Shh."

The voice continues. "Plus, get our bonus program that prevents your answers, which will be converted into meta-particles or tachyons, becoming entangled in parallel universes."

"Sales pitch with scare tactics," I say.

The voice continues, "To get this wonderful bonus that ensures that the answers to your questions arrive from the same universe that they were sent, push the blinking red button that will appear after you begin your Entanglement Insurance subscription. In theory, this should eliminate parallel answers from parallel universes that may or may not make any sense nor relate to your question."

"Should eliminate?" Jersey says. "Either it does, or it doesn't."

The voice says, "All answers are possible when you use

quantum mechanics. So, is that a yes or a no?"

Jersey asks, "How much is Entanglement Insurance?"

The voice says, "Please press the red button in front of you. This makes the quantum wave with the price visible and the waves with the other prices disappear."

Jersey says, "Sounds rigged. Maybe the other prices were lower."

The voice says, "This transaction is processed through the nearest wormhole and is one way only. We have not figured out reversing this to make refunds or exchanges."

"Nice excuse for being cheap," Jersey says. "But I want it."

She pushes the red button.

The voice continues, "Thank you for your purchase. That will be thirteen hundred solars. One thousand for the Extra Light and three hundred for the insurance. Enjoy our free historical presentation that follows this transaction."

Jersey says, "This could be boring, but at least it's free."

"Hopefully it's a cartoon," I say.

The voice says, "In the 1970s, Dr. Nicolas Gisin of the University of Geneva sent pairs of photons in opposite directions. When the photons were forced to make random choices between alternative pathways, the pairs always matched, even though there was no physical way for them to communicate. In the 'many worlds' hypothesis, once a path was chosen, the other paths disappeared."

"You don't have to be a physicist to know that," I say. "When I was dating ten different guys at the same time, the moment I said yes to Cortland, the other nine disappeared."

"Same thing happened to me when I said yes to Trenton, and I never studied physics." Jersey taps her palm. "I'm calling Trenton. Putting it on speaker-palm. Signal me if I say anything I shouldn't."

Jersey connects. In her sweetest voice, she says, "I've thought about what you said, sweetheart, and you're right about being wrong."

Trenton says, "Have you researched the definition of right and wrong and eliminated opposite similes?"

"Every minute. Even added a few more that I wrote in the data bank you snuck into my luggage as a going away present."

I grit my teeth, restraining an eyeroll.

Trenton says, "And you still love me?"

"And I still love you. I'll call after we get into the hotel."

Jersey disconnects.

"That's it?" I say. "That settled the issue of you being excluded from the Android Convention?"

"Not exactly. But if I say the words 'you're right,' somewhere in our conversation, bingo—situation neutralized. I'll bring it up in a new way later."

"That would never work on Cortland."

"Are you sure?"

"Well…"

"There then. Case closed."

Jersey signals a waiter, who ambles over. He wears a dark blue uniform with a gold badge that says, "My Name is Ensanguine Trump."

"Can I help you?" he says.

"Impressive name," Jersey says. "Historic."

He straightens. "Yup. Ensanguine Trump, the first zombie to become a president.

"Can we get those crunchy things that resemble cheese crackers?" Jersey says.

"You mean the ethyl vanillin, aldehyde, gamma decalactone, ethyl butyrate, geranyl acetate, civet, melanol, propylene glycol, vanitrope, diacetyl, benzo dihydro pyrone, artificial buttermilk flavor #3706, artificial cheese flavor #7406, artificial cream flavor #4375 crackers?"

"That's what I said, didn't I?"

3

WE EXIT THE SHUTTLE and enter the spaceport. Most spaceports, like most airports, look the same: walkways, floating signs, fast food courts, bathrooms, newsstands, but Valentine's spaceport is filled with colorful murals and artworks. People sing songs of welcome and play unusual musical instruments. A sign says, "The atmosphere on Pluto looks blue but is not breathable. Nitrogen dominates with carbon monoxide and methane in smaller amounts. Clouds consist of nitrogen, traces of methane, acetylene, ethylene and ethane."

"Sounds like stuff in the cheese crackers," I say.

"Probably is," Jersey muses.

We continue to read. "Pluto's cities are enclosed by clear domes. The outside is made of piezoelectric plastic and it generates electricity from wind. Pluto's radius is seventy percent of Earth's Moon. The gravity has been adjusted to be that of Titan or about twice of Pluto's natural gravity. Without artificial gravity, a one hundred-pound person on Earth is about eight pounds on Pluto. For your safety, do not jump or try to fly when you are beyond the domes."

"Eight pounds," I say. "That's too thin."

"You should know, Molly. You took Mexican Jumping Beans to help you exercise and lose weight."

We walk down a long causeway lined with shops and fast food places. Jersey pulls a pair of sunglasses from her bag and puts them on. The sun looks like a big bright star, its light packed into a diamond-like point making the light somewhat brighter than the light from Earth's full moon.

"Do you really need those?" I ask.

"Style transcends need, Molly. Besides, they were on sale." She throws her shoulders back, raises her chin, and marches on.

"Nice shades!" a man calls over his shoulder.

"See?" she says.

"You'll get nonstop use from them here because the sun rises and sets about once a week. And, the sun is the brightest natural thing—four hundred trillion watts."

Jersey quips, "Who's paying that electric bill?" She points to a holo advertising an azure-colored underground lake with waterfalls that looks as though we could step into it. We walk closer. "I would love to go there." She reads a plaque. "Says it's copied from the Plitvice lakes in Croatia on Earth, and the light there is like being on Earth on a sunny day. Maybe I could convince Trenton to come."

"Well, you have the sunglasses."

We find a cab. The driver smiles like a game show host. "Better tighten those seat belts, ladies. Once we're outside the dome, the gravity will revert to Pluto's natural gravity until we reach Valentine. Pluto is three-quarters the size of Earth's moon or about half the size of Mercury. Don't want you bouncing around."

The moment we leave, Jersey and I say, "Ooh!" as the light gravity makes our stomachs rise.

We spend the rest of the trip in silence until we enter one of the airlocks that leads into Valentine. We cradle our abdomens as our stomachs drop in heavier gravity.

I check the time. It's near noon on Pluto. Valentine glows brightly. It was a big adjustment for me, who was born on Earth, to live in a dome whose flat artificial light glows softly at dawn and grows brighter at midday before returning to a soft glow that signals day's end, without ever seeing the sun. But the majority of the citizens of Pluto know nothing else.

A broad road whooshes us over sky bridges and through tunnels that pass through the bottom of buildings tinted in pale colors and oddly shaped. We turn several times as the taxi hooks on to rails that act as linear motors, using magnetic fields to accelerate us along their length. When we stop at a floor, the rails rotate so the taxi can move off to the left or right rather than continuing up or down.

Most striking is the proliferation of trees and plants that glow with a greenish light that we see almost everywhere.

"How do they make the plants glow?" I ask the driver.

"With an enzyme called luciferase. It's an oxidative enzyme that produces bioluminescence. Energy making the light is generated by the metabolism of the plant, like fireflies emitting light via a chemical reaction."

Jersey says, "Well, it sure cheers this place up."

I give her the elbow and cover my mouth.

***

Our hotel, The Twilight Zone, is small by Mars standards. An attendant behind the front desk is a good-looking man who wears a red and white striped vest in a shiny material. The lobby smells of peppermint. There is a lot of art, but the art seems different from what I remember. I point to one painting and ask the attendant, "That looks like Nicolas Poussin's *Rape of the Sabine Women*, am I right?"

"It's been updated to the *Rape of the Sabine Men*. It's an original copy of a copy of a copy."

"And that statue looks like Rodin's *The Thinker*."

"It's better than *The Thinker*," he says. "It's *The Doer*."

Finally, I turn to what looks like my favorite painting, Matisse's *Piano Lesson*.

The attendant says, "A lot of people want to buy that one from us."

I look at the title: *The Cost of the Piano Lesson*. "I can see why."

A nattily-clad bellhop escorts us to our rooms. He opens the door to our suite and slides the floating platform that holds our luggage inside.

Jersey frowns, eyes narrow. "Is this the best you have?" she asks.

He slouches his weight onto one hip and angles his arm on top of his other hip. "This is our most luxurious one." He points beyond the one bathroom tucked in a corner of the foyer to the main area that has a sofa and a coffee table. Off to the sides are two alcoves with no doors. Each has a bed with no bedspread and a small night table with two draws.

Jersey wrinkles her nose. "Has that new carpet smell."

"It should. We sprayed it on this morning."

He removes our luggage from the platform. We give him a tip, and he leaves.

"Reminds me of a hotel on Ceres," Jersey says.

"You never went to Ceres. When did you go?"

"Trenton and I took a virtual reality vacation there."

"But you didn't actually go to Ceres."

"When you are married to a busy person, Molly, you take what you can get."

As soon as we finish unpacking, I call Tonto. "We're here and can't wait to see Molly's Pluto. How do we get there?"

Tonto says, "The easiest way is to walk. We're both on Valentine's main street, Carotid Artery. Should take about fifteen minutes."

We ask the concierge for directions. He has a straight nose, blue eyes, curly blond hair, clear tanned skin, a winning smile with straight white teeth, and broad shoulders. In short: rivetingly classically handsome. When he realizes I am the Molly of Molly's Pluto, he welcomes me and tells me how much everyone had been looking forward to the opening of a good restaurant.

"But surely you have good restaurants on Pluto," I say.

He shrugs his broad shoulders; says nothing.

***

Carotid Artery is wide and paved in a brown, speckled pavement. A row of glowing evergreen trees in the middle separates the two sides. There is a lane for skateboards and bicycles. Shops sell practical things like arch supports. I point and say, "It's a far cry from Rodeo Dive on Mars, or the Venus's Fly Trap Mall. Look, there's a Neptune's Nuggets, a McBurger, a Saturn Smoothies, and a Brimstone's Barbecue."

"Well, we won't starve," Jersey says. "You know, Molly, so far, Pluto reminds me of Mars before it got crowded and sophisticated."

"And expensive."

On a side street off Carotid Artery, a sign points to "art galleries."

"Let's see what's there," Jersey says.

There are six galleries. We look in the windows. "I may not know much about art, but the work in these galleries is very accomplished," I say. "What do you think?"

Jersey says, "Very accomplished. Don't you think six art galleries is a lot for a city that seems to have so little luxury?"

I point to a small painting in the window of one of the galleries done in the glowing pastel colors of the impressionist's style. "I wonder how much they want for that one?"

"Let's go in and ask."

"Forty starbucks," a smiling salesman says. "But I'll consider any reasonable offer."

"Forty starbucks is an extremely reasonable price for such a lovely painting. I'll take it," I say.

"Shall I wrap it up or send it?"

I palm payment and say, "Send it to the Twilight Zone where we are staying. A painting like that would cost several hundred starbucks on Mars, maybe a thousand."

The salesman says, "Pluto has an abundance of people with art talent. Almost everyone in their family has one person who paints, sculps, sings, plays an instrument, or does them all. As for the price, it's simply supply and demand."

Jersey says, "This is not well known outside of Pluto."

"Plutonians tend to be very private."

We leave and continue to Molly's Pluto.

Jersey says, "Did you notice that the concierge was so good looking he could be a media star?"

"I noticed. In fact, I see a lot of very good-looking people. Even that gallery owner was above average. Compared to them, we're like Quasimodo's children." I point to a striking brunette whose hair is gathered at her neck. "Don't you think she's exceptionally beautiful?"

"Probably works in a car wash," Jersey jests. "I'll ask her."

She has a name badge that says "Meredith Twenty-eight." I think it's a strange name. "Excuse Me, Meredith, but my friend and I couldn't help noticing how pretty you were."

"Really? No one ever told me that before. I think I'm average. I think my sister, Meredith Twenty-nine, is the pretty one."

"That can't be true! We think you're gorgeous. Don't we, Jersey?"

"Stunning. Far prettier than last year's Miss Oxygen Mask. May I ask what you do?"

"I'll give you my card," she says, reaching into a pocket.

I read, "Soapy Sales Car Wash."

"You own the place, right?"

She shakes her head.

"Manager?'

"Just a back-office attendant."

4

IT'S EASY TO SPOT MOLLY'S PLUTO because its blue and white striped awning is identical to the one outside of Molly's Bistro in New Chicago, Mars. My heart flutters as I push the door open.

Tonto greets us. He has a smile that makes others smile. He looks like his hologram. That's not always the case. Many post images of avatars or images that make them look younger, better. I'm relieved that he's not handsome and wonder why. He is tall and willowy like Jersey, a native Martian, and like with most born on worlds with lower gravity than Earth, I have to crane my neck upward to talk to him. His hair is short and brown, eyes brown and his nose slightly droopy. His dark blue shirt is open at the neck and goes well with his tan slacks. We shake hands in his grip till I lower my hand. Then he does the same to Jersey who gives him her new person once over.

"Welcome, welcome," he says with a smile that makes others smile. His teeth are brightly colored—a fashion that replaced tattoos and nose rings of the past, but I don't know if that's a style improvement or a style regression.

"How did you know we were going to push the door open when we did?" I ask.

He points to a small camera inside the door frame.

The jazz music of Dave Brubeck's 'Take Five' plays softly in the background. I know it's Dave Brubeck because my husband Cortland updated it recently for a group he manages.

"Would you like me to turn the music off?" Tonto asks. "With so few people working and no customers, I play music. Plutonians love jazz—in fact, all kinds of music. Unfortunately, the Band Box, Valentine's concert hall, doesn't have the latest acoustics and few want to perform there. Most of us listen to podcasts. Live performances are expensive to produce and have been put on hold."

"Doesn't bother us. Does it, Jersey?"

Jersey shakes her head.

Tonto keeps the music but lowers it. "I wish Valentine could build a great recording studio like the one your husband must have for Molawn Music's artists. Is he coming? What about your daughters? I love all their Lunar Tunes music."

"He didn't plan to come because he thought I would be home soon. The twins are usually very busy." I don't mention that they think of Pluto as a rock in the middle of nowhere.

"I understand," Tonto says, ushering us towards the bar area.

The first thing Jersey and I see when we enter is the bar looking as it does at home, rustic and refined and polished to shine like a fashion runway. The antique-looking mirrored shelves behind it are stocked with all my standard liquors plus the exotic ones like Jupiter Red Spot. The tan buttery stools, that I'm sure I overpaid for but now decide are worth it, look as inviting as the ones in the original Molly's. Jersey sits on one. She runs her hand over the bar, looks at the mother-of pearl-walls embedded with mica chip sparkles, and says, "If you added the snack treats that are always on this bar, I would feel like I never left home." She slides off the stool.

Tonto smiles and touches the tip of my elbow. "Come see the dining room," he says.

Jersey slides off the stool.

As soon as we enter, Jersey and I look up in delight and see light streaming through the vaulted, stained-glass ceiling. The lights behind it add a warm glow to the room. The tables are set with peach-colored clothes, napkins, silverware, and my signature china.

"If you had the fresh flowers I order every day, it would look like you're open for business."

"Let me show you the kitchen," he says.

If I was overwhelmed seeing the duplicate of my restaurant's outer rooms, I'm more overwhelmed seeing the kitchen. Here are the same blue and yellow Portuguese tiles, hanging copper pots, a giant gelato maker, pasta stretcher, espresso machine, and large professional ovens.

I slide my hand over the walk-in refrigerator and say, "Feels like home."

Four staff members are standing to the side, dressed in their restaurant uniforms.

Tonto says, "Thought you would like to meet some of the staff." He introduces a woman who had been Herb Tarragon's sous-chef. "So nice to meet you, Molly," she says. "My name is Nebula Veil." Her flaming red hair is pulled off her face into a bun; blue grotto eyes crinkle at the corners. She extends a hand, and we shake. She would be very beautiful on other worlds, but from what I have seen on Pluto, she is average pretty.

Next to her is a man who would stand out on worlds with light gravity because he is average Earth height—about five foot nine. It's a welcome relief for Earthborn me at five foot five constantly looking up at people like Jersey and my twin daughters, who were conceived and born in gravities lighter than Earth.

"I'm Dante Essen, rhymes with delicatessen," he quips. "Head waiter."

I smile. "Are you from Earth? You're the height of most born and raised there like me."

"No. Pluto native. But I'm asked that all the time. Sometimes I say I was from Earth because it stops questions, and I like the elevated looks I get when I say it."

I nod.

Dante continues. "My mother checked me with doctors, who said it was some kind of DNA glitch that was very difficult to fix but not harmful. As a teenager, doctors tried to stretch me. And when that didn't work, they inserted extensions into my legs, which helped a little." He looks at the man next to him and says, "This is Zee Pope, busboy."

I stare at Zee longer than I should or is polite.

"Something wrong?" Zee asks.

The resemblance between him and the good-looking hotel concierge is striking. I say, "No nothing wrong. I'm sorry I was staring, but you look like the concierge at The Twilight Zone. Doesn't he, Jersey?"

"Dead ringer," Jersey says. "Do you have family here?"

"As far as I know, I'm an only child and have no relatives in Valentine. I come from New Darwin in Cthulhu Regio. I've only been here a few months."

"Well, the concierge is very handsome, and so are you."

Zee smiles. "Thanks, no one ever told me that before. I think I'm average."

Jersey leans toward me, puts her hand over her mouth, and whispers, "That's what the woman we met on Carotid Artery said."

I nod.

Tonto interrupts. "Are you two starved? My small team can whip up lunch."

Before I can answer, Jersey, who would never turn down a free meal, pipes, "How nice."

We go back to the dining room and sit at a table. Dante tells us that although the kitchen is not fully stocked, there are many things they can make. "You will recognize all of them, of course, because all are made from the original Molly's recipes," he says. He recites a list. Jersey selects coconut curry with rice noodles, and I order the lemongrass ginger chicken. We both have watermelon iced tea. After a short wait, Dante and Zee place a warm basket of popovers and pesto toasts on the table. Incredibly delicious. Before we devour them, they bring our orders.

Tonto sits with us as we enjoy dessert, Chocolate Decadence cake.

I say, "Everything was excellent. Why don't you promote Nebula to chef? She seems very qualified."

"She is qualified," Tonto says. "But unseasoned. She's never worked under the pressure of a busy restaurant. A lot of people are great cooks, provided they have lots of time and little pressure. Put them in a busy professional kitchen with orders pouring in and pressure to produce them in limited time, and it's different. No, we need someone with experience who we're certain can handle pressure and cooking. I know because that was a first mistake I made when Interplanetary Foods put me in charge of my first restaurant on Europa."

"Maybe my chef Mario knows someone."

Jersey pipes, "But Pluto is so far away, Molly."

I sigh. "But maybe for more money and a chance to be head chef, they would come."

***

Two days later, as Jersey and I are strolling along Carotid Artery, Mario palms me. "You're in luck. Remember Lucky, one of our sous-chefs? He comes from Pluto and wants the job because he knows it would fast track him to become a head chef anywhere. I hate to lose him. Spent lots of time training him, and he knows the menu."

"He was very good looking. Not easy to forget. What's Lucky's full name?"

"Lucky Luciano the Tenth."

5

I SIT IN THE ONE COMFORTABLE chair in our hotel room, and although Jersey called three times for another chair, it has yet to arrive. Tonto calls. His holo shimmers and stabilizes in front of me.

"That's wonderful news, Molly," he says. "I'll tell the staff about the new chef." He sees me wince. "What's the matter?"

"Lucky Luciano is a top name in the Criminal Hall of Fame. In fact, that family established a scholarship there for those wanting to major in crime with time off for bad behavior."

Tonto asks, "How much do you know about Pluto's history?"

"Not much."

"Well, Pluto, like Earth's Australia, is a place where those convicted of crimes were often sent. Some of Australia's penal colonies were located in an area called New South Wales. On Pluto, they're mostly in Cthulhu Regio, a dark region along the equator. It's known as Pluto's 'Whale'."

"Ah, from 'New South Wales' to 'The Whale.' Is it close by?"

"It's south of us and almost as big as Earth's Alaska."

Jersey asks, "Would that be as in Baked Alaska dessert?

Tonto says. "More likely, global-warmed Alaska. Recent images I've seen show Alaska with palm trees and great beaches."

"Cthulhu Regio is where Zee Pope also comes from," I say.

Tonto says, "One of Lucky's ancestors was probably a convict here. And like so many, when their sentence ended, they stayed to build a new life. Pluto needs people. Still does. There's lots of incentives to come here: great, cheap housing and half-a-percent business loans."

"Are you a native Plutonian?"

"Yes."

"Where were you born?"

"I wasn't born. I was hatched."

"Hatched?"

"Yes, at the Valentine Hatchery. There are other hatcheries."

"Do you have parents?"

Tonto looks puzzled.

"Like one man and one woman responsible for creating you."

Tonto says, "You mean did an egg and a sperm get together to create me? Then yes, I have Parents, but that old process of creating babies is very narrow. A lot could go wrong."

"Well, it usually doesn't. Becky and Lois, my twin daughters, were born from that process."

Tonto frowns. "But it can go wrong. Can't it?"

"Yes, but..."

"Most Plutonians prefer a more controlled reproductive process. Our hatcheries grow embryos in an artificial environment where most DNA imperfections are fixed or screened out. I know Dante is short, but he is a very rare exception. The process is called ectogenesis. It started back in 2015 when a baby named Silas Philips in Los Angeles, Earth, grew inside his mother but was born outside of her in his amniotic sac. It took over a hundred years to completely externalize the process, but once they did, women who wanted a child but didn't want to spend nine months pregnant or use a surrogate signed on."

"Aldous Huxley's 'babies in bottles'," I say.

"Much kinder and more civilized." He spreads his arms like an eagle. "But here I am. If you're interested, you can visit the hatchery."

"I might. Everyone I know, including me, has children the

old-fashioned way."

"As far as you know."

"Yes, as far as I know. Any progress finding out who killed Herb Tarragon?"

"Pluto police are very slow."

"Slow? Why?"

"It's complicated, has to do with our heritage as a penal colony. Many of the original Mafia Families, although they all have legitimate business here, still have a great deal of influence. And the police don't want to make false accusations."

"What kind of influence?"

"Like people are raised not to snitch on anyone."

"Even if they see a murder?"

"Pluto has laws and alternative laws. It's complicated."

"Have Pluto police done any investigating?"

"I think so."

"Who is conducting the investigation?"

"Captain Carmella Soprano. Her maiden name is Ella Passero. She changed it to Carmella when she married Tony."

"I thought the Sopranos were a fictitious family on twenty-first century Earth."

"Fiction then, but real on Pluto now."

"Does Carmella have any theories about the murder?"

"Her theory is that it was a surgical procedure."

"Surgical procedure? How could she say that? He had a knife in his back."

"Like I said, just a theory."

"Would they mind if I called Mars Yard?"

"Mind? They welcome off-planet sources because then they would have to do less investigating and couldn't be blamed if some authorities here didn't like the result."

"You said he was found in the wholesale food market."

"Yes, near Silicone Slings, the bar for androids."

Jersey pipes, "My husband Trenton is an android. Today

they're called enhanced people. I didn't know that Silicone Slings became a franchise. My husband and I love that place."

"The first enhanced person to come as a convict five years ago opened it when he finished his sentence. Now we have lots of enhanced people."

"Did they all come as convicts?"

"No. Most came because they saw economic opportunity and a quiet environment."

"Do you remember his name?"

"Sure, Avery Spelling. The Valentine Inquirer did a feature about him when he came."

"We know Avery. He was the head waiter at Virtual Vitals, a virtual restaurant on Mars. He murdered his boss. Outside of that, he was a nice guy."

Jersey says, "Would you mind if we went to the wholesale market and looked around?"

"Of course not. You could probably learn more than a Plutonian because they would assume that you had no axe to grind other than finding out who did this. Besides, if they didn't like you, you could be sent back to Mars or elsewhere."

"Elsewhere?" I say.

Tonto's pixels fade out.

6

JERSEY AND I TAKE A TRAM to the wholesale market. Like the trams on Mars and other worlds, it's a superconducting magnetically levitating train capsule. Silver and sleek on the outside with caramel colored leather-like seats on the inside, it has less wear and tear than the trams on Mars. The illuminated sign above says the Wholesale Market will be the next to last stop. The last stop is the Hatchery. During the trip, very good-looking people exit and enter. Two who could easily pass for identical twins enter separately and sit opposite each other and make no greeting of recognition toward the other.

Jersey stands. "Let's ask if they're related." The closer we come, the more identical they look. Jersey asks one, "Excuse me, but are you related to that woman sitting opposite you?"

"Who?" she says, adjusting a sleeve on her pale lavender shirt. "I didn't notice."

Jersey points. "Her, in the yellow sweater."

"No way. Never saw her before." She puts her hand over her mouth. "How could you say that? I think she is very unattractive."

I say, "We think you look like her."

"Well, I see no resemblance whatsoever!"

We go to the other woman, and I ask the same thing. She glances and frowns. "I'm offended you would think that. Can't you see that she parts her hair on the right side, and I part mine on the left and her thumbs are totally different than mine?" She holds out her hand.

Jersey says, "But that's not a big difference."

"Big difference to me." She sneers, rising as the tram slows then stops. She shakes her head and exits.

"Something strange is going on, Jersey," I say.

Jersey nods, then says, "Do you think we're noticing these similarities because we're not from here or they don't notice them because they are?"

"Don't know."

We sit in silence as everyone lurches to one side then straightens as the tram resumes its run and moves forward. The Wholesale Food Market is the next stop. When we exit, the first woman remains on the train and watches. Her face shows no emotion.

"Think she's going to the Hatchery?" Jersey asks.

"There has to be more at the last stop other than the Hatchery," I say.

"Maybe a discount shoe outlet."

We laugh.

We cross the platform. A sign says "Wholesale Market and More." The first thing we see is a stall with rainbow-colored hummus, cheese wheels as black as coal, and flaming orange cheese wedges that look radioactive.

I point and say to the salesperson, "I never saw black cheese."

"It's not black; it's navy blue. Never had bleu cheese?"

"Yes, but not like that."

A smiling attendant holds out a tray with samples that could pass for jewels. Jersey asks, "Are these safe to eat?"

"Pluto has its own food and drug administration. We don't always follow regulations set by the Interplanetary Council."

"That doesn't answer my question," she says, popping the flaming orange one into her mouth. "Hmmm. Not bad."

Other stalls nearby are filled with lymonds—lemon and lime combinations—orange and grapefruit combinations, and purple tangerines. There is also a stall selling ice cream in flavors that include licorice and cannoli. One table says "Brass Knuckle Spices: fresh from Brass Knuckles, Pluto."

A large crowd surrounds a table filled with cannabis products that overshadows it. One woman asks, "If I sprinkle dried and ground cannabis over pizza, will it change the taste?"

"Only taste better," the salesman says. He catches my eye and winks. "Can I interest you in some cannabis brownies or cooking brandy infused with cannabis? How about a cup of Leprechaun Delight Plus? It's coffee that'll knock your socks off."

Jersey says, "Let's split a brownie."

"We're here to observe. We need to keep our eyes and ears sharp."

"Okay, just one."

Jersey breaks it in two unequal pieces and keeps the larger piece.

We pass stalls and tables laden with wigs, masks, skin in different colors—with and without tattoos that stretch over various body parts—plus ads for music lessons, dance lessons, and art classes. One stall has a pair of emerald sandals dangling from a hook. "They're Dorothy's sandals from Oz," the sales woman says in an intimidating voice of authority. "Those ruby red slippers cut into her toes. She had to go to a chiropodist every time she wore them."

"Is that a fact?" Jersey says, pulling me away.

Another area has a sign: Deyrolle Taxidermy Shop, first opened in 1831 in Paris, Earth, by entomologist Emile Deyrolle. Current proprietor: Emile Deyrolle IX. We look. There's a stuffed elk, a Goliath beetle as big as a fist, an octopus, stuffed birds, animals, and fish. A striking-looking woman in a snug rainbow-colored t-shirt is trying to bargain the price down on a stuffed blue and yellow panda.

"I thought pandas were black and white," Jersey says.

The salesman snarls. "Not in the USA where I imported this one from. That's why it's so expensive."

"The USA as in United States of America or USA. as in United States of Asteroids?" Jersey asks.

He narrows his eyes at Jersey. "Children know it's the asteroids. Are you on medication you shouldn't take with alcohol? I swear on that copy of a copy of that six hundred-starbuck Samurai sword hanging there that could be yours for two hundred starbucks plus tax, that you're made from inferior molecules."

Jersey reacts. "And you have a chip on your brain."

"It's a chip on your shoulder," I whisper, pulling her away. But not before she says louder, "You have a chip on your brain and on your shoulder."

We continue walking, getting lost in the crowd. A stall sells coffee. A sign says, "Only coffee shop in the solar system that doesn't charge more for iced coffee than hot coffee."

"Want some coffee, Jersey?"

"I'd prefer an Elon Musk Sour."

"If you want an Elon Musk Sour, we can probably get it over there at Silicone Sings. But coffee is a better choice after that brownie. It's probably why you were so sensitive back there."

"But that brownie was so small. And you had the other piece."

"Do you think it's safe for us to go to Silicone Slings, Jersey? After all, Avery did murder his boss."

"He was always nice to us; besides, it was a long time ago. It's not like he was the Venus Flytrap Killer with a string of murders under his wing."

***

Silicone Slings has a large window. I cup my hands around my eyes and peer in. The bar is mostly empty. We enter.

Silicone Slings looks like many popular saloons. Low lit, tin ceiling, brown walls, long bar, small tables to the side near the bar, larger ones in back. Holos of famous enhanced people are on the walls. I recognize Rosie the Riveter and pop singer Mike the Mechanic. Then Jersey and I stop. There is a larger than life holo of Trenton. A sign says, "First Enhanced Person".

Jersey swoons. "Wow! What a great holo of Trenton!" She reaches out to touch it, and her hand jiggles the pixels. She sighs. "I miss him, Molly."

A voice in the distance calls, "Molly? Jersey? I thought I heard your voices. I heard about your restaurant opening a branch in Valentine and hoped you would come."

We turn and see Avery. He looks better than we had ever seen him. He gives Jersey and me quick embraces. "Wonderful to see you both again. I saw an announcement that one of your twins got married, Molly."

"Yes. Becky."

Avery turns to Jersey. "Is Trenton coming? My Oil Spill Champagne will be on the house."

Jersey smiles. "Right now, I would love a Jeff Bezos, shaken not stirred?"

"Of course," Avery says.

"I thought you wanted an Elon Musk Sour?" I say.

"Changed my mind. The Bezos is richer."

"I'll have a coke," I say.

"Real coke or a cola? We have both."

"A cola."

Avery signals the bartender, who brings the drinks.

"At first," Avery says, "I was very upset being sentenced to Pluto for the murder of my boss, but being a prisoner in one of Pluto's correctional facilities was more like serving time in a spa. What Pluto's corrections system shows to the rest of the solar system and what really goes on are two different things." He puts his hand over his mouth. "And everyone here is motivated to keep it that way. The United Council of Planets contributes to the support of the penal system because they send so many here, and Pluto is happy to get them. We need the people and we need the money.

"Everyone was fascinated with me because I was Pluto's first android. They treated me like a celebrity. By the time I was released, I had more friends than I ever had on Mars. I can't get used to androids being called enhanced persons. Sounds pretentious. When I read about Silicone Slings becoming a franchise, I leaped at the chance to open one here. I knew the customer service side of the restaurant business from working at Virtual Vittles, and good service is good service anywhere, so here I am."

"Did you have trouble getting financing?" I ask.

"Not at all. Those old Mafia families knew a good thing when they saw it."

"The Mafia owns most of Silicone Slings?"

"You're making it sound illegal, Molly. They're investors. Investors! Things are different on Pluto. Our Mafia is evolved; they're creative entrepreneurs."

Jersey puts her hand on her hip. "Yeah, everything's under the radar."

Avery smiles. "Well, the radar to most of the solar system."

Jersey says, "Like Mercury, Venus, Earth, Mars Jupiter, Saturn Uranus, Neptune, and Ultima Thule."

"But we do belong to the United Council of Planets, pay our dues, and follow their guidelines."

"Operating at the edge," I say.

"It's complicated. Pluto's laws supersede here."

"Said like a native Plutonian," I say.

"Feel like one, Molly. Best home I ever had. Now that the enhanced human population has grown, I'm very successful."

"Have you heard that the chef at Molly's Pluto was murdered?" I ask.

Avery says, "Never heard murdered. Heard he died from either a surgical procedure or an unfortunate accident."

Jersey rolls her eyes. "Well, if you hear anything, let us know. We're at the Twilight Zone."

7

JERSEY AND I GO TO A CAFE in the lobby of the Twilight Zone for lunch. We order "Bullets and Burgers", hamburgers with a side order of sun-fired Mecurian peas. We bite into our burgers, make faces, and put them down. "Strange ketchup," I say. "But it does drown out the taste of the burger."

"Maybe that's the idea."

We scrape it off.

A waiter overhears and says, "If you want Earth-style ketchup, that will be two extra starbucks. Three for Mars style."

"I'll splurge," I say. "Mars."

Jersey calls Trenton. She taps her palm to speaker mode so I can hear. Trenton answers immediately.

"I miss you, Jersey," I hear Trenton say. "I'll make arrangements to come to Pluto."

Jersey says, "That's wonderful, sweetheart. The Twilight Zone is their best hotel. Pluto's Heartbreak Hotel is a rundown bunker, and the Night Crawler has things that go bump in the night."

"It will be nice to get away from Mars for a while and all the arguing about how to spend the time saved from having Daylight Savings Time. Most think an extra day should be added to the year. Others want to abandon it because they believe it causes global warming like it did on Earth."

Jersey clicks off.

"Maybe Trenton and I can have a second honeymoon at

those underground lakes we saw advertised at the spaceport?"

"But you told me you never had a first honeymoon," I say.

"Back then, there was so much prejudice when a human married an android that it was difficult to find a nice hotel that would take us as a couple. But we made our own fun and called it a honeymoon."

I don't ask more. Jersey and Trenton could live on food supplement pills, stay in windowless rooms, plug themselves into virtual reality programs, and get high drinking tap water thinking they are in a trendy bar in New Paris, Titan.

Jersey says, "If he can hitch a ride on one of those new police transports, he'll be here in about a week. Mars Yard wants to expand its Special Forces Unit and be an arm of the United Council of Planets. Too much happens beyond Mars that is unregulated. Many asteroids, for example, are privately owned with their cores drilled out, becoming huge vaults that hide stolen goods. It's replete with criminals like those shape-shifters, Mona and Lisa Da Vinci."

"No one has ever cracked their code," I say.

The next day Jersey and I discuss what we should do while we wait for Trenton to arrive. I say, "Valentine is boring. Most of the shops sell dreary looking items, the restaurants are neither good nor creative, and theaters play reruns."

Jersey picks up several brochures that are always in our room, looks at a few, and says, "What Pluto does have is abundant natural beauty. Look at these pictures of flowing glaciers, pitted terrains, gorgeous mountains, icy calderas…"

"I would love to see icy calderas. Where are they?'

"Two pits are located at the summits of Wright Mons and Piccard Mons near the south pole."

"Too far. Anything closer?"

Before she can answer, my palm signals a call. It's Tonto. "I just heard from our new chef, Lucky. He'll be delayed because he's getting minor surgery."

"Did he say what kind?"

"He said it was cosmetic."

"Cosmetic? Why? If we're talking about the same person, I remember that he was very good looking. I thought he could have been a model, not a chef."

"No, you don't understand. He wanted the procedure to make him less handsome: put a bump on his nose, change his blue eyes to brown, and tweak other things."

"That's strange, but as long as he's okay."

We scan more brochures. Jersey says, "This one says that there's a beautiful frozen lake just north of Sputnik Planum not far from where we are now. It used to be called Alcyonia Lacus but was recently renamed Lake Vodka."

"I wonder why."

Jersey reads, "Pluto's axis is tilted about one hundred twenty degrees—so far over that its north pole points downward making great seasonal shifts. Parts swing between a half-century of nearly complete sunlight and a half-century of perpetual night. Pluto wobbles. Surface temperatures fluctuate. Its nitrogen, carbon monoxide, and methane atmosphere becomes thicker and thinner over millions of years and goes from a frozen solid into a gas and sometimes high enough for liquid nitrogen to flow on the surface."

"Creating a lake," I say.

"The last time temperatures were sufficiently high to melt nitrogen was around eight hundred thousand years ago. Pluto is now in an intermediate phase between its climate extremes."

"No time to waste, Jersey. Let's go!"

8

THE CONCIERGE ASKS, "Do you want a car, or do you want to take the tram?"

I tell him we prefer to take the tram because we could learn more about Pluto. "Why was the lake's original name, Alcyonia Lacus, changed to Lake Vodka?

"No one wanted to go to Alcyonia Lacus," he says. "Now they do."

He sends us to a room where we are outfitted with bright yellow protective suits that are necessary when we exit the dome.

Like everything else in Pluto's gravity, the bulky suit feels light. "What's the red button on the sleeve?" I ask.

"Press for an emergency."

"Are there many emergencies?" Jersey asks.

"This is Pluto," he says, not elaborating further.

***

We carry our helmets into the tram until it's time to put them on when we reach the station for the lake. After a few transfers, we get one that says, "To Lake Vodka". Two people enter. One sits in the front, the other in the back. Each keeps his helmet on.

"Why are they wearing their helmets?" Jersey asks. "The air is very good in here."

"Maybe they didn't want us to see who they were."

"But we don't know anyone."

We exit at the lake. The other two walk off together and disappear from view.

The path to the lake is clearly marked. A few motion-activated lights turn on as we walk.

"Look at this place," Jersey says. "It's breathtaking! What Pluto doesn't have in amenities and luxury, it makes up with beauty. Those white hills have probably been 'bleached' because the nitrogen ice is shallow here." She sighs. "Mars and Titan used to be so beautiful. At least the Red Party on Mars made sure to preserve vast amounts of the original surface. But Titan is a disgrace. It should be renamed Titan Mall."

As we walk, we see a large sign that says, "If you are a return visitor, the landscape as you remembered it may have shifted. The angular blocks of water ice along the western edge 'float' in the soft dense solid nitrogen ice glaciers and move like icebergs in Earth's Arctic Ocean. Chains of drifting hills happen because water ice is less dense than nitrogen ice."

The lake is ahead. We trudge closer.

"This is farther than I thought," I huff. "It's amazing how a lot of space can distort one's sense of space especially in a world where the horizon is so close."

Jersey points to a small red sign that says, "Caution! Underground thermal vents melt the nitrogen making parts of the lake liquid. Please stand only in marked areas."

"Had it not been in red, we would have missed that sign," Jersey says. "But I don't see any marked area."

The closer we get, the more slippery the ground becomes. Jersey steps ahead and slides forward. "Hey, Molly, ice skating on Pluto!" she calls. "This is fun."

"Stop! Stop!" I yell watching her slide away.

Then she falls on her back. Her arms flail. She slides faster. Faster. And before I know it, she slides into the lake. I can't reach her without losing control and sliding myself. She starts to sink. When she moves, her rate of decent accelerates. She screams.

"Try to relax," I say. "Or you'll use up all your oxygen faster."

"Easy for you to say!"

I lean out as far as I can again but can't reach her. Then I remember a red emergency button on our sleeves. I find mine and push.

"See if you can reach the red button on your sleeve, Jersey."

"Can't reach it. My suit is frozen."

Jersey sinks to chest level. "Our suits have enough air for three hours. I'm sure someone will come before then," I say, trying to restrain rising panic.

"I love you, Molly. Tell Trenton I love him."

Not words of confidence.

Then… "Wait a minute, Jersey, I hear the words: 'park ranger on his way.'"

"What do you mean wait a minute?'"

Suddenly a voice in my helmet booms, "Turn around. I see you,"

I see a gold-colored copter overhead that is descending. I read the words, "Ranger Copter." It lands behind me. A ranger jumps out, pushes something on the side of the copter, and a silver lasso extends toward me and circles me.

"You're standing in a dangerous place," he calls as the lasso yanks me toward him. "You're too close to the edge."

"My friend is already under the ice," I scream.

"No problem."

Why do people say 'no problem' when clearly there is one?

"Jersey can you hear us?" I call.

"Can hear but can't see, Molly."

When I am next to him, I see two bushy eyebrows and beneath it, two dark eyes through his helmet. He removes the lasso from me, adjusts it, and sends it toward the lake.

"How does that lasso know where to find my friend?" I ask.

"All suits have magnetic coding." He points to the sign. "Most people read that!"

"We did read it."

Jersey's head and shoulders slowly emerge from the lake. She slides away from the lake until she reaches us. The ranger moves a hand device over her, melting the ice she is encased in. I see numbers light up on the device that check her vital signs.

"Better?" he asks.

She wobbles as we help her to her feet.

"Wait a minute," I say. "I want to check something." I walk toward the sign.

The ranger says, "Hey come back here. Only one rescue a day. Union rules."

"I want to examine the sign," I continue walking. When I reach it, I look at the ground. "Jersey, come look at the ground near the sign. I think the sign was moved."

Jersey comes. "The bottom of the sign shows two levels of immersion. One higher than the other." I snap a holo. We walk back.

The ranger says, "The land here shifts all the time. Just a moment. I'm getting a call from security headquarters."

We wait.

The ranger asks, "Did one of you make a call to Mars Yard recently?"

"Yes, I did," Jersey says.

"And your husband works for Mars Yard and is now headed to Pluto."

"So?"

"Explains it."

"What?"

"Just explains it. Gotta run. My shift just ended." He turns to go.

"But what if someone else needs you?" I say. "What about the two people who were on the tram with us?"

He stops. A holo of a map floats in front of him. He studies it. "No one else here. Are you trying to blame someone else for your carelessness?" He continues to walk toward his copter and starts to board. He turns and says, "City folk should stay in the city."

9

THE MOMENT I SEE TRENTON, I feel better. He is smart and honest as a day on Venus is long. And for those of you who failed Solar System 101, Venus's day is two hundred forty-three Earth days long, rotating in retrograde, meaning the sun rises in the west and sets in the east, despite the dispute among hard-right environmentalists who think it is a left-leaning conspiracy.

I wait at the spaceport with Jersey, who stands out in her bright pink shirt and shocking green slacks. She shifts from side to side trying to get a better view of the exiting ramp. The moment she spots Trenton, she jumps up and down and waves like a flag in a Martian wind. Then she rushes toward him. They hug so closely you would think they are dancing The Zygote. Finally, they separate, Trenton turns to me, and he says, "So good to see the real Molly."

"What do you mean the real Molly?"

"Well, I just saw the strangest thing."

"Here that could be lots of things," I say.

"Remember when you first came to Mars, you weighed two hundred eighty-seven pounds."

My face flushes. "Do you have to remind me? I work hard keeping those pounds off."

Trenton says, "I saw someone who could have passed for your double back when you were heavy. But I realized that you couldn't have gained all that weight in so short a time. You also looked younger. I called, 'Molly, Molly,' but the woman didn't respond. When I went over and spoke to her, she looked at me as though I were crazy and said that she didn't know any Molly nor did anyone ever say anything like that to her. I showed her a picture of you—that is as you are now—and she said she saw no resemblance. Then I retrieved a file and found an old one where you were fat."

"You have a holo of me when I was fat? Delete that, Trenton!"

"It's part of an official record of immigrants who come to Mars. It's a crime to tamper with it. Anyway, she peered at the holo and added that you both had brown hair, but that's it. And as far as her weight was concerned, she said she suffered with it her whole life, and if we knew some magic bullet to shed the pounds, she would appreciate knowing about it. Then she gave her me her card with her picture and name, Vera Haven. Here. Look."

The full-size life-like image flickers into focus. I blink and stare. It did look like I looked years ago, heavy, unsure of herself. I try to remember what being more than one hundred pounds overweight felt like. I touched my stomach. A small roll. Maybe I should lose ten pounds…okay, fifteen.

Jersey says, "It's you, Molly. It's the way I remember you when we met."

"Demos! Phoebus!" I cry.

"What's with Mars's moons?" Trenton asks.

"Demos and Phoebus mean 'terror and fear'. And that's how I feel at the moment."

***

We go to the Twilight Zone. Trenton checks in.

The man behind the desk hands me a message square. I tap it open. Read and frown.

"Why the face?" Jersey asks.

"It says, 'Go home. Pluto doesn't need a gourmet restaurant.'" I look around. "Who sent this?" I ask.

"Holo Anonymous."

"What's that?"

"An independent messaging company on Charon that has its own encrypting service that hides the identity of the sender. As a moon of Pluto, they are off planet and have their own laws. Those who live there never reveal their real names. They use codes like BW45."

"Does that mean that there is a BW44 and 43 down the line?

"Not necessarily."

"Well, B and W are letters of the alphabet."

"Yes, but it could be a code encoded into a different code encoded into an off-planet language encoded in to a numerical value in a vault on a planetoid in the Oort cloud that leads to another planetoid that leads to…"

"I get it," I say, putting the cube in my pocket.

***

Jersey and Trenton move into their own room. As Trenton works for Mars Yard and is on Mars Yard business, Mars Yard will pay the tab. Immediately, I see the robo-maid down the hall rolling in extra towels and extra bathroom supplies.

When Trenton is unpacked, they come to my room. I program the small food replicator on the wall for coffee and a variety of sandwiches.

Trenton picks one, bites, makes a face, and says, "Tastes stale."

"Probably is," I say. "Luxury and hospitality are not Pluto's strong points. But the longer you're here, the more you get used to the food. You'll be happy to know we found Avery Spelling, who has opened a Silicone Slings. He put a huge holo of you near the front door."

Jersey takes a sandwich. The bread is green. "I hope this is a vegetable concoction and not mold." She takes a bite and chews. "Actually, not bad." I think, for your taste buds.

Trenton says, "Now, Molly, tell me what you know so far about the murder."

And I do.

"That's it? Not much to go on," he says. "And you're saying that a knife in the back is not an obvious felony."

"Apparently not here."

Trenton says, "Let's visit the Pluto Police.

10

WE GRAB A CAB. TRENTON says, "We'd like to go to the police station."

"You mean Sing Sing."

"Sing Sing is the name of a famous prison on Earth," I say.

"Not here. It's what our security station is called. Many of our officers also sing. I guess calling the security facility 'Sing Sing' is (no pun intended) an inside joke."

We arrive and exit the taxi. After passing through a series of doors that scan us, we enter Captain Carmella Soprano's office. It is a large white room. People sit behind gray desks and flick through screens that float in front of them. Carmella walks toward us. She extends her hand to Trenton, then does the same to Jersey and me. She says, "Read about all of you. You've all solved crimes on Mars." She looks at me and says, "I wouldn't mind receiving a case of those delicious Chocolate Moons. We import them, but they are heavily taxed."

She turns to Jersey and peers closer. "And from other reports, your insights have helped close cases." Jersey beams.

And to Trenton, "Mars Yard is lucky to have you. You're their best forensic scientist."

Trenton is about to say something when Carmella adds, "Of course, not on Pluto. We have a superior team."

Trenton says, "Your laws have so many definitions no one can keep track of all the nuances."

Carmella pushes her hair behind one ear, her finger curled

like a hook. "Well, I can." She laughs. "Look, I catch them. I don't try them."

I'm surprised how pretty and well-dressed Carmella is considering the clothes I've seen in the shops. She also looks familiar, but I know we've never met. Although the office is stark, her corner area has a few feminine touches including a pink and gray paisley sofa with a glass kidney-shaped coffee table and two matching chairs. The wall behind her desk holds diplomas, awards, and pictures. I recognize one of the art forger Scheherazade from the time Jersey and I solved the case of the Chocolate Moons. There is a large one of someone with a veil over his face. The caption below the picture reads: Oort Cloud Boss. Another in a black mask has a caption that says third head of security at Cthulhu Regio Prison.

Trenton points to the picture and asks, "What happened to the first and second heads of security?"

"Swimming with the fishes on Encedelus. If you get my drift."

No one asks more.

Then it hits me. Carmella looks like she could be the sister of either the busboy at Molly's Pluto, Zee Pope, or the hotel concierge, both of whom could pass for twins.

"Do you have brothers?" I ask.

"Yes, two brothers, Alto and Mezzo."

"I thought one of your brothers might be named Zee Pope?"

"Why would he be named that? Our family name is Soprano!"

"You look like Zee Pope. Doesn't she, Jersey?"

Jersey nods.

"You people are strange," she says. "Let me introduce you to some of my staff." Carmella motions to four officers who join us. "Meet Carmen, Aida, Don Giovanni, and Tosca. When they are not doing security work, they sing a mean barbershop quartet."

Tosca says, "We call ourselves 'The Cosa Nostra'."

Carmen says, "I see you're frowning. Cosa Nostra means 'Our Thing'. And our quartet is our thing." She steps closer and squints. "Got a problem?"

"No problem," I say.

Carmen says, "Well, that's good because they prepared a short number for you."

They move close to one another and sing in acapella harmony: "We welcome you to Sing Sing. We're mighty glad you're here…"

We listen, impressed that they are so good. We clap.

"That was a treat," I say. "You would be a hit on any world."

Carmen blushes and says, "Here, we're probably average. I know your husband and daughters are in the music business. Are they coming to Pluto?"

"They haven't decided," I say.

"Well, if they come and do a show, I hope your husband can include the quartet."

The quartet smiles and returns to their seats.

Trenton asks, "Did anyone see anything at the wholesale market when Herb Tarragon's body was found?"

"There were security cameras in the area, but they didn't work," Carmella says.

"Didn't anyone report that they were broken?" Trenton asks.

"I didn't say they were broken. I said they didn't work."

"Was the weapon recovered?" Trenton asks.

Carmella says, "We don't say weapon, we say instrument. And we have it and were able to trace its origin." She motions to Don Giovanni, who stops studying his screen. He goes to a cabinet and brings a small box. Carmella opens it.

I gasp.

"Look familiar?" Carmella asks.

"Of course, it looks familiar, I say. "It's the same kind of knife with the same design that was made for my restaurant on Mars." I turn it over. "See there's my initials, MMS: Molly Marbles Somers."

Jersey says, "Yes, but Molly's Pluto has the same cutlery and same dishes as Molly's Bistro. So, it didn't have to have come from the Mars restaurant."

"No, but maybe it did." Carmella narrows her eyes and stares at me.

It works. I'm shaken.

***

We leave. I run through possibilities and can't get a grip. Images of people looking like other people float in my head. It's a mystery I can't solve…for now.

The farther we get away from the police station, the better I feel. We turn a corner and see a woman approaching from the opposite direction. She wears a bright red jacket. A red and blue plaid scarf drapes over her shoulders. The closer she comes, the more we see that she could be Jersey's twin. Jersey moves so the woman must stop in front of her.

"Excuse me," Jersey says. "You look like me."

The woman steps back, gives Jersey the once over. "I see no resemblance whatsoever!" She sneers.

"But you look like each other," I pipe. "Doesn't she, Trenton?"

Trenton's expression indicates that he is triangulating this from every angle. He says, "Except for the clothes that Jersey wouldn't wear, I would absolutely be fooled that you were my wife."

"I see no resemblance," she huffs. "I never saw any of you before. What's the matter with my clothes?" She narrows her eyes at Trenton in disgust. "Your wife! Unbelievable! I would never marry you! You have some nerve!" She turns, scoots off, and leaves us with our mouths open.

11

I palm Tonto and tell him that Jersey's husband from Mars Yard arrived and would like to talk to the staff. Tonto says that the staff is large and asks with whom would he like to talk to first.

"Start with the people I met," I say.

We go the next day. Tonto greets us at the door. Trenton looks at the restaurant. "Amazing, Molly. It's a wonderful duplication of Molly's Bistro at home."

"Like some of the people on Pluto," I mumble.

"What?" Tonto asks.

"Nothing," I reply.

The table is set with fresh flowers. I wonder where they got them. I look at the same spiffy peach-colored tablecloth, dishes, and silverware that would be on my table at Molly's Bistro. It makes me homesick. I introduce Trenton to head waiter, Dante Essen, who pulls out our chairs and unfurls our napkins with a flourish and places them on our laps.

Tonto starts to walk away.

"Please join us," I call.

Tonto turns. "I don't usually sit with guests," he says raising his eyebrows.

"Please, I insist."

Tonto sits.

Zee Pope comes with a warm basket of popovers, pesto toasts, and my favorite cheese twists. I introduce Zee to Trenton.

"Zee could pass for Carmella's brother," Trenton says.

Zee turns his head. "Talking to me?" he asks.

"You look like the police chief," Trenton says.

Zee's eyes widen. "Police? Did I do something wrong?"

"No. You just look like the chief."

I pick up a knife and run my finger over the sharp blade.

Tonto says, "They were recently sharpened."

I put it down.

"Where did all the restaurant supplies come from?" I ask.

Tonto says, "Interplanetary Foods does all the ordering for all their restaurants. Everything was here when I arrived. I think they were shipped from the restaurant supply company your restaurant uses."

"Do you have a receipt?" I ask.

"In my office in my files."

"Why do you ask?"

"I was just wondering if anything was missing."

"Missing? Like what?"

"Oh, a spoon, a fork. Maybe a knife."

"It would certainly be easy enough to count them."

"I know I'm being picky, but would you?"

"Sure."

I swoon when I put a cheese twist in my mouth. Trenton and Jersey devour the rest in the bread basket.

Tonto says, "I'll give you some cheese toasts to bring back to the hotel."

"That would be lovely," I say. "Thanks. Trenton doesn't know much about you. Can you fill him in?"

The veins in Tonto's neck tense. His eyes roam, seeking some diversion. Finally, he gives Trenton a half smile.

Trenton's eyes spin.

"Do you have to do that?" Tonto asks. "It's unnerving."

"Makes recording and processing faster," Trenton says.

Tonto looks away from Trenton and asks, "Why are you

recording this?"

"I'm writing software for my food printer."

Jersey says, "Trenton's been voted the voice of printed food on Twitter."

"I'll quote you as a source on my blog," Trenton says. "Extra Light's CEO is a fan, so I can live-stream it. You should be thanking me for the free publicity."

Tonto looks at me. "As I told Molly, I was hatched at the Valentine Hatchery and grew up in Valentine, studied advanced physics at Valentine University, but I was an average student, so I switched my major to business. I liked the restaurant business but didn't want to be a chef. What I liked was running a restaurant and dealing with people. I applied to Interplanetary Foods and was hired. I've worked on many worlds before landing back on my home turf."

"Why did you hire Herb Tarragon?" Trenton asks.

"He brought an astrological chart done by a descendant of Nostradamus that said the position of dwarf planets were in a favorable alignment with this job. And a letter from a Zen master said he could stir food with one hand while clapping with the other. When I threw the I Ching it said, "The man who stands before you is a superhero because when he turns his apron backward, it becomes a cape.'"

"What else can you tell us," Jersey asks.

"He could also look at a salt shaker and tell you how many grains of salt were in it. But really, it all came down to his cooking skills."

Trenton says, "Do you know if he had any enemies?"

"No. Nor do I know his friends. He lived alone. But everyone liked him."

Jersey says, "Apparently not everyone."

Dante and Zee come from the kitchen carrying a tray with three dishes. Dante says, "We didn't give you a menu because we decided to make one of your specials, Moonburgers on crispy

Saturn Ring potatoes with a creamy mustard/ketchup sauce. Was that okay?"

"More than okay," I say. "I didn't know you could get all the ingredients, but I see you can."

Dante and Zee go back in the kitchen.

Jersey says, "But the food at the hotel is so boring. And all we saw in Valentine were mostly fast food restaurant chains and automats."

Dante brings a pitcher of watermelon iced tea. He fills our glasses and goes back to the kitchen.

Tonto says, "Interplanetary Foods wouldn't have opened a restaurant here unless they knew they could get your ingredients. There are private farms that grow expensive produce and labs that cultivate stem cell animal parts. Some are in greenhouses above ground and some are underground. We get so little light; everything is artificially illuminated so it doesn't make much difference where they grow. They also scan plants to find beneficial genes that create rot resistant raspberries, blight-proof peppers, heat and cold tolerance plants. They barely keep up with the demand for quality food."

Zee Pope brings another warm bread basket and puts it on the table. The hot melted cheese rises from the cheese sticks. We savor the aroma and each take one.

Zee turns to leave. Trenton says, "A moment, Zee. What did you think of Herb Tarragon?"

"We didn't interact much."

"What was the last thing you remember about him?"

"He didn't tolerate anyone being late. He once gave Nebula…"

"Nebula, the sous chef," I say.

"Yes. Nebula once called to say that she was stuck on a tram, but when she arrived, he said that she should have left earlier."

"Well, nothing wrong with that," I say.

"Yes, but it was the way he said it. His response seemed out of proportion to the event. Chefs are artists. They can be moody and picky. He was."

I nod and remember troubles I had with my own chef, Mario Bugatti, when he started.

"Please tell Nebula we'd like to talk to her," I say.

It takes Nebula longer than I thought to come from the kitchen. She and Zee may be discussing the case, getting their stories straight. When she emerges she passes Tonto, their eyes meet. Have I hit on something? I let it pass.

Trenton says, "We're trying to get some background about Herb Tarragon. What can you tell us about him? You were his sous chef."

Nebula takes a visible breath. "I was late once. It was less than five minutes."

"Yes, he told us," I say. "Happens. What else can you tell us?"

"He was very exacting."

"Exacting?" Trenton asks.

"If you moved something a few inches from where he thought it should be, he became very nasty."

"So how does this jive with what Tonto said about everyone liking him?" I say.

"Oh, we did like him. He had a great sense of humor. But those of us in the kitchen were kept on our toes."

I say, "Am I mistaken, Nebula, but do you have an accent from Titan?"

Nebula smiles. "Yes. I grew up on Titan. I can trace my family back to its first immigrants. I went to Titan Culinary. I always wanted to be a chef."

Trenton says, "That's where Herb Tarragon went. Did you know him there?"

Nebula says, "A lot of people went there. No, we met here."

Trenton says, "He must have hired you?"

Tonto jumps in. "No, I hired Nebula."

Nebula turns. "I'm needed in the kitchen."

We question Dante, but he adds nothing new except to say Herb Tarragon seemed to smile even when he was saying something unpleasant. We comment on how lovely the restaurant is and hope it will open to the public soon and be successful.

Nebula comes back from the kitchen with Zee, who holds a silver tray. I immediately recognize one of my signature deserts: an Olympic Mons Soufflé.

"Wow!" I say. "It triples the height of what is made on Mars."

Tonto says, "The lower the gravity, the higher the soufflé."

Nebula turns to Zee and motions him to bring coffee. Then she takes two large spoons from her pocket and pierces the top and scoops some onto my plate. She waits while I taste it. "As good as the original?" she asks.

"After the food we have had in Valentine, a grilled cheese sandwich properly made would have been a gourmet treat, but this is outstanding."

Nebula beams.

Trenton says, "Can you tell us anything else?"

After a short hesitation, Nebula's eyes flash like she is considering adding something, but then she says, "No, nothing."

Jersey, Trenton, and I signal to each other to stop asking questions.

"Maybe we can find some answers if we go to the Hatchery," I say.

12

We return to the hotel. The concierge says, "I hope you don't mind, but sketching is my hobby. Here's some pencil sketches of you that I whipped up."

We look.

Jersey says, "These are wonderful—remarkable likenesses, such detail. Did you do them from memory? We never posed for you."

The concierge says, "Born with a good visual memory."

Jersey says, "Thanks so much. I'm going to frame it. You're very talented. Why didn't you get a job where you can use your talent?"

"So many are more talented. I think I'm average. But I'm glad you like them."

We head to our rooms. I say, "The concierge said that he thought his talent was average. That's similar to what that beautiful girl who worked in a car wash said when we told her she was pretty. That the painting I bought was very inexpensive compared to what I would pay on other worlds. Could talent on Pluto be as common as physical beauty?"

Jersey says, "I thought the barbershop quartet we heard were better than the Crewcuts, barbers from the 1950s on Earth who sang 'Shh-Boom Shh-Boom' while cutting hair, and protesting other things that go boom."

"It was 'The Cutlets' from 2080, butchers who were afraid cellular agriculture that made lab-grown meat would put them out of business," I say.

"And it did," Jersey says.

***

After a brief rest, Jersey, Trenton, and I have dinner in the hotel dining room. The room is dim and half filled with diners. Everyone speaks in low voices. Some sit alone.

Jersey says, "I wonder why they don't turn the lights up?"

"Probably to hide the hospital green paint that even hospitals don't use any more," I say.

I'm wearing my one nice outfit that I packed. Jersey notices. "You look lovely, Molly, and what a beautiful bracelet. Are the stones Uraniums from Uranus?"

"Yes, they are."

"They're the most expensive jewels in the solar system. How could you afford it?"

"I made a killing on Becky and Lois's college education."

"How could you do that? A college education costs at least a hundred thousand starbucks a year, even at New Chicago Community."

"Sold it short."

A call on my palm. "It's Cortland!" I say, smiling and turning sideways. "Miss you, sweetheart."

I listen and hear, "Miss you too. Yesterday I auditioned a group from Pluto. A nice coincidence that you are there now. They came to Mars hoping I would give them a Molawn Music contract."

"Are they any good?" I ask.

"So good they might replace Becky and Lois as the new number one. Don't tell them I said that or I won't hear the end of it. But before I book them here, I want to build suspense and interest by doing a live concert on Pluto. So…"

"So…"

"I'm coming."

"That's wonderful! Everyone, besides me, that is, hoped you would come."

Cortland says, "It will be a struggle to get Becky and Lois there, but I want to find other new talent and build a show around both groups."

"If you find music talent as good and abundant as the art talent I've seen, you'll have lots to choose from."

Jersey shifts in her chair impatiently, wriggles her nose. "Do I smell cheese twists?"

I reach into my bag and remove the cheese twists that Tonto gave me and give her two. "Shh," I say. "I'm not finished with this call."

Cortland says, "What was that?"

"I'm in the dining room with Jersey and Trenton. When will you come?"

"In about two weeks. Pluto has spiked interest ever since Interplanetary Foods announced that Molly's Pluto is opening in Valentine. A new and faster shuttle service has been added to the route."

I click my palm off. "Cortland and the twins will be here in about two weeks. I should have told him that Valentine's Band Box could use an upgrade. But no sense discouraging him."

A busboy hands us menus that we study.

A short time later, a waiter in a dazzling white jacket that fits him snugly approaches. He points to the cheese twists. "That is not on our menu. We don't allow food that our kitchen doesn't prepare. It could be unhealthy or worse, poisoned. Maybe a security breach."

"Cheese twists," I say.

"We're not responsible if you get sick. I have to remove them."

"They come from my restaurant, Molly's Pluto. Want one?" I venture weakly.

"No. I never eat anything that hasn't been analyzed by our

kitchen."

"Well, more for us," Jersey says, taking a crunchy bite.

He reaches to remove her plate. She grabs the cheese twists and shoves them in their mouth.

"Those should be savored," I say, putting my hand over my plate. "Not wolfed down."

Trenton and I make last gulps.

The waiter throws his shoulders back and gives us a look reserved for unruly children. "Would you like to hear today's specials?" he asks.

"Yes," I say.

"The special of the day is pasta with pasta sauce."

"I never heard of that," I say. "What kind of pasta sauce?"

"I bring the food, not make the food."

Jersey raises her eyes from the menu. "And how is the mock chicken prepared?"

"Try it. You'll see."

After dinner, I say, "Did you notice that all the food looked beige, including the chocolate ice cream?"

Jersey says, "Unimportant details."

"Didn't notice," Trenton adds.

Why did I ask, I think? Jersey and Trenton could live on food supplement pills and have Soylant on special occasions.

We leave the dining room and head toward the concierge because he would know about visiting the Hatchery. To the left is library with books.

"Not many places outside of museums that have real books. Let's check it out," I say.

We enter. A lovely young woman with bright hazel eyes greets us.

"I'm delighted you've come," she says, smiling. "So many do their business in Valentine and leave not realizing we have copies of rare books. If any of you are into fashion we have the only copy of *The Chronicles of Narcissism, Volume One: The*

Wardrobe."

We leave without taking any books and find the concierge.

"You'll need an appointment to visit the Hatchery. It is headed by Adam Kools whose family claims to go back to the dawn of time," he says.

"I didn't think they kept records that far back," I say.

"According to Adam Kools, the records are in a hollowed out asteroid in the asteroid belt. A copy was given to King James that became public record and a best seller. Adam Apple, his family's founding patriarch, mistakenly thought he could come and go from a garden he rented. But when he tried to come back, after living it up on the outside of the garden, the garden was locked with a sign that said, 'Paradise Lost.' In time, he made a new home with his wife Eve and opened a restaurant that specialized in barbecued ribs."

Trenton puts his finger to his forehead. "Accessing my data bank for dawn of time and barbecued ribs. Yup, a definite connection. One of man's first foods after apple pie."

Jersey rolls her eyes and says to the concierge, "Please make an appointment for us to visit the Hatchery tomorrow."

***

The next morning, we take the tram to the Hatchery. A few look-alike passengers enter and exit and don't acknowledge each other. Jersey says to Trenton, "See what we mean about similarities?"

Trenton nods.

We pass the Wholesale Market that is filled people pushing wagons filled with produce. Trenton sees the neon sign on top of Silicone Slings of a tipped oil can that looks like it is dripping oil. He blinks an eye cam.

Finally, we hear a bored-sounding automated voice. "Last stop, Hatchery."

"I hate those automated voices," I say.

"Sounds good to me," Trenton says. "It's a baritone."

"That's probably because you're an android and you empathize with it."

Trenton's eyes spin. "If you had android hearing, you could hear what I can hear. Compared to me, you're practically deaf."

We exit the tram. There are two signs. One points to the Hatchery. One points to a shoe outlet.

Jersey says, "I knew that woman on our last trip was going someplace good."

"How do you know she wasn't going to the Hatchery?"

"Maybe she was. But I bet she went to the shoe outlet first."

We see a smooth white building that covers a square block enclosed in an atmospheric dome glowing in the distance.

"I see no windows," Trenton says. "Do you see any windows, Molly?"

"You know I can't see as well as you, Trenton. You have telescopic vision. Stop pushing the envelope."

A sign points toward an enclosed roadway that connects the station to the Hatchery. We enter. It moves when we step on it. The air is as fragrant as mowed grass. We breathe deeply and look through the roadway's clear covering at a dim, barren landscape.

We stop in front of a metal door. A guard holds a pole that looks like a weapon. We don't ask what it is. He looks at his palm. "You're cleared to go in. You're in our database. You were all scanned after you landed at the spaceport. All visitors are scanned."

Jersey narrows her eyes. "We should have been told beforehand that we were being scanned. It's an invasion of privacy."

He shows no emotion and motions for us to proceed.

13

ADAM KOOLS WEARS A BLACK turtleneck and black and white striped pants. I've seen so many good-looking people on Pluto, and Adam is no exception. "Welcome to the Hatchery," he says. "Come to my office, and I'll answer your questions as best I can."

We follow him down a long, well-lit hallway filled with pictures of Mr. and Mrs. Pluto and Miss Solar System, beauty winners. He turns to me. "We consider you a celebrity, Molly. When will that great restaurant open?"

"You must have heard that our chef was murdered."

"Come on now, no one is murdered on Pluto. Yes, we have accidents, but murder? Safest planet in the solar system. We like to think we've evolved beyond that."

None of us say anything. I think of the experience Jersey and I had when we visited the lake, but I say in my cheery restaurant voice, "I think we'll have a new chef soon."

Adam's office is large, bright, and windowless. I scan the walls and ceiling but can't find the source of the light that makes the peach-colored walls and ceiling glow. It illuminates us in a flattering way. The small circles under Jersey's eyes have disappeared; her cheeks are rosier, her mouth pinker. Trenton's skin-color, which sometimes seems a bit off, looks natural. I assume I look better too.

We pass Adam's large brown desk in the center of the room and go to a corner with a sea green sofa, three matching chairs and a Lucite coffee table. It's far nicer than the furniture in our hotel or in Valentine's stores. Hanging on one wall are pictures of animals I have never seen.

"What kind of animals are they?" I ask.

Adam points to each one. "The Komodo dragon, the northern rhinoceros, the Barni dolphin, the Rodrigues fruit bat, a lemur called the aye-aye, and the kakapo—largest fattest least able to fly parrot. All former endangered species, mostly from Earth. We developed them from their almost lost DNA. Now they're no longer endangered."

Jersey says, "That's something to be proud of."

Adam smiles.

A beautiful woman with large blue eyes and dark hair down to her thin waist enters holding a tray with a coffee pot, a plate of macadamia nut chocolate chip cookies, and a bowl of blueberries with whipped cream. She wears a name tag that says, "Sarah Fifty-eight." I admire a sweater she wears. "Is your sweater cashmere?" I ask. "It's beautiful."

She smiles. "No, Wooly Mammoth, another revived species. Their underhair is softer than the underhair of goats used to make cashmere. We just opened a gift shop. Would you like a coupon for the Rodrigues Fruit Bat? We're running a special. Buy one and get one free." She places the tray on the coffee table in front of the sofa, adds three gift coupons, smiles a blinding smile exposing perfect teeth, and leaves the room.

Adam pours the coffee. We each take a cookie and spoon blueberries onto our plates.

"These cookies are a lot like the ones I serve at my restaurant on Mars. Where did you get them?"

"We make them here," Adam says. "Someone who visited Mars brought back a box, and our scientists analyzed them and created the recipe."

"You hardly need a scientist to make these," I say putting mine down suspicious of what they're made of.

Jersey watches. "If you're not going to finish that, Molly…" I push my plate toward her.

Adam says, "Most on the inner worlds don't realize there are more than seven thousand dwarf planets the size of Pluto in the Kuiper belt. Not all of them are round; maybe Sedna, Eris, Haumea, and Makemake are, but certainly not others like Doc, Grumpy, Sleepy, and Bashful."

"New to my data bank," Trenton says eyes spinning as he touches the side of his forehead.

Adam smiles. "Plutonians love our independence and don't feel we have to share everything with The United Council of Planets. And certainly not until they upgrade our 'so called' dwarf planet status." He leans toward us. "Now, what would you like to know?"

"There are so many beautiful and talented people on Pluto," I say. "How is that possible?"

"We've prioritized the genes that develop talents and physical beauty."

Jersey says, "But we couldn't help seeing so many people look like each other."

Adam shifts in his chair and crosses his right leg over his left. "Pluto is sparsely populated and it is difficult to attract colonists. We get tourists but few colonists. Cloning is an easy way to boost the population."

Trenton says, "Why not increase the android population?"

"We have. But regular unaltered humans didn't want to become a minority—fifty-fifty is okay, but not more. How much do you know about cloning?"

"Not much," I say.

"Nothing," Jersey adds.

Adam says, "Clones can happen naturally—identical twins are just one of many early natural examples. Or they can be made in the lab."

"So, my twins, Becky and Lois, are clones?"

"Not exactly but the process that made them is similar to

cloning. They are natural clones. Plants, fungi, and bacteria all use it. The blueberries you've eaten reproduce by cloning."

Jersey and I put our spoons down.

Adam says, "Many people first heard of cloning when Dolly, a sheep, was cloned in 1997. Then China successfully cloned two long-tailed macaque monkeys. It took a while, but eventually humans were cloned."

We listen and say nothing.

Adam continues. "Twins form very early in development when the embryo splits in two in the first days after egg and sperm join. Each half of the embryo continues dividing on its own, ultimately developing into separate, complete individuals."

"My identical twins certainly have different personalities," I say. "I've refereed my share of teenage arguments."

"But they are genetically identical," Adam says. "The DNA may be the same, but DNA isn't everything. A pile of things goes into making a person and their personality, like the physical environment and social interactions, and randomness even plays a role into what genes do what where."

He continues, "The first pet cloned was a cat called Copy Cat, and she didn't even look like the cat she was cloned from, because the genes controlling her fur color were used randomly."

I say, "So the clone isn't an exact replica a but just sort of has the same starting point, then goes off and becomes a unique person after that."

Trenton says, "And you create that process in an artificial womb?"

"Artificial? Nothing is artificial. We say, 'alternative' womb."

"What about the disproportionate number of beautiful and artistically talented people?" I ask.

"We don't think they're a disproportionate number. Who wouldn't want to be beautiful and talented and live on a planet filled with other beautiful, talented people?"

"How do you do it?" Trenton asks.

"We use a genome editing technique that goes back to the twenty-first century called CRISPR-Cas9 to modify genes. The letters stand for Clustered Regularly Interspaced Short Palindromic Repeats as the repeats can be read the same way backward as forward. They are repeated several times but separated by unique sequences."

Jersey claps her hands. "Sounds like a dance—Do the Crispr."

Adam says. "There is certainly some kind of genetic rhythm. Molecular-scissors are used to cut and paste genes. Now we are finally able to use it to create disease-resistant wheat and rice, make biofuels and remove lethal gene defects from egg cells."

"Might there be a Crispr-Cas 10 that could make your IQ jump twenty points?" Jersey asks.

Adam smiles. "That's actually not a bad question. We're still working on that one. Lots of room for improvement. But you may like to know that one of our scientists wants to add it to chocolate and call it a Crispr-Crunch Bar.""

"As long as it doesn't ruin the chocolate," I say. "There is no bad chocolate. There are only some chocolates that aren't as good as others."

Trenton taps his forehead and says, "You're quoting the great twentieth century geneticist, Dr. Raymond Chandler when he said, "There is no bad whiskey. There are only some whiskeys that aren't as good as others.""

Adam continues. "It was truly a golden age of genetics. In fact, historical records say that in the twentieth century, Professor Cole Porter wrote a paper called, 'I've Got You Under My Skin.' A revision was made later by doctors McCartney and Lennon because the skin couldn't contain two people. McCartney and Lennon went on to publish their own work called, 'I Want to Hold Your Cloned Hand' that reinforces the three classic building blocks of the universe: sex, drugs and rock and roll.

"Ray Stevens, scientist and singer whose groundbreaking song 'I'm My Own Grandpa,' became the linchpin for proving conclusively The Unified Field Theory. Stevens won Grammy and Academy Awards; both awards more prestigious than the Nobel Prize.

"But to give credit where credit is due, Dr. He, a doctor in twenty first century China, believed…"

"Doctor He?" Jersey jests. "Are you sure it wasn't Dr. She?"

Trenton says, "Cool it, Jersey. His name is actually Dr. He Jiankui. A report in The New York Times on December 1, 2018, says Dr. He believed he could be China's Einstein."

"Sounds just like you, Trenton," Jersey pipes.

Trenton frowns, thinks about what she says then raises his eyebrows and smiles. He continues. "Dr. He founded two genetic testing companies: Direct Genomics and Vienomics that used gene sequencing for medical purposes. They had a 'do first, debate later' approach that is attributed to creating the first genetically altered human babies."

Jersey says, "But isn't that illegal?"

Adam shifts in his chair, pours more coffee, takes a big sip. "Ethical concerns prompted legislation about human cloning on several worlds, especially Earth. But Pluto is not one of them."

"Sounds like Pluto is the wild west of medical research," I say.

Adam raises his eyebrows. Says, "Let's just say, we get things done."

"Do people from other worlds that don't allow these procedures come here for these procedures?" Trenton asks.

"All the time. It's a major business. Would you like to see a holo about those who grew wings so they can fly or those who grew gills so they can breathe under water?"

Trenton raises his hand. "No need."

"But," Jersey asks, "how do two people who we see as obvious clones not see similarities?"

"Some do. Parents decide if a repellent should be added into the amniotic sac so clones see minute differences exaggerated. If parents don't want the repellent added, we don't add it."

Jersey asks, "The woman who brought the coffee wore a name tag that said Sarah number fifty-eight. Does that mean that there are fifty-seven more Sarahs like her?"

"And possibly at least fifty-seven more after her. She could pick any name if she liked."

"Why didn't she?" I ask.

Adam says, "Some want the kinship, of family, of identity within a group. You might like to get tickets for the Clone Symphony Orchestra. Everyone looks like Leonard Bernstein. Their rendition of Gustav Holst's The Planets, that originally didn't include Earth and Pluto, now does."

Trenton says, "We saw people who looked like Jersey and Molly. How was it possible to create someone that looks like them so fast? They've not been here very long."

"We have bodies with undifferentiated characteristics ready for finishing touches."

Trenton brightens. "The only way I could survive my life-threatening accident years ago and avoid becoming a brain in a bottle was to become an android. I've enjoyed the advantages of not worrying about a carbon-based body, but even if one of my original cells survived, this might offer a viable alternative."

Jersey puts her hand on Trenton's arm. "I love you the way you are, sweetheart."

"Would you like to see one of the labs that does a few of the procedures?"

At first, I think no. Then, as I think, who knows what this Crispr can crisp? Maybe it could evolve into a cooking technique like sous vide or become instrumental in creating crispier crackers that don't get stale and soggy, Trenton jumps in with, "Love to."

We enter a long white room. Young bodies in all sizes lie on tables. Adam introduces one of the doctors. She is, as expected, beautiful, with a small straight nose, large blue eyes, and long auburn hair. Adam says, "These people are from Mars and are not familiar with our work. Tell them some of the ways we use Crispr."

She says, "One way is to fight disease. Much of this was developed years ago, but we have made significant advances. Drops can be put in ears and gels and creams applied to the skin that attack diseased genes while leaving healthy cells intact. Drinkable or edible Crispr is an alternative to traditional antibiotics, especially when there is so much resistance to antibiotics and many bacterial infections became deadly."

Another doctor adds, "We also use skin grafts or skin patches. Great needle-free way to manage what remains of diabetes. Then there's ex vivo gene therapy. We remove certain cells, apply Crispr, culture them in a lab, and then put the edited cells back into the body."

Trenton says, "I'm a little familiar with some of this."

Adam replies, "Yes, but our experiments go further than those on other worlds as scientists here aren't afraid of being persecuted for unethical practices."

The rest of the tour is fascinating, but I'm relieved when it's over. Seeing rooms filled with bodies lying on slabs and body parts and strange colored things growing in unusual-shaped bottles unnerves me.

Trenton and Jersey, on the other hand, love it and are energized.

<h1 style="text-align:center">14</h1>

WE SIT QUIETLY ON THE TRAM back to the hotel looking at everyone in a different way. Jersey smooths her hair with her hand as two beautiful blond women enter who look like each other and head to opposite ends of the car. When we pass the stop with the wholesale food market, Trenton says, "I want to interview as many as I can here later. Herb Tarragon came to this market several times a week. And, someone might have seen something."

"If they'll talk," I sigh.

Trenton says, "I was wondering if there is a black market for 'designer babies'. Not hard to transport them off planet. Almost no one would question an attractive person with handsome children."

Tonto calls. I listen, then disconnect. "Tonto says Lucky Luciano will arrive tomorrow. I want to greet him."

"We should all meet him," Trenton says.

"You just want another free kale and okra smoothie," I say, half seriously.

We go to our rooms. I sit on my sofa and check my palm for messages. There is one from an "unknown sender." I know I should not click anything from an "unknown sender," but I'm too curious. So, I do.

Immediately, vibrating pixels from a smoky looking holo forms in front of me that obscure the sender's features. A simulated-sounding human voice says, "This is a warning for you to stop trying to find out what happened to your chef, Herb Tarragon." The holo's pixels disintegrate.

I call Jersey and Trenton and tell them what happened. Trenton is so upset that Jersey has to spray him three times with WD 4000.

***

The next day we come to Molly's Pluto for lunch. Jersey brings a tote bag.

"What's that for?" I ask.

Jersey pats the bag and says, "I'm taking out dinner to eat in our room. Do you have a better idea, or do you want to keep purging on salt, sugar, cholesterol, and ingredients we can't pronounce from the hotel's dining room?"

"I should have thought of that," I say.

She gives my arm a light punch. "That's why we make such a good team, Molly." Tonto introduces Lucky, who is in the dining room. I introduce Jersey and Trenton. Lucky wears his chef's uniform. Despite surgery to make him less handsome, I think my husband Cortland and most men in the solar system would love to look as good as Lucky.

I smile and say, "You worked so well with my chef on Mars. Mario was sorry to lose you. But we're so glad you're here."

Lucky smiles. "I was hatched on Pluto. Nice to be back."

After a fresh Cobb salad, a seafood lasagna, and apple sorbet adapted from the famed chef Steve Jobs' cookbook, Jersey says she wants take out dinner for four.

"But there are only three of us," I say.

"What's dinner without leftovers, Molly?"

Tonto says, "You told me that you would like to visit an underground farm. I can arrange that."

"Yes, but later," Trenton says not saying more.

***

We go back to the Twilight Zone.

"Any thoughts?" I say.

"Can't wait to eat this dinner," Jersey says, pointing to her bag.

"I meant thoughts about Lucky?"

"He seemed nice, and we know he can cook," Jersey says. "I wonder if his family influences him. Their reputation goes back a long way to Earth. But now instead of crime, the family owns a chain of Luciano-Gambino Pizza parlors."

"I know. Several have opened on Mars and other worlds." I say. "It was rumored that a thumb was found under the tomato sauce. Others said it was a toe. Just a rumor. Could be spread by the competition."

Trenton says, "Isn't Cortland's cousin the owner of Little Green Man Pizza?"

"So...?" I ask.

Trenton says, "Nothing personal. Just an observation."

"Very circumstantial," I mutter.

Trenton continues. "After our tour of the Hatchery, we said how easy a black market would be for designer babies."

"But anyone can go to a hatchery and program a child," I say.

Jersey says, "But maybe not for those off-planet."

We enter the hotel. Jersey asks a front desk attendant if a table can be brought to their room.

"What kind of table? Round? Square? Wood? Plastic? Metal? If it's metal, what kind of metal? Tin, aluminum, steel, iron composite..."

"Doesn't matter. Just something the three of us can eat on."

"We only bring tables with room service."

"We don't want room service. We just want a table."

"I need to know the purpose for the table."

"I have some take-out food, and we want to eat it on a table."

"We don't allow take-out food in this hotel. No room service, no table."

Trenton says. "Let me see a room service menu."

The attendant reaches under his desk and brings out three room service menus. Trenton scans one quickly and orders.

"How did you know that's what we wanted?" I ask.

"Did it matter? We're not eating it."

Overhearing the attendant says, "If you don't eat it, you will never get room service again."

Trenton says, "Did you know I'm here as a representative from Mars Yard?"

"Wouldn't care if you were Red Berets from Solar Flair. Hotel rules are hotel rules. We have our standards! We have our reputation!"

Trenton reaches into his pocket and pulls out fifty starbucks. "Would this help?" he says.

"Maybe."

Trenton pulls out another fifty.

The attendant smiles. "What time do you want that table, sir?"

15

THE NEXT DAY I ASK, "Should we first go to the wholesale market or check out an underground farm?"

Trenton says, "If we go to a farm, we might learn how produce is distributed and have better questions to ask when we go to the wholesale market. I've done research on underground farming. It has a long history."

I groan, anticipating a lecture as interesting as an in-flight magazine.

"Make it brief, Trenton," Jersey says. "Not everyone finds what you think interesting is interesting."

Trenton huffs. "In the twenty first century, in Linköping, Sweden, the first vertical greenhouse was developed."

Jersey says, "Like a skyscraper for plants?"

"Exactly. It was called the Plantagon Greenhouse."

"'Plantagon?' Funny name," I say. "Do they drive tractors? Or do they fly helicopters?"

"No tractors, no dirt, no sunshine. They use nutrient solutions and artificial soil on vertical supports. An automatic irrigation system, monitored and controlled humidity, temperature, breeze, artificial light. Mars has lots of them now."

I say, "I know about that, but on Mars, they're above ground. When did they go underground?"

Jersey sighs, motions for Trenton to speed it up.

Trenton continues. "In 2015, the Earth's first underground urban farm started selling herbs and salads grown in London in unused World War II bomb shelters."

Jersey says. "Bomb shelters? I can't believe they sheltered bombs. Some people can make a business from anything. Like selling ice to Eskimos."

"Do you think I should ask Tonto to come with us?" I say.

"Good idea," Jersey pipes. "We might learn more."

***

A few days later, Tonto accompanies us to one of the underground greenhouses.

We take an industrial elevator three hundred and twenty-five feet down. As soon as the elevator opens, we see a cavernous space that is as lofty as a cathedral filled with vertical plants. Dampness rises. Mist and humidity and the wonderful fragrant smell of fresh growing produce engulf us.

"Feels like Pluto turned inside out," I say.

A dark-skinned attendant with bright blue eyes wearing blue jeans covered in a clear covering who looks like he's in charge approaches. "Welcome to one of Pluto's salad bowls. My name is Ozymandias. You can call me Ozzy."

I look down at his feet. "Look, Jersey," I say. "Do you think his feet are clay or they're just covered in clay?"

"I think they're clay."

We wipe our faces drenched in moisture.

"Would everyone like an airconditioned suit?" Ozzy asks.

"Yes, please," Jersey says.

Trenton steps back and raises his hand. "Not me. I've adjusted my inner thermometer and am very comfortable."

"And for you, madam? You're breathing deeply."

"Actually, I'm enjoying inhaling this atmosphere. I've not felt humidity since I left Earth years ago. It reminds me of a time my school class visited the Amazon River Valley museum. But since we'll be here for a while, I better take the suit. Can the temperature be adjusted so I can feel some humidity?"

"No one has asked that before. But if that's what you want, I'll have one adjusted." He taps instructions into his palm, then leads us to an air-conditioned room where we get our suits.

Unlike the tour of the Hatchery, this tour is fun and beautiful. Continuous lighting produces accelerated plant growth. There are long rows of red tomatoes, green zucchini growing vertically like Christmas decorations, purple eggplants, oranges, apples, plus the usual and unusual hybrids like garlic potatoes and naturally grown candied sweet potatoes. Off to one side, a strange green glow comes from a dark area. "What's over there?" I ask.

"Fungi that glow in the dark. There are about a hundred thousand species but only about eighty of them have bioluminescence emitting a green light. It's nearly the same chemical reaction that illuminates the belly of a firefly or the skin of a squid, but the light is constant in the mushroom, not on-demand as in some insects or marine animals."

Tonto says, "Can you show us the area where the most advanced genetic testing is done?"

"We don't include that on our tours, unless you're a professional in the food business."

"Molly is a professional in the food business," Tonto says. "And Trenton is head of forensics at Mars Yard."

"And I'm his wife," Jersey pipes.

"You'll need to change into stronger insulated suits. We're developing products that expel poisonous gas as they grow but don't absorb poisons and thrive in poisonous atmospheres. There actually are many things grown in atmospheres poisonous to humans. On Earth, in 1986, a cave in Romania was discovered that was isolated for 5.5 million years. At the bottom was a lake whose water was filled with carbon dioxide and hydrogen sulfide."

"Yuck, hydrogen sulfide stinks like rotting eggs and burnt rubber," I say.

Jersey clutches her throat and sticks out her tongue.

Ozzy continues. "Despite no light and a poisonous atmosphere, the cave was crawling with life: scorpions, woodlice, and centipedes. Food came from a frothy foam sitting on top of the water containing millions of bacteria who got their carbon from carbon dioxide just like plants do."

Trenton says, "They can't use photosynthesis like plants because there's no light."

"Right. The bacteria use energy from chemical reactions like the oxidation of sulfur ions into sulfuric acid, the oxidation of ammonium into nitrate and the oxidation of carbon. The methanol bubbles through the cave waters and becomes food."

"I'm trying to understand this," I say. "Bacteria in the cave get all of their nutrition from methane or carbon dioxide?"

"Yes. And there are at least eight types of bacteria that eat electricity. There are also shape shifting Archaea, a group of organisms who have no nucleus that can chain together into wire-like cables."

Trenton says, "If we discover intelligent life living in these conditions, can you imagine what they'll look like?"

Ozzy says, "We've also come a long way manipulating poisonous things so they are no longer poisonous. For example, hemlock used to be a poison. When Socrates Vineyards manipulated the carignane grape, a long despised French grape, in the twenty second century because it was bitter and acidic, they found the side effects not only became an antidote to hemlock, but it created a wine that is now more popular than Merlot. They called it Merlock."

"And it's much more expensive than Merlot, which I think is just as good," Trenton adds.

"We could buy one bottle and try it," Jersey mumbles. "Scientists manipulated the grape that produced that wine for years before they were satisfied with the results."

We exchange our light suits and are helped into heavier ones.

We walk on a narrow hallway until we are in front of the first of two airlocks. We're scanned, our vitals displayed and recorded, and our suits checked for punctures. When the all clear sounds, we hear the hissing of the atmosphere change to one that is poisonous. Then we enter a second airlock that checks our suits again, displays the atmospheric composition, and sounds another all clear. We take a step down when we exit the airlock and wind our way through marked pathways.

Ozzy says. "Lots of slime molds. Everything is in its infant stage."

Trenton says, "Might look like what early life on Earth was like."

After a while, Jersey says, "Mud and slime are not very interesting."

Ozzy says, "It is if you were a scientist. Want to go on or have you seen enough? The rest looks almost the same."

"Enough," Jersey says.

"Enough," I say.

"Definitely enough," Tonto adds.

"Don't I have a vote?" Trenton says. "I think we're leaving too soon. We haven't examined the subtleties in the slime and in the mud."

"Not a big fan of subtleties in slime and mud. Are we Jersey?" I say.

"Give it up, Trenton. You're outnumbered." Jersey says.

We turn and retrace our steps. We walk to the airlock. Ozzy pushes a button next to it. He takes a step up and enters. I pause and turn and take a last look. Ozzy extends a hand to Tonto, then Jersey, and then Trenton, and they get into the airlock.

As I take a step, the door starts to slide closed. "Hey," I yell. "Hold that open."

Trenton tries to help Ozzy, but it slides from their hands and clicks shut. Ozzy pushes the controls. Nothing happens. Ozzy's voice booms in my helmet. "Should just be a moment, Molly.

You have air for half an hour. I'm going to let the others enter the airlock and wait for you outside."

The airlock door opens from the other side and Tonto, Trenton, and Jersey go in.

"Help never takes more than a few minutes to come," Ozzy says, voice sounding a little less certain.

"You mean this has happened before?"

"Well, actually no. The door did close once when it shouldn't have, but it opened again immediately."

I wait. After a while, I see a blinking sign on my sleeve that says, "Danger. Ten minutes of air available."

"Hey, you said I have a half hour of air. The suit says I only have ten minutes!" I cry, banging on the door.

Another five minutes pass. "I have five minutes of air," I scream.

Four, three, two…

The door opens. Ozzy extends his hand and yanks me in. I'm shaking but alright. Ozzy helps me to the dressing area and helps me remove the protective suite. Then we go into his office. He opens a refrigerator removes fresh mangos and a pineapple; cuts them into chunks and blends them into smoothies. When I say I could use something stronger, he retrieves a bottle of tequila from a cabinet and adds a generous shot of it to our drinks. I never learned why the airlock door wouldn't open as it should. But, after drinking our second round Jersey, Trenton and I definitely feel better. And I can't wait to ask Tonto a few questions.

16

I'M RELIEVED TO GET BACK to the hotel.

I say to Jersey and Trenton; "I'm calling Tonto to ask if he knows why with all the wonderful fresh food we saw growing, why is the Twilight Zone's food so terrible."

Tonto's holo flickers into existence. "It's because it's cheap, and they can get away with it. One doesn't come to Pluto to dine. When Interplanetary Foods hired me, they said that Pluto's chamber of commerce begged Titan Treats to open one of their food mall courts on Pluto. But they declined and said to call back when Pluto had more people because now it wasn't cost effective. Those who make money on Pluto usually go into mining or things related to mining not dining."

Trenton adds, "Pluto is also a haven for loosely regulated stocks, bonds, and money funds. And there's lots of inexpensive storage space where no one asks questions."

Jersey chimes, "It's also a haven for unregulated science projects."

"Common knowledge." Tonto shrugs. "Nobody cares."

"So how come Interplanetary Foods wants to open a restaurant like Molly's Pluto? It's an expensive high-end gourmet place," I ask.

Tonto says, "They know it's a risky investment, but Molly's Bistro is a recognized name even out here in the Oort Cloud. Plus, it would be opening in a place with no competition. But more importantly, there are people with lots of money on Pluto who are tired of traveling elsewhere for a great restaurant meal."

Jersey says, "Yeah, hiding out."

"Hiding out or not hiding out, they have to eat," Tonto answers. "Those who can afford it have their own chefs. There is also lots of entertaining at private clubs where the food is fresh and delicious. Those people would be delighted to come to Molly's Pluto."

***

We go to the Wholesale Market mid-morning. It's teeming with bustling throngs who pinch, poke, and sniff the edibles. In addition, there are stalls that sell pots, dishes, and cutlery. There are also cooking demonstrations and book signings.

"Don't get distracted, Molly. We're here to learn about what happened to your chef, Herb Tarragon, not to shop," Trenton says.

"I can do both. Like walking and chewing gum," I say.

Trenton continues. "The holos that I got from Police Chief Carmella Soprano show that he was killed between the stall that sells jackfruit and dragon fruit.

"Jackfruit," I say showing off to Trenton, certain it's something he doesn't know. "On Earth it was native to southern India and is a cousin of the mulberry. It's the largest tree-borne fruit. Never walk under it when its fruit is ripe." I look at my palm and turn to my right. We're right near the stall that sells it. "Look. There." I point. Then I turn. "And opposite is the one that sells kiwis and red-skinned dragon fruit."

I introduce myself to the jackfruit salesman. "I'm the one who is going to open Molly's Pluto in Valentine. You may have heard about it."

"Heard rumors," he says looking at me suspiciously. "What about it?"

"My chef was found near your stand with a knife in his back. Did you see anything?"

"First time I'm hearing about it. Must have been my day off."

The more we ask him about the incident, the less we learn. We turn and walk to the salesman who sells dragon fruit. He says similar things.

We wind our way through various stalls stopping and sniffing along the way. I say, "I smell chocolate."

Trenton points. "It's coming from over there. Must be an area for desserts and sweets."

We follow the scent and find an area with tables laden with all kinds of sweet treats. "We should have started here," I say.

Jersey buys a jelly apple and a bag of gummy bears. I buy a pound of assorted chocolates.

Trenton walks towards a stall that sells Android treats and bargains the man down for a bag of oily munchies.

I point. "Is that Zee Pope?"

"Hard to tell," Jersey says. "So many people look alike. I mean, they look alike to us. Let's see where he goes."

Zee walks toward the area that sells cutlery. He stops at a silverware stall; talks to a salesman who leaves then stands behind the counter and straightens a few items. He looks up. "Molly!" he says, eyebrows arching in surprise. "What do you think of the market? Can I show you some of our products?"

"How come you're working here?" I ask

"Being a busboy is steady work, but I could use the extra money. Tonto recommended me for this job. Actually, I love to sing. If I could make a living from it, I would be a singer. But now, the pay is very low."

I think of the lovely painting I bought for such an inexpensive price. I also think of Cortland coming but say nothing at this time about the possibility of Cortland hearing Zee sing. Instead, I look down at the case that has two levels. "Lots of beautiful silverware." I point to some oversized spoons.

"Jupiter scoops. Big seller," Zee says.

"And what's in the case below?"

Zee hesitates.

"Probably the bargain stuff," Jersey says.

"Let's see," I say.

Zee pulls out the drawer. There are patterns from some restaurants that I recognize like those from The DeMilo Arms on Venus and the Seabreeze Inn on Neptune. Then I freeze. There's the silverware used at Molly's Bistro.

"How did you get that? That's my silverware pattern."

Zee hangs his head. "It's a copy of a copy of a copy," he says. "Big seller."

"If I can't tell the difference, no one else can either," I say. "Let me feel that." I point to a fork.

Zee removes the fork. I take it and run my fingers over it. "Something's different," I say.

"It's silver plate not the sterling silver you use at your restaurant."

"But it's heavier than silver plate."

"They weight it so it will feel like sterling silver."

"Do you pass it off as sterling?"

Zee bows his head. "We say it's silver with a rare metal found on Pluto's moon Hydra."

"Is it?"

"I don't ask questions. Would you like to buy one?"

"Yes. I'll compare it to the real thing."

Zee removes one from the case, puts it in a yellow bag that says "From Molly's Bistro", and hands it to me.

"Does Tonto know you're selling this?"

"Of course. I don't understand why you're acting like we're ripping you off. It doesn't come from the same place you order yours. And it doesn't cost you anything."

"Not in money, in uniqueness."

Zee looks confused.

I sigh. "I guess Pluto has an alternative definition of 'ripping off'."

17

I CALL TONTO. "I'm meeting with Lucky," he says. "He's anxious to start."

When I ask Tonto about Zee selling copies of cutlery at the wholesale market, he tells me that he thought that was common knowledge and asks why it should matter. Other restaurants whose copies are sold say imitation is the sincerest form of flattery and those copies are good advertisements for their restaurants. He asks, "How is that different from selling little copies of Lincoln's horse Fourscore, who won the Gettysburg Derby, or the copies of Magna and Carter's Statue of Liberty?"

I disconnect and turn to Jersey and Trenton. "The knife we saw at the police station might not have come from my restaurant. I never held it when we were there, so it may have been one of the copies."

"That opens other possibilities. Let's take another look at that knife," Trenton says.

We go back to the police station.

Carmella Soprano sits at her desk pushing buttons in the air that only she can see and squinting at several screens. She looks up and smiles when she sees us. "Find anything new?" she asks.

"The wholesale market sells copies of silverware from various restaurants," I say.

"So? I use my copies of the DeMilo Arms' every night."

"Could I have another look at that knife you got out of Herb Tarragon?"

She motions to an assistant who brings a box with the knife. She opens it.

I pick it up. Then I take the copy that I bought at the wholesale market from my bag and lay them side by side. They look identical.

Carmella takes both knives puts them behind her back, rotates them a few times then puts them on the table. "Now pick up the original," she says.

I hold them both rotating them from hand to hand. Then I say, "I think it's the one in my left hand."

Trenton says, "Wrong. I can see it's the one in your right."

"How can you tell the difference?" I ask. Trenton says, "My vision goes from infrared to ultra violet. I just did an infrared scan that indicated that the one removed from Herb Tarragon's back was coated in a substance invisible to most eyes but not mine. Police on most worlds use these scans to keep "evidence straight. Isn't that right Carmella?"

Carmella nods. "Yes. That's exactly what our infrared scan showed."

Trenton adds, "And unfortunately this doesn't prove anything."

***

We head back to the hotel. "There's an Automat," I point. "Let's get coffee."

The automat is a brightly lit with rows of vending machines on the walls. "My treat," I say, sliding into a booth.

I palm pay for three coffees and three cinnamon donuts.

"How did you know we wanted cinnamon?" Jersey asks.

"You and Trenton always order cinnamon. What would you have ordered?"

"Cinnamon," Jersey says.

"With copies of silverware so easy to get, maybe the silverware at Molly's Pluto is not sterling. Someone could easily have switched them, and no one would know," I say, "unless they had reasons to be suspicious. Let's go back to Molly's Pluto and take a knife and bring it to Carmella to test. But I don't want anyone to see me take it."

Jersey says, "You're not good at that, Molly. I'll do it."

***

Trenton pushes the door to Molly's Pluto open. Deliveries are being wheeled through a side door. People are cleaning and polishing things that look already clean and polished. Some tables are set. I hear Tonto, who is standing in the back of the dining room, talking to the staff, most of whom were not here the last time we were here. Zee Pope catches my eye and waves, as does Dante Essen, Nebula Veil, and Lucky Luciano.

Tonto catches my eye and stops talking. "Molly!" he calls. "Welcome! You couldn't have come at a better time." Heads turn as he introduces me. Then he introduces Jersey and Trenton.

Jersey excuses herself to go to the bathroom. It's near where tables have been set. I point to boxes that are being delivered in an opposite direction and ask Tonto questions about what's in them to distract him while Jersey gets a knife. When Jersey returns, she smiles at me and pats her purse. I know that somehow, she has taken a knife. I wonder if I ask for a knife as a souvenir would I get a sterling silver or one that is silver plated.

Tonto ends the meeting. Lucky tells me how excited he is to be head chef. He is joined by Dante and Nebula who also say that they can't wait for the restaurant to open.

Then I say to Dante, "I would like to take a piece of cutlery home as a souvenir because I may not remember later when I'm leaving and packing. A spoon or a fork from the stock room is OK. I don't want you to disturb those tables that were just set."

Dante goes into the stock room and comes out with a spoon. "He's left handed," Trenton whispers.

When we leave, Jersey says, "Why did you ask for a spoon?

We need a knife."

"A knife might arouse suspicion. If someone replaced the real silver cutlery with silver plate, either all the cutlery on the tables would be silver-plate or all of silver. Not a few pieces different from the rest."

Trenton says, "They may have a few silver settings in stock, so if anyone asks, they can bring out the real thing."

"As Dante might have just done," Jersey says.

We return to the police station.

Carmella paces up and down so full of nervous energy that when she touches several things she makes little electric shocks. "This had better be good," she says.

"We want to see the knife again," I say.

"Which one? The one removed from the body or the one you brought?"

"Both," I say.

Carmella motions to Aida to get them. Aida brings them and lays them on a table.

"Jersey has a knife that she removed from a place setting at the restaurant."

Jersey takes the knife and lays it on the table. I take the spoon from my pocket and put it next to it. "This spoon is from the restaurants' stockroom," I say.

Carmella says, "And you think someone at the restaurant might have taken most of the sterling and replaced it with cheaper silver-plate." She turns to Aida. "Test these," she snaps.

Moments later, Aida returns saying that the knife from the table was silver-plate.

"And who gave you the spoon from the stockroom?" Carmella asks.

"Dante Essen, the head waiter."

"Did he bring out a silver-plated spoon like those on the table?"

"No. The spoon he brought was sterling silver."

18

"PROVES NOTHING," TRENTON SAYS. "But I would like to know more about Dante."

Jersey pipes, "Let's go for lunch."

Trenton frowns. "Not so fast. I'll do a search on him and the others and send it to Mars Yard."

"And lunch?" Jersey asks. "Lunch?"

"Brought nutrition supplement pills," Trenton says.

I say, "We can grab a bagel at Square Bagel.'"

"Is 'square bagel' an oxymoron?" Jersey asks.

"Love that word, oxymoron," I say. "It sounds stupid, but you have to be smart to know what it means."

***

When we return, Trenton is downloading information. His eyes are slack and lid-blinded.

We wait for him to finish. Finally, he blinks. His eyes clear. Jersey smiles and puts her hand on his arm. "Learn anything new, sweetheart?"

"Dante, Nebula, and Herb all went to Titan Culinary College."

I say, "But Nebula told Tonto when he hired her that she didn't know Herb Tarragon."

"Well, I found a yearbook holo of Herb and Nebula holding hands and smiling at each other." Trenton clicks his palm and projects the holo.

I look. Nebula is more attractive in the holo when she was younger, and her red hair fell to her shoulders rather than pulled back in the bun she wears at the restaurant. "She and Herb look pretty cozy," I say. "I wonder why she didn't want us to know?"

Jersey says, "Maybe she didn't want to be implicated. What did the reports say about Dante?"

Trenton projects another holo. Dante is standing next to Herb. He comes to the height of Herb's chest. His head is turned upward looking at Herb, whose arm is around him.

"They also look pretty cozy," I say. "Dante didn't mention that he went to Titan Culinary."

Trenton says, "If you don't ask the right questions, you don't get the right answers."

"So," I say, "The three of them knew each other in the past. But we don't know how well."

Trenton says, "We know that Nebula knew Herb Tarragon from the holo, but she may not have known Dante. We also know that Nebula is a Titan native. She has a distinctive Titan twang. It's almost impossible to fake. On the other hand, Dante and Herb were both Pluto natives and could have known each other before."

I ask Trenton. "What about Lucky? Wasn't he was working at my bistro on Mars when Herb Tarragon was killed?"

Trenton says, "I'll palm Mars Yard. They have access to Mars arrivals and departures."

We wait longer than I thought for an answer like watching water freeze into an ice sculpture. Finally, Trenton says, "Lucky boarded an express rocket back to Pluto at the time Herb Tarragon was killed. Says he went to his father's funeral."

I say, "That's legitimate."

Jersey says, "It is, but it's also a coincidence that he was there at that time."

"He could have done both," Trenton says. "When he got back to Pluto, he realized that with Herb Tarragon out of the way, he could be in line to become the new chef."

"Still circumstantial," Jersey says.

Trenton says, "Maybe Carmella will add more. I'll palm her."

Carmella's holo forms. She stands, frowning, her left hand on her left hip. "I could have given you that information. You didn't have to go through Mars Yard," she huffs. "I have more, that is, if you're interested."

I whisper to Jersey, "We really pissed her off."

"Do you want my input or not?" Carmella snarls.

"Please," Trenton says.

Carmella knits her brows. I think of a spinning coin that is that is neither heads nor tails. "Zee Pope comes from Cthulhu Regio along Pluto's equator. He has other jobs besides being a busboy at Molly's Pluto and selling copies of silverware. He works for a catering company that I use when I entertain. They always have him sing. His voice makes teenage girls scream and rip their clothes off."

Trenton asks, "And Nebula Veil?"

"Titan native. Attended Titan Culinary College. Her family runs a large underground farm on Titan and has a controlling interest in one of Pluto's underground farms."

"Thanks Carmella," Trenton says. "Very helpful."

"Professional courtesy. Don't use it all up." Her pixels fade.

Jersey says, "Do you think Nebula and Lucky planned to end up together?"

Trenton says, "Let's get lunch at Molly's and find out."

***

Lunch starts with a mousse made from potons, a vegetable that combines the best of onions and potatoes. It's sprinkled with cumin and hazelnuts followed by a tartare of Enceladus' scall-pops and oysters and a chick-squab breast, smaller than a chicken's but larger than a squab's, glazed with rhubarb and blue apple slices.

I pass on dessert but have coffee. Two small pieces of chocolate sit on the saucer next to the cup. Jersey and Trenton have strawberry and raspberry shortcakes.

When we tell Dante and Nebula that we saw holos of their yearbook and found evidence of them knowing Herb Tarragon at Titan Culinary, Nebula says that although the holo looked as though she and Herb were in a very involved relationship, it was superficial and brief, a regretful embarrassment. She didn't think it worth mentioning.

I ask, "Anything else you didn't think worth mentioning?"

Nebula lowers her head, says nothing.

Dante, on the other hand, says that he did have a long relationship with Herb. He didn't mention it because he was in a new relationship and didn't want his current partner to learn about it and be jealous.

Jersey says, "And those things are more important than solving his murder?"

Dante lowers his eyes and says nothing.

Tonto comes from his office. "I've finally got a great staff again. I hope nothing happens and we can move ahead as planned."

I smile and say, "From what we just ate, Lucky and Nebula make a great team. That was delicious. Did Lucky ever meet Nebula before they worked together?"

"Ask him yourself." Tonto nods to Zee who is clearing the table. Tonto points to the kitchen. Zee turns, goes into the kitchen and returns with Lucky.

"Have you ever met before working here?" I ask.

"No, we haven't," Lucky says.

We leave.

While we are walking, I see several people whiz by on skateboards. Jersey says, "I would love to ride one of those back to the hotel. Wouldn't you, Trenton?"

Trenton nods.

"Not me," I say. "I'm out of practice."

"Come on, Molly, don't be a spoilsport," Jersey says.

We walk to the corner where there is a rack of skateboards. I watch while they insert a few starbucks and remove two of them.

Jersey looks at me and says, "Last chance, Molly."

"No way. I prefer to walk."

Jersey puts her skateboard down and pushes off. Trenton follows her and waves.

I go several blocks, peering into store windows. Suddenly, I feel something jam into my back. A voice says, "Act natural and nothing will happen."

Two men wearing black baseball caps pulled down near their eyes stand on either side of me. I have never seen them before. The one on the right says, "Keep walking."

"What do you want?" I ask.

Silence.

"Turn left at this corner," the other says.

I turn and see a car. "Get in," he says.

"I'm not getting into any car with people I don't know."

I feel pressure on my arm followed by seeing intermittent blasts of light. I collapse like a puppet whose strings have been cut. The world rolls into darkness.

19

WHEN MY EYES FINALLY FLUTTER OPEN, I'm lying on a bed in a white room with no windows. I'm wearing a flimsy blue hospital gown open from the back. I wonder how technology could advance so much over the centuries yet make hospital gowns in the same style as worn by the pharaohs, the secret rumored to be buried in a pyramid somewhere near Mount Sinai hospital.

I struggle to stay awake, but my eyelids are heavy, so I close them and fall into darkness. When I awaken again, I feel for my pulse. Tap. Tap. Tap. It's there. I have a smashing headache. My mouth is dry. I lick my lips trying to bring moisture to them. There's talking in the distance, but I can't make out the words. Something's wrong, but I don't know what. I feel more discombobulated than a caveman clutching a raw turkey drumstick who was suddenly transported to a Baskin Robbins finding a cone of rocky road ice cream in his hand.

Is it possible that I dropped through a portal to another world? I shiver and pull the light covering over me tighter.

The door opens. A man and a woman in white lab coats enter and stand next to me. "So glad you are awake, Ava," the man says, half smiling. "My name is Dr. Bliss, and this is Dr. Hatch. How do you feel? Are you ready to get out of bed?" Dr. Bliss asks.

I realize I am holding my breath waiting for a signal for a better sense of myself. It doesn't happen. I exhale. "I feel fine," I say. "But I don't remember my name being Ava." I roll on my side and push myself up so I can put my feet on the floor.

The hospital gown separates in the back, making me more uncomfortable.

"Steady now, Ava. What do you think your name is?" he asks.

I think. I wait. I think harder. "I don't remember," I say. "But I'm sure it's not Ava."

Dr. Hatch says, "Would you like another name?" She scrolls on her palm. "Alice is available. So is Sarah." I don't respond. She continues scrolling like an optometrist flipping between lenses to find the right one. "How about Lisa, Nora, Paige, Dolly…"

"I think it's Dolly. But I'm not sure."

"Dolly it is then," he says nicely.

"How did I get here," I ask.

"You fell and hit your head when you went to a spa with two friends. But you're fine now," Dr. Bliss says. "How much do you remember?"

"Nothing."

Dr. Hatch says, "It's not unusual for people who were in the type of accident you were in to experience amnesia. When we get you into your old routine and back to work, you should adjust quickly. Do you remember what kind of work you did?"

I think hard. Then, I say, "I think it had something to do with food."

The doctors look at each other and nod.

Dr. Bliss says, "You were a chef at the Chocolate Tower right here in Cthulhu Regio."

"That's along Pluto's equator, isn't it?"

"Yes," Dr. Hatch says. "See, you're already remembering. Now that you're awake, two of your friends and co-workers would love to see you. Do you think you're up to seeing them?"

"Co-workers?" I ask.

"Yes," Dr. Bliss says. "Chocolate Tower is a new restaurant opening nearby. You were helping set it up."

"Is it from Mars?"

"What gives you that idea?" Dr. Hatch asks.

"Something about Mars seems familiar," I say.

"Well, lots of good things come from Mars," Dr. Hatch says. "Nice planet."

"I remember a culinary institute that made Chocolate Moons candy," I say.

"That's right." Dr. Hatch nods. "Love them myself." She reaches into her pocket and pulls out a box of Chocolate Moons. "Here. Want one?"

The minute I put the Chocolate Moon into my mouth, I'm certain something's wrong. But I don't know what. "Delicious," I say. And say no more.

"Ready for visitors?" Dr. Bliss asks, eyes gleaming.

I nod, unsure of the sound of my voice.

Two women enter. I take a deep breath and stare. I feel like I'm looking through the wrong end of a telescope. They look exactly like me. The word "clones" floats to my consciousness. I force a smile that I hope doesn't look forced because the muscles in my back have knotted up.

Dr. Bliss says, "Do you remember Tina and Amy? You were all hatched with them right here at the Cthulhu Regio hatchery. They called an ambulance when you fell."

I don't remember, but I think it best to continue smiling. I say, "I think so."

"We're all anxious for you to get back to work, Dolly," Tina says. "Everyone missed you. No one makes Olympic Mons soufflés as good as you."

The words Olympic Mons soufflé jogs a memory. "Did I learn how to make them on Mars?"

Tina laughs. "You were never on Mars." Amy adds, "Even as a child, you were obsessed with learning how to cook, especially how to make chocolate desserts, Dolly."

I nod, not wanting to show any emotion. I feel light years away from where I should be, but I don't know where that place is.

Dr. Hatch says, "If you're up to it, Dolly, we can discharge you from the hospital immediately. Would you like your friends to take you home?"

Not knowing what else to say, I say, "Yes, I would love to go home."

***

I enter an apartment. Music is playing. I hear a scratchy voice singing, "Hello Dolly, Hello Dolly, this is Louis, Dolly, it's so nice to have you home where you belong."

I say, "Please turn that off. The words bother me."

The music stops. I look at a room I never remember seeing before. The bright living room has lots of fluffy chairs. There is a dining room, a kitchen, six bedrooms, and three bathrooms. Four more women who look like me greet me. "We missed you so much, Dolly," one says. I'm unnerved that they look like me and I can't tell them apart.

I'm shown to one of the rooms that has pictures of me standing with the others at what looks like a school graduation. There are more of us holding flowers dressed in formal clothes. "Remember that day, Dolly?" another says.

I think it best to say, "Of course I remember."

20

FOR THE NEXT TWO DAYS, I spend time getting to know my clones. They won't let me see the news because they said that the doctors told them I should only spend time in stress-free environments. We eat at local restaurants, get our hair and nails done, watch some holos, and rest.

On the third morning, one says, "Do you feel up to going to the Chocolate Tower? We're behind schedule since you were in the hospital. But now that you're back, I'm sure we'll catch up."

The Chocolate Tower is a few blocks away. There is a large sign that gives a date for the grand opening the following week. We go into the kitchen.

"Go ahead, Dolly," one says. "Make your famous Olympic Mons Soufflé."

"It's strange. I remember Olympic Mons Soufflés, but I feel a little rusty."

"Take your time," one clone says, smiling a smile that looks like it could be chipped off with a chisel and makes me feel nervous until she reaches into her pocket, pulls out a box of Chocolate Moons, and offers me one. When I taste it, the memory of me being a restaurant owner, not a restaurant chef, hits me like a moon pie. But where was that?

I make an Olympic Mons soufflé. It falls. I make a second and a third. Same thing happens. "I think I better make something else," I say.

"Try a Chocolate Decadence cake," another says.

But when my cake is pulled from the oven, the texture is leaden and there isn't enough sugar. "Must have lost my touch," I say.

"Don't you remember the recipes?" one asks.

"I know the ingredients, but I can't remember the techniques."

"We were counting on you to share those recipes with us. We hope to build a franchise, based on them," another says.

"I remember how to make chocolate chip cookies. I can make some now."

"Good start, Dolly. Maybe it will jog your memory." She removes a bowl from a cupboard and points to a shelf with ingredients.

When I pull the first batch from the oven, the aroma of dark chocolate permeates the room.

One clone takes a warm cookie and eats it. "These cookies will be a delicious preview until you remember how to make your other specialties."

***

On opening day, the Chocolate Tower team is inundated with people whose mouths are watering in anticipation of the opening. Cthulhu Regio media sends a team to holograph the event that will be broadcast to all stations on Pluto. I stand in the middle of my sister clones holding a large platter of chocolate chip cookies. One clone steps forward and says, "We want to thank Cthulhu Regio media for giving us this opportunity to tell their viewers about Chocolate Tower. Today we have a special on Dolly's Chocolate Chip cookies. But stay tuned for news of our Olympic Mons Soufflé and Chocolate Decadence cake."

There is a rush on the cookies, which sell out immediately.

"See, you haven't lost your touch, Dolly," one clone says, running her finger over leftover crumbs.

"And at least the Chocolate Tower opened and we have

cookie orders for a month," says another. "And we got great publicity. Pluto Media is rebroadcasting our opening all day. I've never been on Pluto media before." I wonder if we'll all become celebrities?

***

The next day, I'm in the kitchen of Chocolate Tower scooping chocolate chip batter on to baking pans when I hear a commotion out front. I peek through one of the double doors that separate the kitchen from the selling area to see what's going on. I think I recognize the two people making the commotion, but I'm not sure.

I hear one of my clones say, "If you didn't come to buy cookies, I insist that you leave."

"Not until we find our friend, Molly," Jersey snarls.

"There is no Molly here. But our wonderful head chef is named Dolly."

"Then, we are not leaving until we meet 'Dolly'," Trenton says.

Hearing that, I push the swinging doors to the kitchen open and emerge.

"My name is Dolly," I say.

Jersey peers closely and says, "I am sure you are Molly."

"How can you be sure?" I say. "I'm not even sure."

Trenton says, "First, when we saw the program about Chocolate Tower, all of you looked like our friend Molly."

One clone sneers. "People who are not from Pluto—and you're obviously not from Pluto—think lots of people look alike."

Trenton continues. "We noticed that you all used your left hand to wave." He points to me. "But the one you call Dolly used her right hand. I want to see everyone's pinkies."

"That's ridiculous," one says putting her hands behind her back.

Jersey says, "Our friend Molly had a scar on her right pinky from removing a tattoo. Hold out your hands, or I'll call the police."

Everyone holds out their hands. Trenton and Jersey look. No one else has any scars on their pinkies. Jersey grabs my hand and pulls me from the group. "You're not Dolly. You're our friend Molly."

"I'm not sure," I sputter.

"See, she agrees with us," one clone snarls.

Jersey hands me a box of Chocolate Moons. "Eat as many of these as you can. Now!" she yells.

"What does that prove?" I ask.

"Just do it," Jersey urges.

By the time I finish the box, a cloud has moved from my mind. "Jersey! Trenton! Jersey! Trenton!" I shout, then burst into tears.

Jersey says, "We're taking you home, Molly. That is, back to the hotel in Valentine."

"But what about the chocolate chip cookies?" one clone says. "You gave us the recipe. Can we continue to make them?"

"I guess so," I say.

"Don't be so nice, Molly. You were kidnapped. I'm guessing that they also altered your memory," Jersey snaps.

"Yes. But they didn't do it."

Trenton says, "But they were probably in on it."

I pause and look at the clones. "Tell you what, I won't prosecute, and you have to give me credit for the recipe. But the name must change from Chocolate Tower to Molly's Chocolate Chip Cookies, and I'll have ninety-nine and forty-four one hundredths percent ownership."

Everyone agrees the offer is generous.

"I'll get a lawyer to draw up a contract," I say.

"And in the meantime?" one asks.

Trenton snarls. "You're closed."

<h1 style="text-align:center">21</h1>

JERSEY, TRENTON, AND I COLLAPSE on the sofa in my room.

Jersey says, "That was a close call. We were sick with worry. Carmella was reluctant to put out a missing person's report because she said most people turn up on their own. Good thing we saw the announcement about the Chocolate Tower on the media. Cortland keeps calling and wants to talk to you. He and the twins will be here soon. We told him that you hit your head and sleep a lot but you're alright. He told me that he has a bad feeling that there's something nasty in the woodshed and wonders if it has something to do with the case we worked on together a few years ago about Avery murdering his boss on Mars."

"I clearly remember that," I say.

"Well," Jersey says. "Cortland told me that he worries that Avery might want revenge for us solving the case and getting him sent to a prison on Pluto. Call Cortland immediately and say you just woke up, which is sort of the truth."

Trenton helps me reconnect my palm that had been disconnected when I was in the hospital. Then I palm Cortland. He sounds very relieved to hear my voice. I reassure him that I'm fine. I mention that the acoustics at the Band Box, Valentine's concert hall, sound primitive, like twenty-first century ones and hope the girls won't be upset performing there.

Cortland says, "Already did research on the place. Maybe I can chalk up renovations as a business expense. I'm sure an upgrade should attract new business to Pluto and increase Molawn Music's visibility in the Oort Cloud."

"Wonderful idea, if you can do it. Pluto has strange laws and regulations unto themselves."

"Know that too. Spoke to lawyers at Shark and Shark and got advice."

"Okay. See you soon. Hugs and kisses. Bye."

"Holographic hugs and kisses don't count, Molly. But good enough for now. Love you. Bye."

There is a knock on the door. The same waiter enters pushing a dolly laden with fried chicken, sweet potato fritters, and a green and purple salad that he tells us that Tonto has sent from Molly's Pluto. This time, he is smiling.

Noting his expression, I say, "Why the changed attitude about having food the hotel didn't make?" I ask.

"Tonto sent the hotel staff a tray of lemon custard moon tarts and a tray of asteroid cream puffs," he says unfurling a napkin and placing it on my lap.

Carmella calls Trenton. Her pixels crystalize. "Everyone is glad you're safe, Molly," she says. "We questioned your clones and they knew nothing about who was in back of this. They were paid to befriend you and get you to reveal how your best desserts were made so they could learn to make them. Each was promised part ownership in a Chocolate Tower franchise."

"Were they from the Cthulhu Regio hatchery?"

"They matured there. Once a hatchery has the DNA, it can be sent to other hatcheries to mature. Lots easier than transporting a baby. It's Pluto's standard procedure to scan visitor's DNA at the spaceport when they arrive. We consider it a security precaution in case something happens to you. In fact, your DNA has been scanned several times. You were recently scanned again when you visited the Valentine Hatchery."

I sigh. "It's also an invasion of privacy to do it without telling people."

"Safety versus privacy: very delicate issue."

Trenton says, "Couldn't scan me. I'm an android."

Carmella says, "We have other methods for androids."

Trenton frowns.

Carmella says, "Many of Pluto's visitors are flattered that their DNA is used to make clones. Some keep in touch with their clones after they have left Pluto—like sending a birthday card."

I say, "I wonder who took my DNA."

Carmella says, "Someone who had access to those files."

I ask, "Would you say that most people on Pluto have a clone somewhere on the planet?"

Carmella says, "It's likely. But clone or no clone, we all lead independent lives. Most who have clones don't know where the others are. Now, our attention is on who kidnapped you and finding Dr. Bliss and Dr. Hatch."

Carmella's pixels dissolve.

Trenton says, "Are you up to talking about what we know so far?"

I nod. "Good idea. I feel weak but in charge of myself."

Trenton says, "Toronto Kim works for Interplanetary Foods and is a Pluto native. Nebula Veil, sous chef, comes from Titan. Head waiter Dante Essen went to culinary school on Titan with Nebula, and Zee Pope just quit his job and went home to Cthulhu Regio."

Jersey says, "Adam Kools, head of the Valentine Hatchery has your DNA. I wonder if others have your DNA. Carmella answered some questions but not all. She never volunteers information."

"I think Carmella feels we are giving her a hard time," I say. "When I worked with Mars Yard, I found the fastest way to a policeman's heart was through his stomach. After I brought the police chief my largest Chocolate Decadence Cake, his attitude improved. I'll call Tonto to tell Lucky to make one. We can pick it up on our way."

***

"What's this?" Carmella asks, eyes narrow with suspicion. Her nose wrinkles. "Definitely chocolate."

"It's a gift for you and your staff," I say.

"How did you know I love chocolate?"

I say, "Everyone loves chocolate."

Trenton says, "But now that I've become an android, Chocolate Motor-Oil-Slicks are more delicious."

Jersey and I look at each other and make a face. "Please, Trenton," I say.

"What did I say? What did I say?"

Carmella removes a switchblade from her breast pocket and slides her thumb forward over the release. A razor-edged blade emerges. She cuts with the ease of someone who had done this many times. The chocolate aroma rises and permeates her office. Everyone stops working. Then, like being drawn by a magnet, they come over to the cake.

Jersey says, "It's not just any chocolate cake. It's a Chocolate Decadence cake, a best dessert from Molly's Bistro."

"Molly's Pluto," I correct. "That is if we ever open."

Instantly plates appear, and Carmella slices the cake with the same speed that she cut the box and put slices on the plate reserving the largest for herself. Then she puts a large piece in her mouth, swallows, and smiles. Chocolate covers her upper lip. "How can I help you?" she says.

Trenton says, "I read a report about the incident but never examined the body. Can I?"

"Of course," Carmella says. "We want to show Mars Yard that we cooperate. The body is in space preserved in our space crypts."

22

Trenton downloads the information about what to expect at the space crypts in Carmella's office. He's ready to go.

Jersey, with a worried grin says, "I'm nervous, sweetheart."

"Nothing to be nervous about. As an android, if I shut most off my programs, I can survive without oxygen for thirty minutes. More than enough time for someone inside the station to send help."

"And if you weren't an android?" I ask.

"It would be about fifteen seconds for you to use up bloodstream oxygen. That is, if you don't hold your breath. Then you could perhaps survive for as long as two minutes. If you hold your breath, the loss of external pressure would cause your lungs to expand and rupture."

I exhale. Trenton looks at me. "You don't have to exhale now, Molly. You're not in a vacuum. But if you were, after that, your tissues would swell as water in your body vaporizes. You won't explode because human skin is strong enough to keep from bursting. If you're brought back to atmospheric pressure, your skin and tissue will return to normal."

"That's a big 'if'," I say, taking a deep breath and feeling air enter my lungs.

"A body without air in space would last for millions of years. Near heat, it would mummify; if not, freeze. If sealed in a space suit, it would decompose, halting any biological process but only for as long as the oxygen lasted. Low pressure would first boil off most of the water, and what was left would freeze."

Jersey says, "Would it be the same for you, sweetheart?"

Trenton says, "Similar. But I would last longer. Of course, the end result would be the same."

Jersey puts her hands to her head and sighs. She turns to Carmella. "Have many others examined bodies in space before?"

Carmella says, "Confidential information."

I say, "Seems like a good place to hide evidence, not just preserve evidence."

Carmella frowns. "My family does a good job with that station," she says out of the corner of her mouth.

"Your family runs that station?" I ask.

"Owns and runs it."

Jersey asks, "Isn't that's a conflict of interest?"

"We call it cooperation, not conflict."

"How many work the station?" Jersey asks.

"Two. But only one at a time. My cousin Igor alternates with his brother Stravinsky. No one else wanted what was considered a graveyard shift."

***

Jersey and I feel better waiting to hear from Trenton in Carmella's office rather than going back to the hotel. We are going to watch from a wall that projects his progress in three dimensions. So far, the wall is a blank milky white.

I say, "Stop pacing, Jersey. We're both nervous."

She sits. She stands. She sits. She stands.

Carmella presses one of the buttons on the wall and walks away. A moment later, the screen comes into focus, a voice booms, "LIVE FROM NEW YORK, IT'S SATURDAY NIGHT." Music blares.

Carmella rushes to the wall. "Oops," she says, rolling her eyes. "Sorry. My staff and I love watching reruns of that American Earth news show Saturday Night Live. Their historical insights tell it like it should be."

If looks could kill, Jersey's was about to.

Carmella pushes another button. The screen clears. Finally, Trenton fills the screen. He's exiting the police shuttle. Jersey jumps and waves.

Then the screen goes black.

"Now what happened?" Jersey cries.

Carmella looks up from her desk and says, "Momentary blackout."

"How momentary?"

Before Carmella answers, an image appears; the scene shifts. Trenton fills the screen again. He waves and says, "I'm peering through the window of the station. There must be hundreds of body pods here."

Suddenly another man's face fills the screen.

"Hi, Carmella," he says. "Nice to have a visitor." His voice drops. "Even though he's an android."

Trenton says, "I don't appreciate remarks that smack of prejudice."

"Just kidding. You're much better than nobody," he says teeth flashing.

Carmella says, "Trenton wants to examine the body of Herb Tarragon who was to be a chef in Molly's Pluto, a new restaurant opening soon. Trenton's with Mars Yard."

"Ooh, Mars Yard. Fancy, fancy. Where's Molly's Pluto? I've been living on rations that taste like stale shredded wheat."

I say, "Molly's Pluto is going to open in Valentine. If you help Trenton, I'll give you a gift certificate for dinner."

"Thanks," Igor says. He goes to his computer. White lights blink and stop. Then different colored lights do the same thing. Repeat. Repeat. Then they all shine together. Igor peers more closely. "We have a Herb Tarragon in area X section Y." He turns to Trenton. "When you get outside, hook your security belt onto the long yellow markers and punch in this number. It's 384958284794SKM7395867YP95849298490946737777777394. When you come to section X, turn right into section Y. Will you have trouble remembering that?"

"No problem. I'm android, remember?"

Igor huffs. Then he helps Trenton screw his helmet in place and checks his spacesuit.

Trenton steps into the airlock, waits, enters the second compartment. Waits.

The screen goes black again.

Jersey wails, "Now what?"

Carmella says, "You were supposed to fix the outer cameras, Igor. We only have audio."

"That was Stravinsky's job. I found a black bra with the initials PF floating in the bathroom. He may have taken Petrouchka Firebird with him. I'll call him."

After a long pause, Igor says, "Stravinsky told me that she came to help fix the cameras. She used the bra as a tool."

Carmella says, "Is that a fact?"

Igor says, "I think I can do it by using one of the bra hooks."

There is silence for what seems like a long time. Then Igor says, "Visual on."

We see Trenton in the second air-lock. There is a hissing sound that turns into a loud roar as the door opens to space and Trenton pops out like a cork from a bottle. The airlock door closes behind him. Trenton says, "Don't see any yellow markers, only red markers."

Igor says, "The color doesn't matter. It's the markers themselves. They all go from here to there."

Trenton says, "From here to where?"

"From here to out there."

Trenton hooks his security belt to the first red marker and punches in the code. The markers move forward, sliding Trenton with it.

After several minutes, we hear Trenton say, "I'm at a body pod that matches those coordinates. But four body pods light up: Herb Tarragon A, B, C, and D. Each contain identical-looking bodies. How do I know which body pod is the one I want?"

Igor says, "It's probably body pod A."

"What do you mean probably?"

"They're clones. If one is murdered, we retrieve any other of the clones who have died to see if there is anything that might help the investigation. You're lucky there are only four bodies. Sometimes there are more than fifty."

"Have they all been examined?"

"Let me check." Pause. "Nope. None have been examined. You can try to examine them there or you can bring them back into the station. You have air for one hour and fifteen minutes."

"I'll bring them back to the station."

We watch Trenton unhook body pod A and try to hook the extension wire onto one of the hooks on his belt, but the hook doesn't click in. He tries several times. Finally, it clicks. Trenton gives it a tug and then releases his grip. Body pod A floats next to him. Body pod B and C are easier and float behind pod A.

Trenton says, "So far, not hard." But when he hooks body pod D, his elbow nudges the wire that is attached to body pod C causing pod C to spin. Trenton tries to reverse the process, but it only makes the other body pods spin and twist around him.

Igor says, "I'll try to yank all of you to the station together. When you get close, I can cut each pod lose and haul it into the airlock. Then I'll do the same for you."

Trenton says, "Don't you think you should do me first? I'm the one with a limited supply of air."

Igor says, "It will be easier to get you this way. I don't want to risk you floating off in case something happens."

Then the holo goes black. Jersey jumps to her feet. "What happened?" she yells at Carmella.

Carmella says, "It's best you don't watch."

"How many times has someone drifted off?" Jersey sobs.

"That's confidential information."

23

Half an hour later, the holo projects Trenton and Igor inside the station bending over one of the bodies.

"See," Carmella calls to Jersey. "No problem."

Jersey wipes her brow.

Igor says, "Start with a scan, Trenton. If the first one fits the criteria, you don't have to go further."

Trenton says, "He's in body pod D."

"How do you know?"

"He has a knife wound in his back."

Trenton opens a case that he had brought and removes a small, sharp, curved tool and inserts it into the wound and moves it around. He removes it, shakes it twice. The handle lights up. "I have a reading."

"And that is?"

"The residue around the wound was made with a knife used to scrape chocolate curls for desserts. Also, the person who did this was left handed."

"How do you know that?" Igor asks.

"By the angle from the way the knife was inserted into the body. I'm doing more tests and taking more samples. I'll send the results back to Mars Yard for further analysis."

Carmella interrupts. "Don't you trust our scanners?"

"I trust them, but Mars Yard's are very advanced."

Carmella huffs. "I wouldn't be so sure about that. Our forensics are more advanced. They just called and said they want the body sent down to their laboratory."

***

At breakfast in the hotel dining room, I ask, "Is it a coincidence or a clue that the knife was used for scraping chocolate?"

"Clue," Jersey and Trenton say together.

Trenton says, "It might suggest that someone who worked in Molly's Pluto took it and followed Herb Tarragon to the market where they stabbed him."

"Carmella showed us that knife," Jersey says. "We knew it was a copy of the original knife made for Molly's Bistro. But we didn't know that it had a residue of chocolate. So, it wasn't washed and was probably used not long before Herb Tarragon was murdered. Of course, just having chocolate on it is not evidence. Lots of people could have used that knife to scrape chocolate elsewhere. In fact, Herb Tarragon could have used the knife himself and someone else picked it up. Call Tonto, Molly, and ask who made the desserts that day."

I call. "Tonto says it was Nebula. That puts her in the kitchen early in the morning and access to the knife. We don't know what happened between her and Herb Tarragon that morning. We know he could be difficult."

Jersey says, "If Herb was in the kitchen, he could have said something that infuriated her. If he wasn't in the kitchen, he may have called her and upset her. Either way, she knew he would go to the wholesale market. She may not have planned to take the knife but grabbed it in anger and went there to threaten him."

"All or any of the above," Trenton says. "By the way, Carmella did dust for prints but didn't find any."

Jersey says, "But she didn't dust for chocolate."

"Carmella doesn't think in chocolate," I say. "I do. Let's see what Nebula can tell us."

I palm Nebula, who my palm indicates is home. When her

holo materializes, I see people in the background, "Did I disturb you, Nebula? I see you're not alone."

"Hi, Molly," Dante Essen says stepping closer. "Just came to Nebula's place to discuss having a private party for one of my friends at the Twilight Zone. Didn't want to do it at work."

Another person steps closer. It's Adam Kools. He says, "I also came to discuss this party."

I say, "Why didn't you meet at the hotel and talk about it there?"

Adam laughs and says, "Those walls leak news."

Trenton says, "Nebula, we called to ask where you were on the morning Herb Tarragon was murdered."

Nebula pauses and says, "I was at the wholesale market that morning. But I went to get blue beefsteak tomatoes. They're much sweeter than the red ones, especially the tiny ones that are like blue cherries."

I say, "Anything else?"

Nebula says, "Who can go to that market without browsing and buying something you didn't plan on buying?"

"I can," Trenton says.

Jersey and I shake our heads.

"Did you walk where Herb Tarragon was murdered?" I ask.

"No, not unless the body was moved."

I disconnect. "Do you think she was telling the truth? Was saying 'moving a body' a slip of the tongue?"

"I was thinking the same thing," Jersey says.

"I wonder what Lucky will say about the blue tomatoes," I say.

"Blue beefsteak tomatoes?" Lucky says. "Never buy them. I break out in blue spots if I touch them! Like peanuts, a lot of people are allergic."

Jersey says, "So Nebula was lying?"

"No, not necessarily," I say. "She may have bought them and used them herself or given them to someone else. But if she bought them for the restaurant, she most likely paid on a restaurant expense account. Not hard to check on that."

"I'll have Carmella send me those holos. I believe I can do a finer analysis," Trenton says.

"But don't tell her that," Jersey says. "She doesn't like us being here and interfering with Pluto police procedures. She's sensitive about everything related to us. No need to put more than her nose out of joint."

I say, "Did you notice that when I said I was kidnapped because someone wanted to learn the secret of my recipes, no one, not Tonto, not Nebula, not Lucky, not Dante, reacted. In fact, everyone seemed to clam up. Don't you think that's strange?"

"Strange for Mars; maybe not strange for Pluto," Jersey says. "Do you think that others might be in on a plot to kill Herb Tarragon?"

I say, "Hard to know at this point. When I was abducted, my clones wanted to open a place that served desserts from Molly's Bistro. It was reasonable to think I knew the recipes. A restaurant such as Molly's depends on a team of specialists. Those who grill meats and fish usually don't always know how to make fancy desserts, and those who make the desserts don't know how to make all the sauces. The only one who knows how to make all the recipes with professional panache is the chef, Lucky. Could he be in danger?"

"Or could Lucky be part of a plot to take the recipes and open a restaurant independent of Interplanetary Foods?" Jersey asks.

I say, "My Mars Bistro chef, Mario, invented these recipes and has exclusive rights. He made the kitchen staff sign disclosure agreements. Lucky signed when he was Mario's sous chef. I know because I witnessed it. Many recipes are not hard for a skilled chef to figure out. But dishes like Golden Calf and Olympic Mons Soufflé are complicated and use special equipment. Did you know frozen nitrogen freezes alcohol?

Mario once showed me how he ladles liquid nitrogen on honey that coated molds. After the honey froze in the shape of the mold, he filled the honey shapes with ice cream."

Trenton says, "I can do that."

"But you didn't think of it," I say. "Mario's the cooking genius. He told me that secret to making fantastic burgers is to first slow-cook them to medium rare, then dunk them in liquid nitrogen to freeze a thin layer of the exterior and, finally, deep-fry them. The deep-frying creates a perfect brown crust and thaws the frozen layer but does not overcook the interior."

Jersey says, "I'll never make that!"

"I will," Trenton says with the authoritarian certainty of a dentist who says "open wide."

Jersey says, "It would be best if we spent more money on better ingredients. You can't make a silk purse out of a sow's ear."

Trenton smiles. "Gave you one on your birthday, sweetheart. You loved it."

Jersey frowns. "Made your point, Trenton."

"So where does that leave us?" I ask.

Jersey says, "Does anyone know why Zee Pope went back to Cthulhu Regio? That's an enormous place. So many cities: New Melbourne, New Sidney, New Perth, New Hobart…"

Trenton interrupts. "He lives in New Darwin. Just accessed his biography. I have an address."

I say, "What do we really know about him?"

Jersey says, "He worked at Molly's Pluto and sold silverware copies at the wholesale market."

Trenton says, "He looks like Adam Kools, who heads the Valentine Hatchery, as well as Carmella Soprano, but he says he's not related to them."

"As far as he knows," I say.

Jersey says, "He also sings and worked for a catering company that Carmella used."

"Maybe if I call Zee and say that Cortland is coming and he

could audition for him and get a Molawn contract, he'll be more forthcoming?"

"Wonder why he wanted to leave?" Trenton asks. "And when can we check out New Darwin?"

"I'll have lots of time after Cortland and the girls arrive and start rehearsing. Also, Tonto told me that Nebula did not charge the blue tomatoes to the restaurant account. She bought them for herself."

24

The Twilight Zone promises to upgrade me to a suite when my family arrives. I remember Nirgal Palace, the luxury hotel on the space station that circles Mars with its swimming pool that creates the illusion that you are swimming in space and where Becky was married. After being on Pluto, I could spend a month luxuriating there by getting a floating weightless massage every day.

Cortland calls and makes it very clear that he wants me to go home after he finishes auditioning singers and arranging a concert at the Band Box. He mentions for the second time that he's worried about Avery having it in for me because I helped catch him and send him to prison on Pluto for murdering his boss. He also hopes every mother who thinks her child is a wunderkind doesn't apply for a place in the show nor any three-headed singers, four-armed guitar players, or singing animals.

I tell him about Carmella's four officers who are in a barbershop quartet and would like a spot in a show and say that Carmella is very important being the head of Pluto police.

Cortland says, "I'm not coming all this way to put on a show with a barbershop quartet no matter how good they are. I'm looking for music that rocks the solar system." He pauses for a moment. "Wait, maybe there is a way they can perform but doesn't interfere with the spirit of the show. I'll let you know when I've worked out the details."

***

Cortland and the twins finally arrive and enter the lobby of The Twilight Zone.

Lois covers her mouth and whispers, "Are you sure this is Valentine's best hotel?"

"Checked them all and this is it. I'll treat you to a deluxe room at Nirgal Palace for a week after we get home."

Becky and Lois toss their long blond hair and eye roll each other. "Make that two weeks," Lois says.

"Who gave you those hats?" I ask.

Lois puts the red one on her head. It says, "Make Pluto Great Again." Becky puts the blue one on. It says, "Pluto for the Plutonians." Becky says, "We got them at the spaceport. There was a demonstration about the Pluto Constitution. The hats were free."

Cortland says, "There were groups that supported more cloning and others that wanted to restrict cloning. I thought the downgrade to Dwarf Planet cooled political activity."

"No," I say. "It only made it worse. Take those hats off, girls. You don't want to start riots."

A handsome bellhop approaches and slides the luggage onto an anti-grav platform. I watch the girls straighten up and smile. They walk on either side of him and can't take their eyes off him. Cortland and I follow behind. He brings us to two adjoining rooms on the top floor whose door is open between us. It's an improvement over my former room, albeit in excessively bland good taste. The girls say Mars Charity probably gives the homeless better accommodations. I sigh and say they're spoiled. Cortland doesn't care as long as the bed is clean and firm and the bathroom has a strong shower because he's exhausted from the trip.

Becky calls through the doorway from her room, "There's hardly any closet space."

"Most don't have much luggage because they don't stay very long," I say.

"Can see why," Lois says, her mouth a flat line.

Becky adds, "I hope I make it home for my wedding anniversary. I miss Burton."

Lois says, "We're only here because Dad dragged us here and says it would be good for our careers. By the way, did you notice how good looking the bellhop was?"

I laugh. "Get used to it, girls. What Pluto doesn't have in amenities, it makes up for with beautiful and talented people. Wait till you see the concierge; he's more handsome than that rock star, Mohamad Moons." I look at my twins and think, very pretty, but not blindingly beautiful as so many are on Pluto. I hope they won't be intimidated when they see how many are prettier.

Becky turns and says, "I'm going to the bathroom. I'm very tired and don't feel well." Lois remains. Soon we hear retching coming from the bathroom.

Lois says, "She started throwing up, halfway through our trip here."

Cortland says, "I didn't want to say anything until we unpacked. Can we get a doctor?"

"Trenton can do a scan," I say.

Becky comes from the bathroom. "I must have eaten something that didn't agree with me. Are you okay, Lois?"

"Feel fine," Lois says.

"Sweetheart, I would feel better if you let Trenton scan you. It would only take a moment. He and Jersey may have something that might make you feel better. If not, I'm sure the hotel has a doctor on call."

Becky says, "I would rather have Trenton than a doctor from this place. Call him."

Trenton and Jersey come in with two huge bags. "Thought you told me that Trenton was only going to bring the bare necessities to Pluto," I say to Jersey.

"He did," Jersey says.

Trenton says, "You can stand or sit, Becky. Whatever's comfortable. This will only take a moment and you won't feel anything.

Becky sits.

Trenton scans. Reads the scan. Then he scans again.

"Anything wrong?" I ask.

Trenton smiles, eyes bright. "I want to scan one more time. I keep getting a positive result."

Becky's voice quivers. "What kind of positive result?"

"You're pregnant! In fact, you're going to have twins."

Becky jumps up. "Pregnant? Twins? Burton and I wanted to wait another year before we had children."

Trenton says, "Doesn't always work that way."

"It does if you live on Pluto and have children through the Hatchery," I say.

"What's the Hatchery?" Becky asks. "Is it a place to buy eggs?"

"Something like that, depending on how you define eggs."

***

The next morning Cortland and the twins can't wait to get to the Band Box and start rehearsing because the sooner they do a show and have a recording ready to distribute to Galaxy Media, the faster they can go home. Becky and Lois are nervous meeting the two Plutonians who arrived a few days ahead because Cortland told them they were almost as good (rather than better) than they were.

I get a call from Cortland as soon as they're at the Band Box. "There's a line around the block waiting to audition. How did they know we would be here?"

"No secret you were coming, Cortland. The Plutonians must have told everyone you wanted to do a show with them and Becky and Lois. In fact, I met someone you should audition, Zee Pope."

I hear Lois calling into Cortland's palm. "Mom! When are we

going to go home?"

Becky chimes, "Mom, I'm pregnant. I miss Burton."

Cortland says, "These auditions are going to take much longer than I thought."

"In that case," I say, "I'm going to New Darwin with Jersey and Trenton. A former employee at Molly's Pluto moved there, and we want to ask him some questions. I'll be back tonight."

***

Jersey, Trenton, and I take a cab to the tram. Suddenly, the traffic slows until we stop. We hear shouting.

"Problem?" I say.

The driver says, "I forgot that today university students are having a protest march."

Jersey says, "What are they protesting?

"Protests 101, a required course. Who do you guys support?"

He takes out a red "Make Pluto Great Again" hat and puts it on. Takes it off and replaces it with a blue "Pluto for the Plutonians" hat. "Never know who's in my cab and I need the tips."

***

The tram to New Darwin is cramped and uncomfortable. We are offered nothing to eat or drink. Jersey says she wouldn't eat or drink anything they would serve. And that's saying a lot. She opens her mouth and pops in a nutritional supplement that she doesn't offer knowing that I usually refuse. She leans toward Trenton. "Thinking about something, sweetheart?"

"Processing information about New Darwin. It's near Elliot Crater on the eastern edge of Cthulhu Regio where a canyon and a crater meet. Beautiful place and it's booming. Lots of condos being built as well as a new art museum. The museum will draw big crowds because it's going to display a splinter from the true cross that was found floating in the asteroid belt etched with the words, 'True Cross made in China.' Also, I have to use a privacy setting because real estate agents would see that we're coming and would flood us with ads."

We exit the tram and step on a moving roadway. It's a relief to be out of the tram, smell the healthy odor of growing plants, see bright blue sky, and breathe fresh seventy-two-degree air, albeit artificially recirculated. I always marvel how the piezoelectric plastic that covers the domes is so clear it looks as though we are in open air, and except for the gravity and lack of clouds, it makes me feel as though I'm back on Earth on a very clear day.

People who came from places that had clouds and now live under domes, whose uniform light glows brighter toward noon and darkens toward night, all say the same thing. They miss clouds, even dark stormy nimbus ones. And although Titan has rain and sleet, it's made of hydrocarbons and is very cold so no one walks in it very much. And, needless to say, hardly anyone off Earth has ever held an umbrella or know what an umbrella is used for having lived in domed cities all their life.

We transfer to an automated seated walkway that goes to the center of New Darwin. An automated voice says, "If you wish to transfer to the north, south, or western domes, please push one of the appropriate buttons floating in front of you and your seat will move into the connecting roadway. If not, exit now."

The town square has colorful mosaic sidewalks, a large splashing fountain, and trapezoid- shaped buildings with cute shops on the ground floors and apartments with terraces above.

Jersey says, "I wonder if all new cities are like this. Valentine is so dreary."

Trenton says, "The oldest cities were built quickly and needed to be practical not beautiful. When urban problems eat up funds, beauty is a low priority."

"Or no priority," I say. We walk a little farther. "Look, a Darwin Diner. Let's go."

We enter and are shown to a booth with brown banquet seating on the right side. I sit and look around. On the opposite side, I see someone who resembles Zee Pope sitting with people who resemble Nebula Veil, Dante Essen, and Tonto. There is also someone who looks a lot like Herb Tarragon standing with his arms around two waitresses. I've learned not to jump to conclusions because there are so many clones on Pluto and I, like most not from Pluto, have trouble telling them apart.

Jersey says, "What are you staring at, Molly?"

"I think I see Zee Pope, Nebula Veil, Dante Essen, and Tonto on the other side of the room. I also think I see someone who looks like Herb Tarragon. He just sat down with the others."

"That's impossible," Jersey says. "Herb Tarragon is dead."

25

"Let's say hello," I say.

"I'll stay here," Trenton says, "and adjust my lenses and hearing. I may learn more this way. Besides, I want to record this."

Jersey and I saunter over. The waitresses watch. "Herb? Zee? Nebula? Dante? Tonto?" I looking from one to another. No one looks up.

The man who looks like Herb Tarragon raises his eyes and says, "Are you talking to us?"

I say, "Are you all from Molly's Pluto in Valentine?"

"Valentine?" the man who looks like Zee says. "Never been to Valentine."

"Me neither," says the woman who looks like Nebula.

"What's Molly's Pluto?" the man who looks like Herb Tarragon asks.

"You look like people we know in Valentine. Sorry to have bothered you."

We walk back to Trenton. "They must be clones," I say.

Jersey looks back over her shoulder. "They're getting up and leaving."

"Stop looking," I whisper.

We sit. Jersey says, "Strange that…"

Trenton puts his finger to his lips. "Shh, I can barely hear them."

One waitress approaches. She has chin length brown hair

flipped under with bangs. Her name tag says, "My name is April May." I wonder how her parents arrived at that name.

April says, "The special of the day is meatloaf with mashed potatoes. Any takers?"

"Just coffee," Jersey says. Trenton and I nod in agreement.

"Okay, three coffees. Anything else?"

Trenton says, "Please, you're interrupting me. I'm working."

"You must be a food critic if you think ordering coffee is work." She turns and leaves.

"Could you hear anything they said, Trenton?" I ask.

"I heard the man say, 'That was a close...' and then the waitress interrupted."

"Well, what are they saying now?"

"They're talking about building supplies, but they just passed out of range."

April returns with three coffees, two different pies, and a chocolate cake.

I say, "We didn't order dessert."

"I know. I decided to bring you a few complementary desserts because I saw you talk to some of our owners. There's apple and plum pie and a new Chocolate Nemesis cake."

Trenton asks. "What are their names?"

"Herb Tarragon, Tonto Kim, Nebula Veil, and Dante Essen. They told me that they are part of a group that bought the Darwin Diner. I think they also bought a few other places."

"Are you sure?" I ask.

April narrows her eyes. "Something wrong? They're big tippers."

I ignore her question, tap my palm, and display a holo of Avery Spelling. "Ever see him?"

"Sometimes. He comes in with the others. He's an enhanced person." I show her one of Lucky. "Nope, never seen him."

Trenton asks, "How did you know Avery Spelling is an enhanced person?"

"My brother had the procedure after a near-death accident. Become a brain in a bottle or become an enhanced person. Easy choice. He wanted to become a German Shepard, but that is still experimental and very expensive."

Trenton says, "I've never heard of that procedure."

April says, "Pluto has many things other worlds don't have."

Jersey says, "Some of Pluto's medical procedures are not considered ethical on other worlds."

"I had a rare genetic disease. It didn't manifest for twenty years; then it did. A hatchery could rebuild my genetic code, but it was a long, drawn-out process with possible unpredictable changes. Seeing how well my brother did, I decided to make the transition."

Trenton peers more closely at April. "You're the first enhanced person I've not been able to spot immediately."

Jersey and I zero in. "Amazing," Jersey says. "And is the other waitress also enhanced?"

"June May, my clone? No. She didn't have my genetic disease. Clones have many features in common, but there are many differences. We don't even have the same fingerprints. Twins don't you know."

I make a mental note. I never checked the fingerprints of Becky and Lois to see if their fingerprints were identical.

April turns and calls. "June, some people want to meet you."

June May comes from the kitchen. April stands next to her and smiles.

"Wow!" Trenton says.

April shrugs. Then she peers at Trenton longer than is polite. "You could certainly use an upgrade. You have so many old-fashioned features."

Trenton winces. Jersey defends. "And I think they're charming. Besides, upgrades are so pricey."

April says, "Pluto has the best and least expensive hospitals that do these procedures. People travel from everywhere to get them. Some clinics combine with luxury spas in vacation sites. You should consider it."

Jersey frowns.

April gives me the once-over. "More old people like you are getting the procedure because they want to live longer and it's not possible in an organic body that breaks down so easily."

She and June go back to the kitchen.

"I don't think I'm old," I say, frowning. "I'm not even close to one hundred, and I can be healthy until almost two hundred."

Trenton says, "But I can be healthy until three hundred."

We try our desserts.

"This plum one is delicious," I say. "Let me taste yours."

Jersey and Trenton cut small pieces that couldn't be smaller and still have flavor and put them on my plate. I put Jersey's apple sample in my mouth and run my tongue over it. Then do the same to Trenton's chocolate cake. "The apple pie tastes a lot like the pie served at my bistro, and the Chocolate Nemesis cake is almost as good, and I mean almost as good, as my Chocolate Decadence cake. I wonder where they got the recipes." I push my half-eaten plum pie away.

Jersey eyes my plate. "If you're not going to finish that, mind if I do?" I slide it toward her. She digs in. "What are you looking at, Trenton?"

"Looking at holos of Nebula Veil I took when we were at Molly's Pluto. I'm trying to see if there is something that could distinguish her." He pauses, cuts a piece of chocolate cake and pops it into his mouth. "Ah, in this holo, the she has two tiny piercing on her ears inserted with two small earrings. In the holo I just took, the person who might be her clone has three piercings, no earrings. But it only takes a few seconds to get a third ear pierce, and people change earrings daily." Trenton finishes his cake and adds, "We came to find Zee Pope. I have an address and number. I'll call."

We wait. No answer. He leaves a message saying we'll be

in New Darwin until the evening. Ten minutes later, Zee calls.
"Sorry I missed your call. Why are you here?"

"We wanted to talk to you and see New Darwin," Trenton says. "It's so much nicer than Valentine. Would you like to meet us at the Darwin Diner?"

There is a long silence. Then, "No. Not there."

"Why not?"

"Let's go to Silicone Slings. It just opened a branch here."

"We know the owner, Avery Spelling. Because he worked at virtual restaurant on Mars that was near Molly's Bistro. We visited him at the Valentine Silicone Slings near the wholesale market."

"No problem," Zee says.

26

Silicone Slings in New Darwin looks like the one near Valentine and the one in New Chicago, Mars. Trenton is pleased seeing his holo near the front door. Jersey puts her hand through and jiggles the pixels. "You're famous, Trenton," she says.

We are shown to a table. Zee eyes a waitress and orders three coffees and a large plate of poton chips.

"Love poton chips," Zee says. "Combines the best of fried onions and fried potatoes."

The waitress takes his order and says, "You're in luck. Avery is in town. I'll call him and tell him you're here."

She returns shortly with coffee and poton chips. "Avery's on his way. He said that whatever you order is on the house."

I take a chip and crunch. "Delicious," I say between chews.

"Pluto used to import them," Zee says. "Now our hydroponic farms grow them."

Trenton says, "They're so much better with a motor oil dip."

The waitress hears and says, "I'll bring some. Extra or regular?"

"Extra," Trenton says.

"We have some new items on the menu: a spiral galaxy wrap with mozzarella cheese and megahertz malted and Ursa Major Colas."

I say, "I'll have the spiral galaxy wrap and a megahertz chocolate malted."

"Same thing," Jersey pipes.

I turn to Zee. "Well, Zee…" I start to say.

But then the floor shakes.

"What was that?" Jersey asks.

"The reason that happened," Zee says, "is because we're building a subway. The heat it produces causes the surface ice to melt and refreeze. Nothing like a real quake."

"Does Pluto get large quakes?" I ask.

Zee says, "Nothing to worry about. At least not here."

Trenton's eyes spin. He says with the concern of someone who fears he's going to fall into a large hole, "No tremor is minor! As long ago as 2015, the New Horizon spacecraft investigated Charon's surface and noted similarities to Earth's huge plates of crust that floated on a taffy-like mantle, crashing into one another. Much later they found a similar thing on Pluto. Icy surfaces always have stress. No tremor is minor."

Suddenly the floor buckles. My chair rocks and tips over. I fall on my side bending and twisting my arm until it resembles a Calabi-Yau shape. "Ow!" I scream in the only four dimensions that I know. I think: Richard Feynman, where are you when I need you?

Trenton and Jersey help me up. Trenton says, "Let me see your arm."

He looks and pokes. "Does that hurt?

"No."

"And how about that?"

"No."

He pokes another spot. I scream.

"That's the place," he says. "And it's broken."

"That diagnosis technique hasn't changed since man left the cave," I say.

"Works, doesn't it?"

I sigh.

"I have an anesthetic patch in case Jersey needs it. It lasts for a week." He taps the spot on my arm again, this time very gently.

I wince as he applies the patch. Instant relief.

"All the hatcheries have clinics," Zee says. "The one in New Darwin can do the job."

"Let's go to the one in Valentine," I say. "I'm not in pain. Besides, it would give us an opportunity to talk to Adam Kools."

Trenton takes the last poton and dips it in the oil. "As long as we're here, can I add a Carburetor Tune-up, a flat tire sandwich on whole wheat, and two chocolate silicone shakes?"

Zee signals the waitress and places the order.

I turn to Zee. "We came to ask you about something we saw at the Darwin Diner."

Zee gives me a long, piercing look. He measures his words in voice as flat as a nature documentary. "I could tell by the way you were asking questions that eventually this would come out. But I had nothing to do with murder."

"Back up, Zee," Trenton says. "Was that or wasn't that you, Herb Tarragon, Nebula, Dante, and Tonto and that we saw at the Darwin Diner or were they clones?"

Zee looks down again and studies a crack in the floor. I knew he would say nothing as it was not common on Pluto to give extra information. We wait.

Trenton urges. "We're going to find out about Herb Tarragon sooner or later. Forensics on Mars are looking at the evidence from the body I examined in space."

Zee shifts in his chair. The moment stretches.

Trenton says, "If you're not going to say anything, I'll call Mars Yard. Most of the major tests on the body should be done by now."

Zee sighs.

Trenton calls, listens, nods. "Mars Yard forensics said that the body I examined was not Herb Tarragon. It was a clone."

Jersey looks at Zee. "So, the man we saw with you at the Darwin Diner was not Herb Tarragon's clone but the real Herb Tarragon. And the woman who I thought was a Nebula clone was Nebula. As well as Dante and Tonto."

"Yes," Zee mumbles.

"Was that so hard?" I ask.

Zee shakes his head, sighs.

"My husband is at the Band Box auditioning people for a concert. Carmella said you have a great voice. If you're interested, I can arrange an audition."

Zee brightens. "That would be wonderful, Molly."

Then we hear Avery Spelling's voice. "Sorry I couldn't come sooner. Did you guys feel that rumble?"

Trenton says, "Molly broke her arm, but I patched it."

Avery says, "A hatchery clinic will make you better than new."

I pat my arm. "New is good enough," I say.

Avery looks at the food in front of Trenton. "I see you're enjoying my complementary offer."

Trenton drains his second silicone milkshake and points to his glass for another. Then says,

"Are you the silent enhanced person partner in that new restaurant conglomerate?"

Avery brightens. "Yes. I jumped at the chance to join them and help them expand into the enhanced person market. Opening an enhanced person cafe is very expensive. Carburetor Tune-up drinks, flat tire sandwiches, and most of the other foods that enhanced people love are processed in refineries. I already have two mortgages."

Jersey says, "As long as you're offering complementary food, you have something on your menu called a lemon cumulous. What is it?"

"Lemon meringue pie with our mile-high merengue."

"Make it two," I say, willpower gone. "After all, my arm just broke."

Jersey asks, "Are there any other partners that you know about?"

"I only know the people from Molly's Pluto," Avery says.

"There may be others I don't know."

We look from Avery to Zee who had been listening with a blank expression. Zee stretches his legs in another direction and says, "This was Herb Tarragon's idea. He was the one who found the backers. When Molly's Pluto came close to opening, everyone could see Herb was acting strangely, but no one said anything. Then when he didn't show up for work, I was told he died."

I say, "When did you learn that he was alive?"

"Don't remember. Tonto told me he wasn't dead. I was shocked. Then Tonto said Herb was in touch with a group who wanted to open restaurants in the Cthulhu Regio area because it was easier to get backing from Mafia families who still lived here. And, assuming correctly, knowing I was from that area, was related to one of the original families and must have been raised with their code of behavior, and therefore could be trusted. Besides, they made me an offer I couldn't refuse."

"Like what?" I ask.

"Either give me a one-way ticket to Nix to work in a cheese factory for the rest of my life—"

"Nix?"

"Pluto's moon, Nix. It's the green cheese capital of the solar system."

"You mean, there really is a moon made of green cheese?" I say.

"How come you don't know that? I thought you were a smart person with a good education."

"And your other option?"

"Be sent to Ultima Thule to scrutinize life insurance policies for preexisting conditions."

27

WE GET BACK TO THE HOTEL. Jersey and Trenton go to their room. The person at the front desk tells me that Cortland and the twins haven't come back yet. I'm relieved. I have time to pull myself together with my broken arm.

When my room door releases, I see a note on the floor. I pick it up. Its edges glow red, meaning that it was made on a timed-sheet that destroys the message a few moments after it's handled. I read quickly before the words disappear. "This is a warning for you and your friends. Leave Pluto."

I call the front desk and ask who put the note under my door.

An attendant says, "A robotic delivery service called Our Lips Are Sealed. Would you like to send someone a message using their service? Answered messages are half price."

"No."

I palm Jersey and Trenton. They both pick up their speaker palms.

Jersey says, "We were just going to call you, but we didn't want to upset you. We got the same message. Maybe answers are closer than we think."

Trenton says, "This is a threat. I'm calling Carmella." I wait while Trenton talks.

"Well?" Jersey says. "What did she say?"

"She says that it wasn't a threat. You need more on Pluto to make it a threat. It's advice."

A half hour later, Cortland and the twins return. The twins

are tired and in a bad mood. When I ask how was their day, they say in chorus, "DON'T ASK!" They slam the door connecting our rooms.

"Does that food replicator on the wall work?" Cortland snarls. "Too exhausted to go to the dining room or out to eat."

I go to the replicator. "It's best to get something simple," I warn.

Cortland says, "Anything as long as they have cold beer."

I scroll and tap a button. Two cold Mars Malts appear. I tap for two more. Then I see the sandwich I remember Jersey saying wasn't bad. I choose two.

"What kind of sandwich is this?" Cortland asks.

"Not sure, but Jersey ate one and liked it."

Cortland shakes his head and takes a bite. "Tastes like a tuna fish and okra wrap."

I sit quietly while we eat and Cortland regains energy. I don't mention my broken arm.

Finally, I ask. "So, how did it go at the Band Box?"

"You want the good news or the bad news first?"

"Good news."

"The good news is there's so much talent on Pluto that the Plutonians, the group that caused me to come, is just average compared to the others. I've heard so much great jazz, experimental, and alternative music that I can't understand why more of Pluto's performers aren't well known."

"Plutonians can be very secretive. And many don't like to travel off planet."

"Even for the good stuff?"

"Seems to be learned from childhood."

"Well, their isolation and introspection may have contributed to so many musicians creating sounds that push the boundaries of genres that I heard. But most should be performed in a large space with echo chambers. Which brings me to the bad news."

I sigh.

"The Band Box's acoustics are terrible. A concert there wouldn't do justice to my work or theirs. That hall needs extensive renovations. I could tell contractors what's needed, get estimates, and let the locals handle it, go home, and come back when it's finished. Or...or..."

"Or what?"

"Stay."

"Stay? What do you mean, stay?"

"Stay until the construction is finished and a concert is done and recorded. Becky and Lois's last album didn't sell as well as I expected. I have some half-finished music that would benefit from jazz accompanists. This would update Becky and Lois's sound and help them reach a new fan base. I only heard a small percentage of those waiting to audition, but so far, those I heard are excellent and so good looking. If I didn't know they were here for a music audition, I would say they were here for a beauty contest."

"That could have affected Becky and Lois. They are used to being the prettiest, and here they're average."

"If I can show the twins how a new sound would expand their visibility and boost their popularity, maybe they would soften on the competition and be willing to stay."

"But Becky is pregnant?"

"There must be lots of good doctors and hospitals here. What about that Hatchery place?"

"I don't know."

Cortland continues. "Maybe Becky's husband would come. If Burton had a reason to be here, she would be willing to stay."

"And what would be the reason?"

"I know that Burton's parents want to expand Club Mood, their Virtual Reality Travel Agency. It should be a big success here because so many never leave Pluto. Besides, I don't want word getting back to my competition at Sun Studios, Abbey

Planet, or Trident Titan that there's so much talent on Pluto before I have time to develop new venues. If the concert is a success, it might help restore Pluto's status to planet from dwarf planet and ending bad jokes like 'why did Micky Mouse go into space?'"

"You got me. Why?"

"To find Pluto."

28

THE NEXT MORNING, CORTLAND goes to the Band Box to continue the auditions. Becky and Lois decide to explore Valentine's shops. I try to dissuade them, knowing that they are hopelessly out of fashion and try to encourage them to see some of the beautiful natural resources, but they say, that they don't want to look at rocks unless they're diamonds, sapphires or rubies.

I meet Trenton and Jersey in the dining room. They are eating breakfast and discussing why imaginary numbers are imaginary if they are imaginary. I have coffee. I add milk, stir, and sip.

"I don't know if the coffee is getting better or I'm getting used to it," I say.

Jersey says, "You're getting used to it."

***

After breakfast we go to Molly's Pluto to ask questions about what happened in New Darwin.

Tonto is in the middle of the dining room and turns to us when we enter. "Zee called and told me what happened. How's your arm?"

"Broken but not hurting. Is Lucky here?"

Tonto says, "His day off."

Trenton asks, "Are Dante and Nebula here?"

"Yes. I'll get them."

Dante and Nebula come from the kitchen.

I look at them and say, "I feel betrayed."

"We are so sorry," Nebula sighs. "We were offered triple our salaries and artistic freedom."

I sigh. "You could have set up Molly's Pluto and after a year told me that you wanted to open your own place. It would give me time to find qualified replacements."

Tonto says, "We were going to do that. Our plans are not finalized. We never expected to see you and your friends in New Darwin. When we saw you, Herb said it was difficult for non-Pluto natives to tell clones apart so we should act like we were our clones. And it almost worked. Didn't it?"

"You've probably managed to keep this off Interplanetary Food's radar," I say. "Don't you have contracts?"

Tonto says, "Only Herb Tarragon had a contract. Interplanetary Foods gives contracts to everyone else if the first year is successful."

"Where's Herb Tarragon now?" I ask.

Tonto says, "Don't know. I spoke to him, and he thought we could answer your questions."

"Does Lucky know that Herb Tarragon is alive?"

"He does now. We told him when we got back from New Darwin."

"There's been a murder," I say. "Just maybe not Herb Tarragon's murder. Do any of you know anything about it?"

No one volunteers. I'm not surprised. We leave.

Trenton's palm rings. "It's Carmella," he mouths. "What?" we hear him say. Pause. Then he clicks off. "Carmella said Pluto forensics found the chocolate on the knife was the same as the chocolate from your restaurant. And the knife was silver plated not sterling silver. They also found that Herb Tarragon was left handed. She keeps saying that the Pluto police and its forensic team are the best in the solar system. I wonder how much she know about forensic teams on other worlds."

"Pluto does have a disproportionate number of prisoners who remain on Pluto when their sentence is over, share information with the police, and open legitimate businesses," Jersey says.

"Jack the Zipper Ripper now makes designer knock-offs. The Saturn Ring opened a chain of Saturn Ring Donuts."

"But other worlds have larger populations with excellent forensic teams," Trenton says. "I'm calling her back. I want to visit their forensic lab and see what she's talking about. We could go there first if it's near the hatchery; that is if you're not in pain, Molly."

"I'm not in pain, Trenton. That patch is wonderful. I never told Cortland I broke my arm, and he didn't notice."

Carmella is happy to oblige. And, the laboratory is near the hatchery.

We tell the concierge that we want to go to the Police Forensic Laboratory and then go to hatchery. He says the fastest way is on a tram that passes through the newly completed hyper-loop.

"How many have used it?" Trenton asks.

"You would be the first."

Jersey says, "We prefer if you would book us a car."

The concierge taps a screen. "Well, you're in luck. The new Dow Jones is available." He taps Again, and a holo of a sleek blue sedan appears. "I wouldn't recommend the Standard and Poors; it's very volatile."

The car is waiting for us in front of the hotel. Trenton keys Pluto Forensic Laboratory into the dashboard. Its big upholstered seats recline, and there are amenities like a holo for viewing hit shows. I key "The Lunar Tunes". Becky and Lois's image appear, waving and blowing kisses. A flat automated voice asks if we would like anything from its food replicator. We have fresh orange juice. It must be from fresh oranges because mine has pits.

"So many places could use a replicator like that," I say.

Jersey says, "Yeah, like our hotel room."

***

The pathology department is in a ten-story gunmetal-gray building. We enter a small room on the first floor where we are scanned. I am wondering what's on the other floors when a door slides open to a central area with branching corridors paved in a shiny speckled material. A woman with curly brown hair, the straight nose, and blue eyes that we have seen on so many sits behind a high desk. She looks down at us and introduces herself as one of director Professor Bacitracin's assistants. She climbs from her perch. "Follow me," she says.

We follow her through one corridor, up and down several ramps past supply rooms. The acrid smell of formaldehyde, alcohol, and other competing chemicals becoming stronger as the corridor widens into the laboratory. About fifty technicians using computerized equipment peer at screens and microscopes. Some shake tubes of varying sizes and colors and make notes. No one looks up as we pass. Glass cabinets to one side are filled with the tools of the trade like scalpels, hacksaws, and tweezers.

A man in a light green lab coat with frizzy brown hair crosses the floor. He extends a hand. "My name is Professor Bacitracin. Carmella called and said you're from Mars Yard. You're our first Mars Yard visitors. She told me that you examined Herb Tarragon's body when it was stored at our space crypts."

"Yes, I did," Trenton says. Then he introduces us and shows Professor Bacitracin his Mars Yard credentials.

"Impressive. Follow me."

We enter a long bright room. Rows of bodies are on slabs. Jersey pauses at one whose head is half gone and turned one hundred eighty degrees. "Some of these guys were in fierce struggles," she says.

Herb Tarragon's body is near the back. A clear box under his slab holds his clothes and personal belongings.

Professor Bacitracin says, "We found something tiny and red near the shoulder of his coat."

"Nebula has red hair, and the uniforms that April and June May wear at the Darwin Diner are red," I say.

"Let me check to see if the results from the infrared spectrophotometer is completed. He palms a code and reads, "The amount of infrared light absorbed matches a fabric."

"A hair would be easier to track," I say. "Fabric could come from anywhere." I look at Jersey's red scarf and the red sweater I'm wearing. "Oops!" I say.

"Any prints on the knife that killed him?" Trenton asks.

"Unfortunately, no. We don't have much to go on. I sent some samples to other labs on Pluto and labs on Charon."

Trenton says, "Labs on Charon?"

"Have you ever been to Charon?"

"No. Why?"

"Charon is less regulated than Pluto. Not only do they work with experimental procedures even we won't touch, but their casinos attract the solar system's biggest gamblers."

"Bigger than Las Venus?" Jersey asks.

"Las Venus is amateur night compared to Charon's casinos."

We get back in the car. Trenton programs, The Hatchery. The car's motor engages and we move forward. The car offers us generous samples of green cheese from Nix that Jersey and Trenton love, but I would have preferred brie or brilliant savarin.

29

ADAM KOOLS GREETS US. "Sorry about your arm, Molly. It's easy to fix." He watches us look at the butterflies perched on his head. He brushes them off. "Beautiful, aren't they? A gene called optix controls the color in a butterfly's wing. We turned it off in some species to get black and silver colors, and iridescent blues in others."

Some fly around us.

"Our new wing is finished," Adam says. "Now we have space to use a newer version of Crispr-Cas gene editing." He turns to Trenton. "Our advances come from studying the Mexican Walking fish, a salamander-like creature called the axonotl. It regenerates multiple structures like limbs and the spinal cord. It has ten time more genes than humans. It took years before we learned how to make adjustments for humans."

Trenton is about to comment, but two doctors stop and interrupt him. I think they look and sound familiar. Then it hits me. They look like Dr. Bliss and Dr. Hatch, the doctors who tried to convince me that I was Dolly not Molly.

They finish talking to Adam briefly glance at us and walk on.

I say to Adam. "When we were here before, you said certain chemicals are added to the amino sacks of clones so clones can see differences."

"That's right," Adam says.

"And those two doctors that you were talking to may have many clones."

Adam says, "You mean Dr. Nucleus and Dr. Trademark?"

I say, "Yes. They look like doctors I met who had different names."

"That could be. If you want to experience what many of us experience, we can give you hormones that create perceptual differences, but there might be risks. We can give a small shot so effects would be temporary, unless of course if you wanted a complete transformation."

"Would the process work on me?" Trenton asks.

"Definitely not. Enhanced people have a different chemistry. There are places that can build another 'you' and implant your memories."

Jersey chimes in. "One Trenton is enough."

"Any risks?" I ask.

"Blindness, chills and hot flashes, tremors, deafness, IQ dropping thirty points, and an inability to taste chocolate."

"The chocolate is a deal breaker," I say.

Jersey says, "I'll try it, Molly. It might be easier for Trenton to monitor my progress. Right, sweetheart?"

Trenton nods, turns to Adam. "Is there an antidote?

"No. But it wears off in time. It's different for every person."

"Give me the formula. I'll feel more comfortable if I work on an antidote."

Adam palms a message to a doctor's doctor who sends Trenton the formula.

Trenton's eyes spin and turn colors. "This formula is a very complicated. The majority of things download immediately." His eyes spin again in the opposite direction.

We wait. Jersey crosses her arms, frowns.

Finally, "Got it!"

"Are you sure, sweetheart?" Jersey asks.

Trenton says, "We'll soon see."

"Not the right answer, Trenton. Yes or no?"

"Yes."

One of the doctors gives Jersey a shot. At first, nothing happens. Jersey yawns. "I don't feel anything. Maybe tired."

Adam makes a call on his palm. A few moments later, I see three identical women enter the room.

Adam says, "Do these women look the same or different to you, Jersey?"

Jersey says, "Completely different."

"They look the same to me, Jersey," I say.

Trenton adds, "Looks the same to me also. How are they different?"

Jersey says, "The one on the right has Asian looking eyes, the one in the middle has a small bump on her nose and the third has a straight nose and bow shaped mouth."

Jersey looks at me. "Is that you, Molly? I can tell it's you by your voice, but you look different?

"Better or worse?

"Just different."

"Explain."

"Your nose is shorter. Your eyes are larger."

"Does that make me prettier?"

"Well, actually it does."

Trenton asks, "What about me?"

"You look the same."

Adam smiles. "Convinced?"

"Impressive," Trenton says. "Can I administer the antidote immediately?"

"Only after a week. Otherwise, it will be toxic and kill her."

"You said it would be temporary!"

"A week is temporary."

Jersey wrinkles her brow and says words that tempt fate: "I'm sure nothing bad will happen."

I pull Jersey over and whisper, "Tell me about the two doctors over there."

"The one on the right has a mark of a tattoo removed from

his neck. Other than that, they look like two different people."

Adam Kools escorts us to the hospital area. A woman wearing a white coat and blue badge over her left breast that says "Nurse 47" asks if Jersey and Trenton want to wait in the waiting area or accompany me. They accompany me. She takes us to a small windowless room and tells us that the technician will be with us shortly. She leaves and closes the door behind her. The room is freezing. It feels like we are waiting a long time, so Trenton opens the door and peers down the hall. "I don't see anyone coming," he says.

Jersey says, "Just like doctors' offices back home. They call you into a room, close the door, and you wait. We could have stayed in the waiting room. At least there's old magazines and a holo turned to a station no one wants to watch."

Finally, the door opens, and a white square box about four feet tall with red flashing lights and black circles in varying sizes on the sides and top wheels itself in. A voice from it says, "I'm Osteogenesis 89. I understand that I am to repair a broken arm. Correct?"

I say, "Correct."

"Will the patient please put her arm into the circle that has just turned yellow? It is important that you do not remove your arm once the process has started."

"I don't want to do this," I cry, my voice cracking like a thirteen-year-old boy's. I thrust my arm behind me.

"Courage, Molly," Jersey says. "Courage."

Trenton says, "If worse comes to worst, remember the hatchery can grow you another arm in two years."

"What do you mean if worse comes to worst?"

"Just an expression, Molly. It doesn't mean anything."

The word "worse" rings in my head over and over like an alarm. I brace myself, take a deep breath, and insert my arm.

"What do you feel?" Jersey asks softly.

"Nothing. I feel nothing." Then. "Ooh. I feel a warm tickling vibration, but it doesn't hurt."

After ten minutes, which feels like an hour, Osteogenesis 89 says, "Please remove your arm."

I slowly remove my arm. I run my other hand over it. It is smooth and red.

Osteogenesis 89 says, "The red color will fade when the arm is completely healed. Would you like me to check on any other part of your body?"

"No," I say, moving away, relieved that it is over.

Osteogenesis 89 rolls out, and a nurse enters. I ask, "What would have happened if I removed my arm during the process?"

"It would have come off," she says in a flat voice. "You could have replaced it with a wing or a fin. Some do."

I cradle my arm.

"Then, please follow me. Adam Kools is waiting."

As soon as we enter Adam's office, he comes from behind his desk and says, "How did you like the procedure?"

"Impressive. Why do you think it isn't commonplace on other worlds?" I ask.

"Their medical lobbies are strong and don't want to put doctors out of business. Each year Mercury and Titan require new and more elaborate tests to pass this procedure. Mars and Earth never seem to finish the paperwork."

Trenton says, "Interesting point. But we really want to ask you something else. We want to ask about your relationship with Herb Tarragon."

Adam's face falls, making two parallel creases between his eyes. We say nothing, not wanting to reveal too much before we get some answers.

Adam clears his throat. "Our relationship was brief. He broke up with me," he says in a flat matter of fact tone. "He told me that he's been with women and men in equal number. But then he said something that completely surprised me."

We wait. Adam shifts in his chair and watches us watching

him. "Herb said that he was having an affair with an android woman. I never suspected anything when he took me to Silicone Slings. You know, that bar for androids."

Trenton says, "Enhanced humans."

"Enhanced humans," Adam repeats. "Herb said he was curious. But I never thought much of it. Strange drinks like an Oil Refinery on the rocks; but they have good beer. I was aware that humans were marrying enhanced humans, but never met any till I met you and Jersey."

Jersey and Trenton look at each other and beam. Trenton says, "We were the first. We've been married twenty years. Today Mars has a large diverse population. There was lots of prejudice toward enhanced humans at first because people were afraid we were taking their jobs and destroying their neighborhood's property values, but after a while when everyone saw that didn't happen, people relaxed."

"Well, this is new to Pluto."

"You're advanced in some sciences, but a cultural catch-up is long overdue," Jersey says.

Adam says nothing.

"What else can you tell us about Herb Tarragon?" I ask.

"Besides loving food and being a great chef, he loved jazz. But he also had a dark side. Loved gambling. Not only did he go to the Pluto casinos, but he went to Charon where the highest rollers play."

Then he stops talking. We wait. We look at each other and don't want to push for more at this time.

30

WHEN I GET BACK, CORTLAND IS waiting for me in our room. "Picked up something to eat at Brimstone's Barbecue, one of the better food franchises in Valentine," he says unwrapping a package. "Hungry?"

"Starved. I was with Jersey and Trenton, remember. I had one of their food supplement pills. Nutritious but not satisfying."

"Where did you go?" he asks.

"The Hatchery."

"Did you go to find out about Becky having her babies there?"

"No. But something related to Herb Tarragon's murder. I know you don't like me getting involved, but it was only a few questions."

"That's how it starts with you, Molly."

To change the subject. I ask, "Did you have time to call Burton about coming and setting up a branch of his family's virtual travel agency here?"

"Yes. He and his parents had already thought of expanding Club Mood to Pluto without me suggesting it. Elvis and Lulu won't come, but Burton will. He can set it up without them."

"Does Becky know he's coming?"

"Yes, Burton called her after he spoke to me."

"So, she must be happy?"

"Not exactly happy, but happier. She wants to go back to Mars, not stay here. Burton, however, thinks having the babies born on Pluto is a cool idea."

"And Lois?"

"Ah, Lois…"

"What do you mean, ah, Lois?"

"Lois met a drummer. I think his name is either Shooting Starr or Ringo Starr. Says he descended from a beetle."

"We should get his DNA checked before she gets more involved."

Cortland says, "Don't be silly. He can't mean a real beetle."

I shrug and say nothing.

Cortland repeats, "Can he, Molly?"

"Probably not. But there's lots of strange things here regarding one's heredity. In any event, looks like we'll be here longer than I first thought. Maybe we can get a better deal on our rooms."

There is a bright flash out our window. It happens again, then grows dark.

"What could that be?" Cortland says. "I'll palm the front desk."

Cortland calls and mostly listens for a long time. He finishes the call by saying, "No problem." And disconnects.

"So?" I ask.

"The flashing light is from a solar mirror system in space that Pluto is experimenting with to create more light. So far it has only produced occasional flashes. The red hats are for it; the blue hats aren't. They'll be a vote to see if they should continue developing it."

"Someone named Kim Stanley Robinson wanted to build one on Mars called a soletta, but it never worked out," I say.

"The Band Box needs serious renovation. I'm overwhelmed with messages from musicians wanting to do concerts and donate their proceeds toward the work. I'll offer contractors free concerts when it's finished if I can get them to give wholesale prices on the construction. Also, a new hall could use a new name! I'm thinking of 'The Blue Note.' It's the name of an ancient jazz club on Earth in a village called Greenwich, a place known for playing great beats in mean time."

"Good idea," I say.

"You know, Molly, I still worry about Avery. You did get him sent to Pluto for the murder of his boss."

"Yes, but his boss wanted him to donate to organizations that were prejudiced against androids and would have fired him if he knew he was one of them."

"Be careful. I don't like you having anything to do with him. Makes me nervous."

***

A few days later, in Jersey and Trenton's room, I say, "We're getting nowhere until we talk to Herb Tarragon."

"Nice work if you can get it," Jersey says. "Who do you think murdered Herb Tarragon's clone?"

"Could have been Herb Tarragon," I say. "The clone's murder happened the same time Herb Tarragon disappeared." I look at the wall with the food replicator and point. "Do you ever use that?"

"It had nothing we liked."

"See if they added anything new?"

Jersey pushes a button. "Grilled cheese from Nix," she says. "That's an improvement." Jersey pushes a button. A few moments later a grilled cheese sandwich appears. Jersey takes a bite. "Not bad," she says. "You know, I was wondering if Herb Tarragon would meet with us?"

"I was thinking the same thing," I say. "I'll ask Tonto to ask him."

I palm Tonto.

"Sure Molly," Tonto says. "I'll call Herb now."

We wait a few moments. Jersey finishes the grilled cheese sandwich. Tonto calls back.

"Sorry, Molly," Tonto says. "Herb Tarragon said no."

I disconnect and think for a moment. Then I say, "Maybe we could entice him if we offer something he may want."

"He's a chef," Jersey says. "Maybe an expensive spice like saffron. It can be more expensive than edible gold and white truffles."

"Good idea," I say. "I remember learning in college that it's an ancient medicinal plant. Cleopatra used it to make the first paella that she smuggled inside a piñata that she served to Mark Anthony to cure his toenail fungus."

Trenton adds, "I think it's also mentioned in histories about Alexander, the Great Chef, who was born in Pella, the capital of the kingdom of Macedon also known for great paella. Should I check?"

"Don't," Jersey snaps.

Trenton frowns. "You never know when such information might come in handy."

Jersey sighs.

Trenton continues. "Saffron comes from the stigma of the blue flowering crocus. It must be handpicked and it takes two hundred to five hundred stigmas to make one gram of it, which explains the price."

"I remember when we were at the wholesale food market, I saw a booth called Brass Knuckle Spices. Tonto must know about it," I say.

Tonto says, "Saffron? Can you really afford that? It's not sold in Valentine. It's only sold at the Brass Knuckles Spices along the equator. The people who grow it are still connected to some of the original Mafia families who I think get a cut from every transaction. They are very secretive and control the market as they do for all luxury foods like white truffles, Beluga caviar and edible gold. Good cooking joins several families together. The price varies; last time I checked it was eleven hundred starbucks an ounce."

"But what about the Brass Knuckle Spices at the wholesale market near the Valentine hatchery?"

"Oh that," Tonto says. "All they sell are parsley, sage, rosemary, and thyme. If you want something like saffron, you can only get it at their main facility. You need a letter of recommendation, proof of a sizable bank account, and a medical report that shows your DNA and any other identifying things before they will consider letting you in."

Trenton says, "That rules Jersey and me out, Molly. We don't have a sizable bank account."

"Or any bank account," Jersey sneers.

"Is it near New Darwin near the equator?" I ask.

"No," Tonto says. "It's where there are skyscraper-sized methane ice blades. A dangerous place. You'll have to copter down into the gorge where it is."

"Maybe you should give me the money, Molly, and I'll go," Trenton says. "If something happens, most of me can be repaired."

Tonto says, "They only deal with who has the money not who will be given the money."

Trenton says, "In that case, we'll go with Molly and wait while she buys it."

***

The transport is small and cramped and takes a little over an hour. I look with mystical awe at the beauty and danger of the skyscraper-sized methane ice blades below.

Trenton says, "Methane ice changes shape as conditions change. When it's warmer, it never becomes liquid but goes from a solid state to a gaseous state. Like dry ice."

"Somehow that information doesn't make me feel any better, Trenton," I say.

Suddenly the transport rocks back and forth. There is a tug. I grip my seat. There is another, stronger. We slow and circle one of the ice blades and descend cautiously, in the dim light, avoiding dangerous jagged methane protrusions. I hope the automated driver works properly.

Finally, we stop. A voice, clearly synthetic and devoid of emotion, sounds in our helmets. "Please exit the transport on your right and continue down the corridor. Once you enter, you cannot speak of what you see. More instructions later."

Jersey exits first. She turns and says, "Why do we need instructions to walk down a corridor?"

When she disappears around a curve into the darkness, my stomach feels queasy. Trenton stays close to me. The corridor twists and rises several times until it abruptly descends. We follow a long way before we start climbing higher again. "Good thing the gravity's light," I say. "I could never do this on Earth or Mars."

After the next turn, we see Jersey. She's standing in front of a narrow suspension bridge. It links two sides of a terrifying-looking ravine. The voice in our helmets says, "There is a small button on the back of your boots that magnetizes your boot to the path of the bridge. Press to activate. One foot on the bridge is strong enough to support five hundred Earth pounds."

I take a deep breath and search for the button. "Where? Where?" I cry.

Trenton reaches over and presses my button.

Sweat prickles over my neck and brow. "I never liked heights," I say.

"Just look straight ahead, Molly," Trenton says, "and think you're shopping on Rodeo Dive."

I try to think of the shoe department at Mars Marcus, but it makes it worse because I look down at my feet.

Jersey says, "Looks like fun. I'll go first. You come next, and Trenton can walk in back of you in case you fall."

"Fall?"

I watch Jersey hold the handrails, put one foot in front of the other, and cross to the other side. She turns. Her voice in my helmet says, "Come on, Molly. You can do it."

I put my foot on the bridge and feel the magnet grip my boot. Then I lower my other foot on the bridge. Emptiness surrounds me. I grip the handrails till my palms almost bleed, take a few steps. Then more.

I'm sweating so much by the time I get to the middle I can hardly open my eyes. When I do, I look down. I'm so dizzy that I can't see the bottom. I lift my left foot to take the next step, but it goes to the side of the bridge. The next thing I know, the bridge twists and I flip over and over. I'm aware that one foot keeps me from falling.

Then it slides.

31

I DON'T KNOW IF IT WAS Trenton's version of a mind meld, a rescue, or my own adrenaline that got me to the other side because everything from that point is a blur. All I know is I'm on the other side and safe.

A blue arrow points ahead. It's so faint that if it weren't for Trenton's infra-red to ultraviolet vision, we would have missed it. We see a narrow corridor that can only fit one person at a time. Trenton walks through, then I go, then Jersey. Jersey and Trenton are so thin they can pass with no difficulty, but I have to go through sideways.

Jersey says, "Good thing you're not the two hundred eighty-seven pounds you once were when I first met you, Molly. You would be stuck in here until they blasted you out."

"Is that supposed to make me feel better, Jersey?" I say in the dim light, happy she cannot see my expression.

The passage becomes a little brighter. We make several sharp turns until my sense of direction, not that great to begin with, is completely destroyed. I feel that we're circling back to our original place. After the next hairpin turn, and a moment before I panic, the passage grows wider and is punctuated on either side by doors in different colors.

After passing through the passage for five minutes, Jersey says, "Let's open a door."

We struggle to open a blue one; an ammonia smells greet us. We struggle more to close it. We try a yellow one. It opens more easily. Hot steam pours through. We jump back. It closes by itself. The white door's handle turns easily. Icy air engulfs us. I rub my arms to stop shivering. Finally, the corridor gets brighter and much wider. In the distance, we see a large transparent building glowing with colored plants. We walk closer. The automated voice says, "Please step on the green square on the floor while we scan you." I scratch an itch on my nose.

An automated voice booms, "Remain steady or you won't see the surface again."

We freeze. Time slows.

The voice says, "Now remove your protective suits. A vapor that will engulf you ensures you don't carry dangerous germs."

We wait.

Jersey starts to say, "Looks like it's not…" when a thick vapor billows from the center of the ceiling, so thick that we can't see each other. When it dissipates, I touch my sleeve. I'm amazed. I'm not damp.

We hear, "Continue until you stop at the next door a few feet ahead."

When we reach the door, it automatically opens. Aah! The fresh wonderful smell of organic life.

The director, who says his name is James Gandolfini, greets us. I think he looks like Tonto. I say to Jersey, "Do you still have those hormones in your system that lets you see differences in clones? Does he look like Tonto?"

"Tonto? He's totally different: longer nose, wider chin…"

"Okay. Got it."

James says, "You'll find that we have everything from anise to prepared condiments like Za'atar. Ours, of course, is made from fresh thyme, oregano, marjoram mixed with toasted sesame seeds, and sumac. We grow saffron in a separate area. Want to keep it away from the other spices and as pure as possible. Will you want venti, trenta, or grande size? Do you want it ground for cumulous, nimbus, stratus, or cirrus? Do you want it mixed as in saffron coke or saffron meth or pure?"

"What would a great chef like Herb Tarragon like?" I ask.

Silence. Blank stare.

I prod, "You know, Herb Tarragon? The chef who was murdered in Valentine's wholesale market?"

"Murdered? No. You must mean found dead. The story was in The Oort Cloud News. Everyone was amazed that a chef of his caliber wanted to work on Pluto. Great chefs want larger audiences."

"Unless they have something to hide," Trenton pipes. "So, in your opinion, what would a great chef like Herb Tarragon like?" I repeat.

James wrinkles his brow. "Only the purest and freshest saffron. The going rate this morning was eleven hundred starbucks an ounce."

He holds out his hand and wiggles his fingers. "Pay in advance." He taps a code into his palm. "Send it to this address."

I check my palm. "I never saw an address like that."

"It's off planet."

I push send and don't ask questions.

His eyes narrow, checking the transaction. Finally, he smiles. "How about hot chocolate while I get the saffron? We make our own blend."

"I could use some," I say. "I'm still recovering from the way we got here."

James snaps his fingers. A moment later, a drone approaches with three steaming cups.

Trenton asks, "Have you created new spices for the enhanced human market? Carburetor scrapings don't have much punch."

"Not here. Check Silicone Slings."

A man comes with a green package that has been put into a small shopping bag that has a picture of a fist with brass knuckles on the side. Under it are the words, "Please recycle or else."

"If you have any problems," he says, "tell them that you got this from Tony Knuckles and you won't have any trouble." He hands me the bag and cracks his knuckles. I wince.

Trenton turns to James and peers more closely at him. "You're an enhanced person. You must be a new model."

"Just upgraded. You're the first to notice," he says. "I'm lucky to live on Pluto. Scientists here get the fast results. Now, would you like to exit by the way you came, or would you like to take the elevator?"

I gasp. "You have an elevator? Why didn't you tell us?"

His explanation is so convoluted, you would have to be the famous veterinarian and taxidermist, Schrödinger, who could turn a cat's nine lives into ten, to make sense of his answer.

32

WE MAKE ARRANGEMENTS TO MEET Herb Tarragon and give him the saffron. Herb wants to meet at Silicone Slings in Valentine because he trusts Avery Spelling, who is a graduate of the Pluto prison system. I look at Jersey and say, "Does that mean it's off the record?"

"Isn't almost everything here?" she says.

We take the tram, and as usual, I see so many who look like each other not look at each other. But Jersey thinks everyone looks different. I miss being home in New Chicago where the people are much less attractive, but smile more often.

Avery greets us and offers us coffee and a cherry motor soda currently available only on Pluto to Trenton who is delighted to try it. I think I spot Herb Tarragon sitting at a corner table. He looks coiled, ready to spring. The dark wall behind him highlights his slicked back auburn hair. I lean into Trenton and whisper, "I hope it's really him and not a clone."

"It is," Jersey says.

"Who do you think that man is over there in the other corner? The one with the black baseball cap pulled down over his eyes? He's pretending to read a tablet, but he hasn't moved his finger to turn a page since we got here? He just looked at us."

Jersey looks. "I have no idea."

Herb rises, looks me in the eye, extends his hand. "I'm sorry to have put you through this, Molly. I really thought being a chef at Molly's Pluto would work out. Tonto said that you had saffron. I love those exotic spices, but they are too expensive for me to buy, so I appreciate getting some."

I hand him the bag with the saffron.

"There's a lot of the fake stuff out there," he says, taking a small pinch and rubbing it between his fingers, which turn an orange/reddish yellow.

Jersey watches and says, "Is that good or bad?"

Herb smiles. Then smells it. "Ah, that dark sweet scent. The good stuff," he says putting it in his pocket. "Thank you."

"I'm glad you like it," I say. "Tony Knuckle gave it to us."

Herb's eyebrows rise. "If I knew Tony gave it to you, I wouldn't have checked it. His stuff is the best." He sits.

"You have a lot of explaining to do," Jersey snarls.

We pull out chairs and sit opposite him.

Herb Tarragon breaks off eye contact. "I never killed anyone," he says, suddenly intent.

We say nothing, hoping it's a promising start. Jersey and I lock eyes. I know we're thinking the same thing: maybe he's not telling the truth.

"That day, as usual, I went to the wholesale market. I saw a crowd standing in a circle looking down. When I went closer, I saw a man face down with a knife in his back. Someone rolled him to the side and turned his head. I was shocked when I recognized one of my clones. I quickly turned and walked away."

Trenton asks, "How many clones do you have?"

"I'm one of six, a small number for clones."

Trenton says, "I examined four of your clones who were dead at the space crypts. You make five. Where is the sixth?"

Herb Tarragon says, "I have no idea."

Jersey asks, "Did you grow up together?"

"No. I was told that there were six of us, but as far as I know, we grew up in different places. It's one way to spread genetic codes to other cities with other hatcheries. We all had different lives. Some were like distant cousins; others were strangers."

I say, "When you saw your clone with a knife in his back, what did you think?"

"At first, I was shocked, then felt panic realizing that maybe I could be implicated. But then I thought that if I disappeared and let everyone think the body was mine, my contract with Interplanetary Foods would be null and void, and I would be free to do what I really wanted, which was start my own restaurant."

"But you must have realized that sooner or later the authorities would figure out that the murdered person wasn't you," Jersey says.

"Yes, I knew that. But I also know things like that move slowly on Pluto."

"We've learned," Trenton says.

Herb continues. "I hoped that it would buy time to move elsewhere and get a new identity. I wanted cosmetic surgery but feared my DNA would show up in old records. I knew Zee Pope came from Cthulhu Regio and thought it a good place to hide and start my own restaurant."

I lean in and peer at him. "Did you have anything to do with my kidnapping and memory loss and people who tried to learn the secrets of my recipes?"

"Are you referring to someone probably called Dr. Bliss and Dr. Hatch?"

Silence. Wide-eyed looks.

"Yes. How do you know?" I say.

"I might as well tell you because it's easy to find out." He clears his throat. "Can I have a glass of water? My throat feels dryer than a saltine cracker."

Avery brings a glass of water. Herb gulps quickly. "We're cousins. Their real names are Prozac and Viagra Tarragon. Besides using Dr. Bliss and Dr. Hatch, sometimes they use Dr. Novocain, Dr. Pavlov, and Dr. Adderall to disguise themselves further because many of their procedures are considered unethical, even on Pluto."

I say, "Yeah, like wiping a person's memory clean."

"Would you believe that people pay them lots of money for such procedures?"

Jersey says, "I bet." Trenton asks, "Do they work at the Valentine Hatchery?"

Herb says, "Not likely. Much more money in private practice. After I got to New Darwin and found a place to live, I called them and asked about getting cosmetic surgery because I wanted to alter my appearance. But they were booked for months. Then I never heard back from them."

"But they knew about Molly and Molly's Pluto restaurant," Jersey says.

"Everyone knew; it was all over the media. That idea was theirs. There was nothing in it for me. All I want to do is have my own first-class restaurant with my own recipes."

"What was so bad about your contract with Interplanetary Foods?" I ask.

"I never realized how much I wanted to create my own recipes until I had that job. Then the reality that I had to follow a rigid menu designed by your chef on Mars day after day sunk in. Interplanetary Foods wants to build a franchise empire of Molly's Bistros. Everything about the place, the decor, the flowers, the food must be the same. You don't go to a McBurger to order shrimp scampi and another to get veal parmesan."

Trenton chuckles. "Yup! Restaurant clones. It's burgers all the way down."

I ask, "How do you explain the knife from Molly's Pluto with chocolate on it?"

"Can't. That's what happened and that's all I know."

There is a long silence. We wait. But it's clear that Herb Tarragon is not going to say more. We all get up and start to walk out. The man with the tablet also gets up and leaves.

Jersey says, "Did you notice that man with the tablet?"

I say, "I did. I wonder who he is."

"I can't shake the feeling that there's more to Herb's story or he's hiding something," Jersey says.

"I agree," Trenton says. "But from his expression and body language, he's told us all he's going to for now."

33

NEWS OF RENOVATING THE BAND BOX moves faster than great gossip. Everyone is filled with excitement and loves the hall renamed The Blue Note. Frank and Lloyd Wright, clones who carried the DNA of famed architect, Frank Lloyd Wright and oversee the project, tell the Pluto Press that The Blue Note will outshine Carnegie Hall in New York, the Royal Albert Hall in London, The Sun Dial on Mercury, the Koncerthaus on Mars and the Esplanade on Titan.

Bets are placed that performances will outdo those in time worn and still standing Madison Square Garden in New York that hosted rock legends Led Zeppelin, Freddie Mercury, The Grateful Dead, and Lady Gaga's Monster Ball.

Workers descended on Valentine offering services in exchange for free concert tickets causing construction to move ahead of schedule.

The mayor thinks the area surrounding the new hall should be renamed 'Greenwich Valentine' because he hopes identifying with Greenwich Village, once home of artists, bohemian types, the avant-garde and other hipster groups will boost tourism.

The red hats and blue hats, sensing economic opportunities, unite in their support of the name Greenwich Valentine but are divided naming its main street Penny Lane or Tin Pan Alley because many think those names sound too cheap. They finally agree to 'Titanium' Alley because they liked that titanium has a high strength to density ratio and resists corrosion.

Economists want to float a cryptocurrency called the Plutocoin to accelerate funding copying the bitcoin, the Marscoin, and Titancoin. But most, even after hundreds of years, don't trust their value nor fathom how they work. So, starbucks as the currency of Pluto and the rest of the solar system remains.

Ugly abandoned warehouses are converted to trendy lofts. Shops selling crafts and hip clothes open in spaces vacant for years. New Orleans, a restaurant with a spicy cuisine and late-night jazz, papers its walls in old *New Yorker* cartoons that people don't understand. Some pretend they do; others insist they are Zen koans that lead to one of the other hands clapping in a parallel universe. A coffee shop called Jelly Roll Blues is packed the moment it opens. Real estate prices soar. Real estate agents multiply.

Cortland auditions so many wonderful musicians that he has enough for two shows. He hasn't had time to work out new musical arrangements for Becky and Lois, who unfortunately feel overwhelmed by those who are prettier. I am upset when the girls consider nose jobs and eye enhancers. Becky feels unattractive because her growing pregnancy has caused her to lose her figure.

Nor does it help that Burton is delayed. The equipment needed to set up the virtual travel agency on Pluto was sent to Neptune's moon, Triton, that along with Ganymede, Calisto, Titan, Io, Europa and Earth's moon are all larger than Pluto and also want to be called planets. They insist size matters.

Burton says that a virtual travel agency will be a huge success there because Triton has a lot of geezers.

Becky says, "Don't you mean geysers, sweetheart? Ever since you got there, I did a lot of research about that world."

"They have both," Burton says. "In fact, the capital of Triton, Asmann City, sits between two geysers, Old Faithful and Old Unfaithful. But they also have a lot of old people, who, because

Triton real estate is so cheap, have retired there, but they still want vacations. So, as long as the virtual reality equipment for the virtual travel agency is already on Triton, I might as well stay and set one up. I'll order more equipment sent to Pluto."

Burton's delay makes Becky depressed and grumpy.

I want to ask Nebula Veil, my sous chef, more questions. I call her. She says she is happy to comply and could I come to her home tomorrow as it is her day off.

***

Nebula lives half way between the Hatchery and the center of Valentine. I check the address to make sure I have the right place because the building looks like so many others: light slate gray devoid of decoration, probably an amalgam of plastic and concrete.

Nebula greets me with a crying baby in her arms. She looks younger when not dressed in her cooking uniform. She usually gushes energy, but not now. "You'll have to excuse me, Molly. Ever since I got this baby from the Valentine Hatchery, she won't stop crying. She's one of three clones. I've called Adam Kools and asked if I could return her."

"I didn't know you had a child."

"I always wanted to be a mother. I thought I would marry Herb Tarragon. We had an affair and even registered as a couple at the Valentine Hatchery. But Herb broke it off, said he couldn't go through with it because his desire for men was stronger than his desire for women. I had no clue he felt that way. I always wanted a family, so I decided to become a single mother."

The baby squirms in her arms and cries again. Nebula rocks her. "I didn't think being a mother was going to be that difficult."

"It can be. Do you have help?"

"I have a great nanny so I can go to work, but today is her day off."

The baby stops crying. Nebula sighs and puts her in her crib that's in a corner of the living room. She turns and sighs. "Tea? Coffee?"

"No, thanks."

We sit on two pink club chairs opposite each other.

"You may have heard that I have a reputation for being something of an amateur sleuth," I say. "Once I get the bit in my teeth about a crime, solving it becomes irresistible."

"Like Lucky with new recipes. He wants to try a new recipe as soon as he gets it."

"Have you known Lucky a long time?"

"Yes. He was devastated when Herb Tarragon didn't pick him as his sous chef. Almost on a whim, he applied to your bistro on Mars. He was very surprised he got the job. Molly's Bistro on Mars is more prestigious than working at Molly's Pluto. His plan was to work there a few years then return to Pluto. He's a small planet guy. Found the hustle and bustle of Mars unfriendly. When he heard that Herb Tarragon died, he jumped at the offer to replace him as chef."

"I saw you at the New Darwin Diner with Dante, Tonto, and Herb Tarragon and know you all had plans to invest in new restaurants. Were you surprised that Herb Tarragon wasn't dead?"

"Yes. Totally surprised."

"Was Lucky included in this deal?"

"No. Lucky hates business. All he wants to do is cook. Tonto said he would tell Lucky that Herb Tarragon was not dead and reassure him that his job at Molly's Pluto was secure since Herb did not want to come back and had other plans."

The baby cries. Nebula gets up and goes to the crib, picks the baby up, cradles her in her arms. She stops crying. "I haven't slept since I got her. I was going to call her Andy. Short for Andromeda."

"I remember feeling that way after my twins were born."

"What Hatchery did they come from?"

"They were born on Earth's moon, and I had them naturally."

"The Hatchery is natural."

"No, I mean I carried them for nine months inside my body."

"I read about that. Sounds risky. No one I know would do that. Weren't you uncomfortable?"

I take out my palm and show a holo of me nine months pregnant.

"Why would you let yourself look that way? And your twins were born with no problems?"

"Yes, thriving. In fact, today they're the pop singers, 'The Lunar Tunes.' My husband wrote Moon Rover that they turned into a hit."

"I love that song! And you're really their mother! If I had a baby that way, would my child become a rock star too?"

"Probably not."

"Then I'll stick with The Hatchery. It's safer and faster."

"My husband, Cortland, is here. He's helping renovate Valentine's old music hall and producing a show."

"Everyone knows that."

"My twins are here too. Becky didn't realize that she was pregnant when she left Mars. She's about five months along with twins. Would you like to meet her?"

"Yes. I never met a pregnant woman. Does she know her options at the Hatchery?"

"No. I haven't told her."

"What if she finds out? Wouldn't she wonder why you never told her?"

I sigh.

My palm signals a call. I raise a finger to Nebula. An automated voice with sounds of background music says, "Stop snooping. Go home."

Nebula says, "You look upset."

"Do I?" I say. "Too much to do. Thanks, you were helpful." I leave.

***

Before I go back to the hotel, I call Dante and ask if we could talk. He suggests meeting at the Robo-Coffee Café because it's between the Twilight Zone and Molly's Pluto.

We gaze at a list of floating selections and make our choices. We push through the crowded room and find a table in the back. A moment later, a drone delivers two steaming cups and hovers, projecting an ad with a jingle for the Artificial Intelligence Olympics. It won't stop repeating the ad nor give us our coffee until we pay and send a donation to its website.

Dante blows the top of his coffee to cool it, then takes a sip. He puts it down carefully. His shoulders hunch as he leans forward on his elbows. "I still feel badly about the trouble we've caused you."

I take a sip of coffee. It's weak but not bad.

"Herb Tarragon and I were in a relationship. He called me little Dante."

"Nebula also had a relationship with him, but he broke up with her because he preferred men."

Dante nods, runs his index finger around his saucer like a moon around a planet. He calculates his words. "Ours was more than a relationship. We considered marriage."

I say nothing, hoping he will fill the silence. His eyes show emotion. "I don't know what I did wrong, but we remained friends."

"That's hard to do."

"We wanted to work together."

"Still, hard to do."

"He broke off his affair with Adam Kools because he told me that Adam was demanding and very high powered. I thought we would get back together, but we never did."

I laugh. "Well, everyone I've spoken to says that Herb Tarragon was also demanding and high powered: puffed up like loaves of bread with too much yeast."

I return to the hotel and go to my room. What I learned about Nebula Veil, Dante Essen, Adam Kools, and Herb Tarragon is a mental mobius strip: back to the same place but upside-down.

I palm "childbirth" and see what comes up. I find a natural birth clinic started by women who felt that the Hatchery was too impersonal called Inside-Out. I feel relieved knowing it exists.

34

CARMELLA SITS BEHIND a shiny new Lucite desk that has more keys than a Jupiter style triple-level synthesizer. Her staff sits behind her with similar but smaller desks. Various sized screens line one wall. Codes below blink in alphabetical order. Another wall has a beautiful holo of a waterfall. When she sees us, she stops what she's doing and stands.

We comment on the new digs.

"Long overdue," she says. "It is a graduation project from this year's Miss Incarceration and the inmates of Rikers Pluto, one of our prisons. How can I help you?"

I tell her what we learned about Herb Tarragon.

"Know that already," Carmella says.

"When did you find him?" Trenton asks.

"A while ago. But we didn't pick him up for questioning. We just followed him."

I say, "There was a man pretending to read a tablet who wore a black baseball cap when we met with Herb Tarragon."

"I sent Don Giovanni to follow you. Maybe protect you if need be," Carmella says.

I see Don Giovanni reaching under his desk and get a black baseball cap. He puts it on and waves.

"You're supposed to be working with Mars Yard," Trenton says. "When did you plan on letting me know?"

She cocks her head to one side and frowns. "How about now?"

Jersey says, "And if we hadn't come in?"

Carmella says, "Look, I didn't want to report with inconclusive evidence. We have no eye witnesses and no proof that he did it. All we definitely know is that the murdered person was one of his clones."

"What do you know about Prozac and Viagra Tarragon?" I ask. "Did you know they were Herb Tarragon's cousins?

She walks to the waterfall, thrusts her hand in. The waterfall shimmers and becomes a menacing holo of fire complete with the smell of smoke. She removes her hand, puts two fingers together, and taps a code. The fire hisses. A flowing wall of small triangles appears. Carmella touches one triangle and a file slides out. She takes it and brings it to her desk and inserts it into her computer.

She reads aloud. "Prozac and Viagra Tarragon. Brothers and medical doctors. Arrested several times for unethical practices like administering untested viruses, memory wipes, altering a patient's DNA when they thought they were getting their tonsils removed."

"Well," I say. "We think they were the ones who kidnapped me."

Carmella says, "Any proof?" She pauses and reads. "Seems they were in the same prison at the same time Avery Spelling was. What do you know about Avery?"

I say, "Avery is an enhanced human."

Carmella says, "Enhanced human, android, whatever."

"We knew him on Mars. He murdered his boss, the owner of Virtual Vittles, a virtual restaurant. He was sentenced to prison on Pluto and remained here after his sentence was finished. He owns two Silicone Slings. We just saw him in New Darwin."

"Worked at Virtual Vittles, a virtual restaurant?" Carmella huffs. "We don't need those."

"They say virtual restaurants are the latest in food technology," I say.

"Don't make me take an antacid. That's a toy for the rich. Smoke and mirrors. Pluto needs real restaurants." She peers at me. "That's why you're here. Remember?"

I offer her a Chocolate Moon. She takes the whole box and puts it in her pocket. I ask, "Could you see if the Tarragon cousins show up near a Molly's Chocolate Chip Cookie shop?"

She taps several fingers together. A holo of Prozac and Viagra Tarragon reaching into large bags of cookies and munching on them projects in front of us.

Jersey points. "Enlarge over there and search for unusual features." Everyone squints. "It's silly, but their eyebrows grow straight up."

"Enough of an identifying feature," Trenton says. "I'm palming the Valentine Hatchery and asking Adam Kools to check holos of Dr. Nucleus and Dr. Trademark to see if they have the same eyebrows to make sure they are not Prozac and Viagra Tarragon."

Adam responds immediately. They have different eyebrows.

Carmella says, "I can easily pick up Prozac and Viagra Tarragon for questioning."

We leave.

"Now what?" Jersey asks.

I say, "Let's get a snack."

"You always want to get a snack."

"If you came from Earth as I did and your parents owned an ice cream factory, you would understand."

Jersey's brow wrinkles. "I never wanted to go to Earth. All that gravity is bad for my health. But I would love to visit the ring they built around Earth so I could see it better."

"The building of Earth's Ring was a big success," I say. "It's still being expanded. People who don't want to move far from Earth but want to live in light gravity have bought condos. It has great duty-free shopping plus a lot of things Earth doesn't allow to be imported."

Jersey stops walking. She takes a deep breath and touches her forehead. Then she grabs Trenton's arm.

"Something the matter, sweetheart?" Trenton asks, sounding concerned.

"Those chemicals I took feel strange, different. Suddenly everyone looks like you."

"Really?"

Jersey grips Trenton's arm harder. "I feel lightheaded." She takes a step but staggers.

Trenton says, "Maybe you should sit down."

"No, wait. It's passing." She looks at me. "Molly! You look like the old Molly."

"I don't know if I like being called the old Molly, but I know what you mean."

Trenton says, "Sounds like the effects of the chemicals are worn off. I'm relieved." He kisses her on the cheek and points ahead. "Let's go to Saturn Ring Donuts. But I can never decide between a Daphnis, an Atlas, a Titan, a Hyperion, an Enceladus, a…"

"Stop!" Jersey protests. "You always get the Titan because it is the only one with the sugar glaze atmosphere."

We slide into a booth. A flat screen on the wall plays the news.

Jersey says, "No holo? Only flat pictures? This must be what listening to the radio was like in the twenty-first century."

"Radio only had sound, no pictures," I say. "This is more like their TV."

"Unbelievable! One step above smoke signals!"

An announcer says, "Police have arrested Bernie the Madoff, president and CEO of Universal Bernie. His company, Bernie's Space that had thousands of investors and was going to build a Dyson Sphere was a Ponzi scheme. Yours truly just lost thirty thousand starbucks."

"What's a Dyson Sphere?" I ask.

Trenton says, "A megastructure that was supposed to be built to surround a star and capture a large percentage of its power output."

"There is no technology even close to doing that."

"You know it and I know it," Trenton says. "But throw lots of technological words and concepts around and offer high returns on money and greed trumps caution."

"People are smarter than that," Jersey says.

"Really?" Trenton says. "You think so? Investors are always looking for the next big thing. In 1964, a Soviet astronomer, Nikolai Kardashev, created a method of measuring a civilization's level of technological advancement. Bernie the Madoff combined this information with false information to lure investors citing the Kardashev method."

Jersey asks, "Are you talking about the Kardashians who were twenty-first-century pornography historians?"

"Them too."

"I wonder if we know anyone who invested in this?" Jersey asks.

I shrug my shoulders and finish my donut. I watch Jersey and Trenton continue to slowly savor one half of their donuts and wrap the other half in napkins for later. They could win a food torture Olympics.

***

When Nebula visits the twins and me, her hair ripples down falling to her shoulders.

She wears a trendy yellow top with cut outs on the shoulders and jeans that have rips at the knees, a retro style from the past that somehow has endured, making her look fresh and young. She brings Becky two stuffed bunnies for her unborn twins, which Becky cuddles, and a chocolate strudel that she made at home.

Nebula can't take her eyes off Becky's swollen belly. "Can I touch your belly?" she asks Becky in a very soft voice.

"Sure," Becky says.

Nebula's eyes glow. She places her hand on Becky's belly. Her belly rises and falls. Nebula is startled. She removes her hand quickly. "Your belly jumped," she says.

"That's just the babies kicking. Happens all the time. It's a sign that they're healthy."

"Does it hurt?" she asks.

Becky laughs. "No, that part feels fine."

I serve coffee and the chocolate strudel and say, "This is delicious. I'll ask Tonto if it can be added to the menu as a special."

Nebula smiles.

"I found a natural birth clinic called Inside-Out," I say. "The twins and I were going to visit it. Would you like to join us?"

Nebula says, "Would love to. Could I bring a friend?"

"Of course," I say.

Becky says, "Lois and I did research about childbirth on Pluto because we wondered about the disproportionate number of beautiful people here. Mom, do you know about The Hatchery?"

Nebula mumbles, "Told you so."

I say, "Yes. I've been there. It's a medical facility that is both a hospital and research center. They do a lot of genetic manipulation."

Nebula says, "Genetic enhancement."

Lois asks, "For example?"

I say, "If you want a child with blue eyes or a higher IQ, it can be arranged. Also, if you didn't like the feelings of being pregnant, the fetus can develop in an alternative womb."

We all look at Becky as she circles her abdomen with her hands. No one says anything for a long time. Then Becky says, "I want to go to The Hatchery and see for myself."

I call the concierge. The first available date for The Hatchery is the following week. But we can visit Inside-Out tomorrow.

Bottom line: Becky, Lois, and I love Inside-Out. It is a bright happy modern facility with an intelligent professional staff who make us feel welcome. Pictures of mothers holding babies and fathers standing next to them radiating with love line the walls. We meet several women in various stages of pregnancy who Becky bonds with. One invites her to join a class that teaches deep-breathing Lamaze techniques during labor.

"Labor?" Nebula cries. "They call the process of giving birth going into labor? Sounds like work. I don't like that."

The more Nebula and her friend see, the more distressed they become.

"Cruel and primitive," Nebula says to her friend who agrees with her and can't wait to leave Inside-Out.

***

The following week Becky, Lois, and I go to the Hatchery. We take the tram. Becky and Lois lower their heads and peek at the beautiful people who enter and exit the car. They are clearly unnerved and feel unattractive compared to them. I try to cheer them up as we pass the wholesale market asking if they would like to go, but they are not interested. We exit at the last stop where there are two signs: one points to The Hatchery and the other to the shoe outlet that I forgot was there.

Lois points and says, "That's more like it."

Adam Kools welcomes us and introduces us to several people, all of whom stare at Becky's large abdomen and ask if they might holograph her.

"Why?" she asks.

Adam says, "You're the first pregnant woman they ever met. Are you ready for the tour?"

The tour is mercifully short, a very toned-down version of the tour that Trenton, Jersey, and I were given earlier.

Adam offers refreshments. But like Nebula and her friend

when they visited Inside-Out, the twins' unsmiling, grim faces
signal they're anxious to go and we do.

35

EACH EVENING CORTLAND COMES BACK to the hotel rejuvenated and exhilarated, just like when he was young and started Molawn, his music agency. Years ago, many predicted that he would become bigger than Gordy Blueberry who managed the Subprimes. And when groups like Max and the Planks and Niels and the Bohrs left Gordy and signed-on with him, he did.

Every day he watches construction on the music hall progress and hears musicians rocking and rolling and jamming it all the way up as they audition for a spot in a show. The new hall has attracted many backers who have given lots of starbucks and want their names prominently displayed on its walls.

He's also working with the architects to design a rotating stage, like the one we have on Mars, that lets one act finish and fade off while the new act moves center. It will create a seamless spin to the show without pauses and losing energy. He is a perfectionist with dramatic stage lighting that if not done well, makes a young person look old and an old person look scary.

*****

I'm glad Cortland is so busy because Carmella calls Trenton and tells him that she wants to question Herb Tarragon, but she says he might be more forthcoming if we do the questioning. He turned up in a security holo at Venture Land, a large recreational facility with a woman whose biometrics registered as android.

She sends complementary passes to our palms. If it's anything like Mars Disney, this could be fun. I tell Cortland that Jersey, Trenton, and I got free passes to Venture Land, and as long as he's so busy, I might as well go. All he mumbles is, "Enjoy your day. Too busy for fun."

Our tram goes through several airlocks before it stops under the clear dome that encompasses Venture Land. We scan our passes and exit into an area filled with ads for winter and summer activities. There are two roadways: one goes to Summer Land the other to Winter Wonderland.

We start with winter. A floating infomercial tells us that the area is 22,500 square meters of indoor ski slopes and 3,000 square meters of a Winter Wonderland, with sled and toboggan runs, an icy body slide, climbing towers, giant snowballs, an ice cave, and more.

A moving walkway brings us to the winter dressing room. Attendants ask our sizes and give us warm clothing. We put our clothes in a locker and dress. A florescent sign says we can buy the clothes at their gift shop, but they are expensive, and I'm not likely to wear mine again.

Trenton says, "I'm glad clothes and equipment are included in the admission price."

"It doesn't matter, Trenton," I say. "The Pluto Police are paying."

"Details." Trenton smirks. "Details."

We step on another moving roadway that grows colder the closer we near Winter Wonderland. A door opens, and a blast of freezing air hits us. "I forgot what winter feels like!" I say, my nose instantly cold. "I've grown so used to living in controlled environments and haven't felt real winter since I left Earth." I rub my hands together and see my breath. Then my eyes light up. My mouth waters. "Hey, hot chocolate!"

Jersey says, "You know, Molly, you could easily put back those hundred pounds you lost when we were security guards at the Culinary Institute."

"Some things are worth it. Come on, the hot chocolate is my treat."

"Well, in that case…"

We all sip our steaming cups of hot chocolate and see a mountain to our left. A floating sign says it's eighty-five meters high and has slopes of varying steepness. We watch skiers on the quad lift and tow lift carry snowboarders and skiers up.

Trenton says, "They're paying, and I'm going."

"When did you learn to ski?" I ask.

"Never learned. I'm adding a skiing program to my database so I'll know by the time I reach the top of the mountain."

Jersey asks, "Don't you think you should start on one of the smaller slopes?"

"Nonsense. I'll be fine."

We go to the quad lift. Trenton is helped into a seat and a security belt fastened. We watch him move up and away.

Jersey says, "Trenton can be overconfident because he can adjust his pain sensors and ninety percent of him can be rebuilt."

"A good reason to be confident."

Trenton palms Jersey. I hear. "I'm on the top and ready to go. See you on the bottom."

We wait. We watch. We're impressed. Trenton skis gracefully to the bottom. Jersey jumps up and down in relief. We run over to him.

"I have to do that again," Trenton says.

"We're here to find Herb Tarragon, not ski," Jersey says.

But before she can stop him, he slides into another quad lift and calls, "Well, maybe Herb Tarragon will be on the next run." He waves and rises.

Jersey says, "Look! Over there. Doesn't that look like Herb Tarragon with a woman who just got off the other lift? I think it looks like April or June May. I can't tell which one from here."

"Hard to tell with this clothing. But yes, close enough."

"They're walking in the direction of the ice cave. I'm palming Trenton to tell him that we're going to follow him."

Jersey palms Trenton. He doesn't answer.

Suddenly an announcement booms: "Skier registered with the name Trenton down on Alpine slope three." Everyone's head turns as two drones fly to the area pick up Trenton and fly him to the recuperation area.

"You'll have to follow Herb Tarragon alone," Jersey cries in a high-pitched nervous voice. "I have to see how Trenton is."

***

I trudge a safe distance behind Herb Tarragon and the woman. They stop and buy hot dogs. I resist. They finish eating them and continue toward the ice cave. A large sign says, "Dark Ice Maze—twenty rooms filled with bone chilling terror." I watch as they pause and talk to the attendant who scans their palms. They enter and disappear into darkness.

I walk over and say to the attendant, "My friends just went into the ice cave. I really don't like going though scary mazes."

"It's all illusion," he says. "Nothing to be afraid of."

"I know," I say trying to think of a way to avoid this. "If the entrance and exit is in the same place, I can wait for them here."

"We change the exit location every day. If you want to find them, you have to go through."

I palm Jersey. "They went into an ice cave of horrors. I have to go in or I could lose them. I always get lost in these places and am the last to get out."

Jersey says, "Don't be ridiculous. It's all fake. Trenton is fine. Don't worry. We'll find you."

I step inside. I hear the sound of a squeaking door closing behind me. Everything is black. I couldn't find the door again if I tried. I'm trapped. I smell smoke. "Does anyone get lost in here?" I cry.

"You'll find out," a voice booms followed by laughter and

blood-curdling screams.

The light is very dim. Fog envelops me. I cough and walk into a wall of ice that I thought led to a hallway. This may be smoke and mirrors, but it feels real.

The ground shifts. I grab a nearby rail. I slide forward and see a rotating tunnel spinning ahead. I take a deep breath and walk toward a descending wall that moves down toward the ground position. I think it best to crawl through on my hands and knees because if I fall, I'm already down. I make my way through as I ignore the distracting strobe lights, air blasters, gory images of vampires, werewolves, and ghosts who reach out to grab me.

The moment I exit and stand, a dark cloak drops over my head. I can't see anything, and it smells musty. I sweat as I struggle to get it off. A moment before I panic, it rises. A dark image about my size is ahead. The only place I can walk is toward it so I am facing it. When I reach up, it reaches up. When I turn sideways, it turns sideways. When I step forward, it steps closer. I scream. The dim glow grows brighter. It's a mirror. I can't believe I was afraid of my own reflection.

After following more dead ends that play havoc with my sense of direction, someone dressed as the Hulk and doesn't scare me points toward the exit where I'm relieved to find Jersey and Trenton, who is not seriously hurt, waiting for me.

Jersey says, "You disappeared from our scanners when you went into the ice cave, and I had to call Carmella to track you. You spent so much time in there that Carmella says Herb Tarragon and the woman have likely gone to Summer Land."

"Likely? She found me easy enough. Why can't she track them?"

Trenton says, "She can, to a limited degree, but there are blind spots in the security system that can be activated for privacy if one pays extra to activate them. They did."

<h1 style="text-align:center">36</h1>

I LOVE THE HEAT in Summer Land. We enter their dressing area and are given bathing suits, t-shirts, and towels. "No sunscreen?" I say.

The attendant in a Hawaiian shirt, shorts, and open-toed sandals rolls his eyes. "No sun," he says.

"I'm relieved that Carmella put a trace on us," I say. "I hated the ice cave."

Trenton says. "They have a surf pool that makes three-point-three-meter-high waves every ninety seconds. I'm definitely going. They also have bungee jumping."

Jersey says, "You're not bungee jumping."

Trenton frowns. "These indoor recreation sites are copied from those in Old Dubai, a city in a desert on Earth."

"Earth had deserts?" Jersey asks.

Trenton says, "They used to. Now if you want to see a desert, you have to go to the Moses of Arabia museum. It's run by the Environmental Protection Agency best known for refreezing Earth's North and South Poles."

"My history class at Armstrong U. said that Moses may have had poor health and financial difficulties. His doctor, a brilliant scientist famous for living in a house that burned but was not consumed (and never got the price he wanted for the retardant he discovered) made him take ten tablets. Then, he never got into a land he was promised."

"That's sad," Jersey says. "What about Dubai? Is it still there?"

"It flooded when they redirected some of the ice from the north pole to make the Sahara Sea," I say. "I'm surprised you didn't know."

Jersey frowns. "Everyone doesn't know! You know because you're from Earth."

"Well, time to surf," Trenton says. "It's 'The Endless Summer' with its perfect wave."

"If you go, Molly and I can go whitewater rafting."

"We're here to find Herb Tarragon," I say. "Shouldn't we stick to that?"

"You're afraid to go whitewater rafting. Aren't you, Molly?"

"Maybe."

Trenton starts to march off. "See you guys later. Time to hang-ten."

Jersey looks at me. "I guess you don't want to go bungee jumping either."

"No, but I can watch."

We go to the bungee jumping area, passing a stand that sells frozen yogurt that we don't buy. It's easy to spot the few people from Earth because Earth is the largest world that people live on with the strongest gravity making them the shortest and heaviest in the solar system. They never win beauty contests, but some win sporting events that depend on muscles easier to develop living in heavier gravity. I try to imagine, without success, what someone conceived and raised on Jupiter might look like, but no one lives there.

I call Carmella and ask if she can access security and find Herb Tarragon. She says she followed him best she could, but he moved from one blind spot to another. However, some activities have no blind spots for safety concerns.

A moment later, Carmella says, "Hey! Trenton is water skiing. He's not bad."

We say nothing.

"Wait," Carmella adds. "I just found Herb Tarragon and a

woman at the bungee jump putting on jumping harnesses."

"On our way," I say.

By the time we get to the bungee jump, we see the images of Herb Tarragon and the woman projected onto a screen showing them waiting their turn to jump from a high platform. The woman is in back of him with her arms around his waist. He turns to say something to her and she moves to his side. Attendants tie them together and connect a large elastic cord. They look at each other and appear to be counting down.

They jump.

First, they free fall. Then the cord stretches and grows taut as they hit the point of maximum decent and then they are yanked upward as the cord recoils. They oscillate up and down until all the kinetic energy dissipates and they are slowly lowered to the ground. The woman unstraps herself and gets up.

She bends down and say something to him. Then she shakes him. He slumps down. She reaches toward him again and his head lolls to one side. She touches his head, moves it and says something.

Herb Tarragon doesn't move.

She screams. Two workers wearing white outfits that say "medic" rush over. They unhook him and lay him on the ground. One bends over Herb with a hand-held scanner then holds Herb's nose and breathes into his mouth. Then the medic bangs on his chest and takes a device and puts it on Herb's chest that makes it rise and fall. He repeats the procedure several times. Finally, he stands and signs thumbs down.

Carmella palms and says, "I saw the whole thing. Can you find out more?"

I hear sirens and see flashing lights as an ambulance arrives. Two more paramedics jump out and lift Herb onto a stretcher and slide him into the ambulance. The woman goes and sits in the front with one of the attendants. She's sobbing hysterically.

Trenton finds us. He shows the bungee jump staff his Mars

Yard credentials.

One sneers. "We don't have to talk to you."

Another adds, "Or talk to anybody."

Trenton palms Carmella, who says, "Well, it was worth a shot. I'll send you the results of Herb Tarragon's autopsy when I get them."

Hours later, Carmella tells Trenton, "A preliminary report said that the body was definitely Herb Tarragon and not a clone and the woman with him was April May. They also found a note in his palm phone that said, 'Let's talk more. I still love you.' It was signed Adam. I'll question Adam Kools to see if it was him. Could be another Adam."

Trenton says, "Of the six Tarragon clones, we definitely know four are dead and now Herb Tarragon makes five. One clone is still unaccounted for."

***

Back to the hotel, an attendant at the front desk says that Cortland and the twins will be late and are having dinner at a new restaurant. We go in the elevator. It bounces to a halt between the fifth and sixth floor. Trenton presses the emergency button. No response. We bang on the door. Silence. Jersey palms the front desk, who tells us that they know the problem.

Suddenly the car shakes. We rise seven floors. We stop again. When Trenton pushes the emergency button again, the elevator falls and bounces to a stop on the second floor. I fall and hit my head. I see colors in whirling cascades. There's banging beneath us. Someone calls, "We're going to drill through the floor to get you out."

Five minutes later, we feel strong vibration and see the tip of a buzz-saw cutting a hole in the floor. Soon the hole is large enough for us to be pulled through. We're given a free glass of champagne and escorted in another elevator to our rooms.

I lay on the bed and try to nap so I won't be exhausted when Cortland comes, but I can't relax. So, I get up and decide to go to the Twilight Zone's library.

The librarian is happy to see me again. I browse through what I'm told is the first and only edition of *The Maltese Chicken*. It looks well done but tough. Then I find *From Eternity to Here*. Most of the book is in chapter one and looks very repetitive. The librarian tells me that *Twenty Thousand Leagues under the Encedelus Sea* had just been added to their collection.

"Nice," I say. "Do you have the other one by Jules Verne? It's about another sea?"

I get a strange look. "Another sea? Encedelus only has one sea. Maybe you would like a romance like *Atlas Hugged* by Ayn Rand. It won the Fountainhead award. Or a biography of Don Quixote, who struggled with wind turbines."

"Maybe later," I say, finally feeling sleepy.

***

The next morning, I meet Jersey and Trenton at the hotel restaurant. They each order the full moon pancakes. I look longingly at the pancakes but order yogurt and fruit. Trenton pokes his palm and checks the news. "Going to project this," he says. "Let's see if Pluto media is reporting this accurately or if was fake news added to attract headlines."

A holo of Summer Land appears in the middle of the table. A reporter standing in front of the bungee jump says, "April May and Herb Tarragon were two of over a hundred people who bungee jumped yesterday. Herb Tarragon was dead when the jump ended. April May is fine. Bungee engineers checked the ride several times by harnessing five fat circus clowns together and having them jump. No problem. The clowns want to go again, but the engineers don't want to push it."

Trenton holds his fork that has a large piece of his pancake dangling. How can he hold it like that and not eat it, I wonder.

"I'm sure the police are questioning April," he says. "I'll ask Carmella for her sister June May's palm code. We might learn something new if we can talk to her." Finally, he pops the pancake in his mouth.

Carmella gives Trenton June May's code. She tells him that after finding the note on Herb's palm she questioned Adam Kools. Adam admitted he sent the note to Herb Tarragon trying to revive their relationship but Herb wanted a clean break as he had fallen in love with someone else. She adds that Pluto forensics reported that Herb Tarragon had a substance in his system never seen before and they have hit a wall identifying it. Plus, remnants of saffron were also found in Herb Tarragon's pocket.

"Know anything about this?" she asks.

Trenton tells her he knows nothing about a substance that can't be identified without examining it himself. But that he and Molly and Jersey gave the saffron to Herb Tarragon, hoping to elicit more information and they got it from Tony Knuckles.

"Tony Knuckles, I love that guy. Our families are related. We grew up together. Well, this is very good work," Carmella says, words I never thought I would hear, followed by, "How about another Chocolate Decadence cake?" Words I was not surprised to hear.

Trenton clicks off. There is no answer when he calls June. A message says she went to Charon Maximus, a hotel on Charon.

Jersey says, "We should find her. If she's involved in one of the deaths, she can hide on Charon or go farther into the Oort cloud and be out of reach. Family and close friends are the usual suspects and should be questioned."

"Maybe we can combine a little work with a little fun," I say.

"Didn't we just do that?" Jersey asks.

Trenton says, "Charon is half the size of Pluto and tidally locked, keeping the same face toward each other like Earth and its moon."

"Handy if you want to hide on the dark side of the moon like Molly's old boyfriend Drew did when we solved the case of the chocolate moons. Right, Molly?" Jersey says.

"When we lived on Earth's moon, Cortland put advertising on the side that didn't face Earth, and we went bankrupt because Earth never saw his ads. We were fortunate his cousin offered him a job on Mars with Little Green Man Pizza."

Trenton interrupts. "The Pluto-Charon shuttle leaves every morning and comes back every evening. Let's go tomorrow."

37

CORTLAND IS SO BUSY AUDITIONING singers, and since the twins found the shoe outlet and Becky started classes at Inside-Out, I don't think I'll be missed for the day. When I tell each of them I'm going, no one looks up but just says, "Bye. Love you." or, "See you later."

As soon as I sink into a wide comfortable Pluto-Charon shuttle seat, a holo coalesces in front of us advertising Oort Cloud vacation spots. Jersey says, "Looks like fun."

"Why would you go there when there is so much closer to home?"

"First class deluxe is so inexpensive, Molly."

"There's a reason for that." The holo fades. One that shows how to adjust the chair's angles, vibration settings, and order refreshments replaces it. Jersey says, "The gold button on the left lets you play with a virtual slot machine."

"Already won seventy-five starbucks," Trenton pipes.

We peer out of the window and watch Charon grow larger. I see a dazzling oasis of light circle its equator. The closer we get, the bigger it shimmers and grows. I say, "That must be the strip with all the hotels and casinos. Those dark areas nearby could hold lots of secrets."

We dock. Artificial gravity makes our stomachs drop. A porter in a shiny gold jacket walks through the car, smiling a four-aces smile. He shakes clinking pouches. "Fifty free starbucks to start you off," he says. "Compliments of Charon Casinos.

Good luck with your luck." The door slides open. A voice booms, "Please stand clear of the closing doors," followed by, "TIPS NOT INCLUDED. Please drop one into the box near the door or you may be delayed indefinitely."

We each drop a starbuck into the box, exit, and follow signs to the taxis. We climb into the first one in line.

"Where to?" the driver asks.

"Charon Maximus," Trenton says. "It's on the Vulcan Planum."

"Know where it is. Charon's not that big." He pulls onto a road that runs parallel to the edge of the dome. We see lots of construction on the outer side.

I ask, "What are they building out there?"

The driver says, "Not building. Digging. Pluto wants to add volume to make itself larger so it will no longer be a dwarf planet. They're getting the materials from any world willing to sell. Also, there's a big vote next month to decide if Pluto and Charon are planet and moon or a binary. Like Earth and its moon, the mass of the moon is exceptionally large compared to the mass of the planet."

"I didn't think that was something one could vote on," Trenton says.

The driver smiles broadly. "Here we can," he says.

I ask Trenton, "How did you know June May is at the Charon Maximus?"

Trenton says, "Carmella texted me."

Jersey says, "Did she learn where June May was from a scan?"

"No, she asked April."

The taxi pulls up to the hotel. It looks like an enormous circus tent. Two ferocious lions on either side of the front door growl. I clutch the taxi door. "Is there another entrance? I don't want to get out."

The driver laughs, "They're robots. Those teeth are as soft as foam rubber." He shows us a picture of his head in a lion's mouth. Nevertheless, when I exit the taxi, I run when the lion growls and lunges at me. Trenton and Jersey pat its mane and laugh at me.

The lobby of Charon Maximus has a glass ceiling that rises fifty feet. As we are on the back side of Charon, stars in the night sky shine beyond making the lobby dramatic and spectacular. The framework and beams are sculpted in green metal floral patterns. There is so much marble a quarry might have been emptied to build it. One side has a wide spiral escalator filled with well-dressed people.

The other side has a huge circular bar and lounge with a glowing installation of dancing lights that spin continuously while changing colors. Boisterous voices come from inside.

"If I drank and watched those lights, I would fall off my chair," I say.

Jersey laughs. "Want to try?"

In the distance, there are hundreds of slot machines, poker-machines, plus an enormous wheel of fortune. An arrow blinks and points: Whales and Dolphins casino. "I wonder why they gave the casino that name?" I say.

"Whales and dolphins never sleep," Trenton says. "They switch off one side of their brain at a time and keep going."

"That's a half-brained idea," Jersey quips.

A waiter holds a silver tray with free champagne cocktails in crystal flutes. A drone floats with canapés. We take one of each. Jersey sips and says, "The Twilight Zone in Valentine could learn a thing or two from this place."

A man in a navy jacket with the words Charon Maximus over the left breast pocket approaches. "I see you're impressed with our lobby. Will you be staying long?"

Trenton says, "Depends." He shows him his credentials.

His eyebrows rise. "We've never had anyone from Mars Yard before. We can give you a good deal on a suite."

Jersey pinches Trenton's arm. "Go for it, sweetheart! It's a

Mars Yard business expense."

I say, "We brought no luggage because we thought we would be going back tonight."

"Thousands come without luggage. Just ring for room service and ask for the 'no luggage special'."

We are shown to a two-bedroom, two-bathroom suite with a sitting area and a large food replicator in one wall. The furniture is sleek, modern, and black lacquered. Each bathroom has a double-sized stall with a teak shower and black tiles. Blinding light comes from the strip below.

"I'll never sleep with that light," I say.

Jersey finds a switch, presses it. The windows turn black. "Now you will." She presses again, and the lights return then grow dimmer. A voice says, "Welcome. Anything you want, please just say 'Room Service'."

Jersey says, "Room Service, we need a no luggage special for three."

The voice says, "I'll scan for sizes then project holos of clothes. Point to your choices."

Trenton chooses new jeans, a blue western shirt, underwear, and silk pajamas and charges his purchase to Mars Yard as a business expense. Jersey and I, upon seeing the prices, decide to wear the clothes we came in but go for pajamas and new underwear.

Trenton puts Carmella on speaker palm. "We're here," he says.

"Know that," Carmella says. "Scans indicate that June May is spending most of her time in the kitchen."

"So much great stuff here even if you don't gamble. Why would she go there?" Jersey asks.

"Find out," Carmella snarls. "That's why you're there."

I text to Cortland and tell him I will be back tomorrow.

"Before we go, let me try the food replicator." I tap a menu that has pictures of food. "Look at this. It's incredible! This replicator makes a T-bone steak, poached sea bass in a light curry sauce, linguine in white clam sauce, and so much more! Usually you're lucky if a replicator makes fresh coffee and a simple sandwich."

Trenton comes over. "Let me see that." He pokes around. We wait. Pokes more. "No wonder it can do that. They call it a replicator, but it's not. There are tubes that connect to the restaurant kitchen. Just another way of having room service."

"Order me a grilled cheese and tomato on whole wheat and coffee," I say.

"Make that three," Jersey says. "I wonder why they do that? They have room service."

Trenton thinks and says, "Probably for privacy."

"We need to find the kitchen. I wonder if they will let us in. Only the kitchen staff is allowed into Molly's Bistro. This may be the same," I say.

"They may let me in because I'm with Mars Yard," Trenton says.

"But I should go," I say. "I'm a restaurant owner that will open a branch on Pluto. They might, as professional courtesy, let me in."

"Great idea," Jersey says. "And I'll come as your head waiter."

"Mind if I use those starbucks they gave us?" Trenton asks. "No reason for them to go to waste."

Jersey says, "Who said anything about them going to waste?"

<h1 style="text-align:center">38</h1>

The elevator to the lobby is crowded even though there's only three other people in it; but their large wings fill most of the space. "You could have flown down," I quip.

Silence and a nasty look.

Trenton heads to the casino. Jersey and I go to the front desk and ask for the manager.

"Any problem?" an attendant asks.

I tell him that I am a professional restaurant owner and ask if we could see their kitchen. I access Molly's Bistro and show him a holo and say that it will open in Valentine soon.

The attendant makes a call. Soon, a striking-looking woman with long blond hair in a body-revealing black and silver gown approaches. She puts out her hand. "I'm Platinum, hotel manager. I've read about your bistro coming to Valentine. Taking a while, isn't it?"

"It's not easy getting a professional staff," I say.

"Know what you mean. We recently hired a new chef. One of our six restaurants needs a head waiter. His girlfriend has good credentials from a restaurant in New Darwin. Bronze from hospitality will accompany you." She taps her palm. "Are you enjoying your stay?"

Before we can answer, a woman in a navy suit and white blouse that looks like Platinum with golden brown hair approaches.

"You're clones?" I say looking from one to the other.

"Yes," Bronze says. "I'm seven of nine. Platinum is eight of nine. Our kitchens range from deluxe to casual. Any preference where to start?"

"Deluxe," I say.

We follow Bronze to the kitchen in a restaurant called Gold Rush. It is large and bright and filled with fragrant cooking aromas. Bronze moves her arm in an arc. "As you see, there are stations for different jobs: one makes salads, one grills, one fries, and so on."

And, although I have a similar layout at my bistro's kitchen, I am overwhelmed by size of the kitchen and the number of people prepping, cooking, plating, cleaning, and the consistently swift preparation of the volume of dishes.

We cross the room. The chef is standing in the center. The closer we come, the more he looks like Herb Tarragon. June May is next to him, stirring a pale-yellow sauce in a large pan.

June May smiles and looks up. "Hey, Bronze, who are the visitors?"

"You probably don't remember," I say trying to look as nice and interesting as possible, "but we met a while back at the Darwin Diner."

June May squints. "Sorry. Don't remember."

"It was brief," Jersey says.

Bronze says, "You and your head waiter keep staring at the chef, Molly. Does he remind you of someone?"

"Yes," I say.

"Then let me introduce you to Sage Tarragon."

Jersey looks at Sage. "You must be Herb Tarragon's sixth clone."

Sage has a downturned mouth and an indifferent gaze that shifts to a piercing look. "Sixth clone? I could be the first clone. Most Plutonians have clones. I was never interested in learning about the others. We grew up separately and have different educational and environmental backgrounds."

Bronze stiffens and frowns. I can tell she thinks that the meeting is not going well.

Sage continues, "Never met Herb Tarragon, but his death when bungee jumping at Summer Land was all over the news. I would never bungee jump. I'm sure we're very different."

I say, "Not that different. You're both great chefs." I turn to June. "You knew Herb Tarragon was a great chef. In fact, you and April were going to invest in a new restaurant with him."

Sage's eyes narrow at June. "How come you never told me that?"

"I didn't think it was important," June says.

Sage glares.

I ask, "Where did you two meet?"

June answers. "We met at a cooking convention in Valentine. April and I were two of the hosts. Sage was demonstrating a quantum cooker that makes several meals at the same time. When you pick the meal to serve, the others disappear. No trace, no mess."

Jersey says, "But are probably in parallel universes where our other selves are eating them."

I say to June. "April has had a hard time. Have you spoken with her? The Pluto police are questioning her."

"She called immediately but said I didn't have to come. She gave Carmella Soprano her statement and now all she wants to do is sleep."

Sage interrupts, "If you don't mind we have hundreds of dinners to prepare."

Bronze, anxious to move us out asks, "Would you like to see the kitchen of Penny Change? It's our casual café."

"No," I say. "Thank you. We learned a lot and don't want to take more of your time."

We leave. Jersey palms Trenton. "Where are you? We finished touring the kitchen."

The noise is so loud I can hear it through her palm.

"Can't hear you, sweetheart."

"Now he's texting. He says he won a hundred thousand starbucks at the Wheel of Fortune." She disconnects.

"That's wonderful," I say.

"Wait. New text. Oh, oh. He said he just lost the money. That was fast." Jersey sighs. "We've got to get him out of there."

We go to the casino and find Trenton. I grab his right arm; Jersey grabs his left. His eyes are spinning faster than the wheel of fortune. We push him from the casino.

Jersey turns to me. "I shouldn't have let him gamble. I forgot how easy it is for androids to become addicted."

We get back our suite. Jersey calls room service. "Do you have something for an android coming off a gambling addiction?" She listens and nods, then continues. "Well, send one Bill Cosby, a double silicone milkshake, two steak dinner specials, and a bottle of Merlock. Charge it to Mars Yard under the name Trenton." She disconnects and turns to me. "We have the room and clothes, so we might as well enjoy a good dinner and drink that expensive Merlock wine. Trenton will be out cold until the Bill Cosby I'm going to give him wears off."

"What's a Bill Cosby?"

"The operator I spoke to said Quaaludes produces a drunken sleepy high. But in an android's system, it clears addictions. After eight hours, Trenton should wake up refreshed and remembering nothing. I'm taking a holo of him taking this in case he asks."

"Any idea who Bill Cosby was?"

"I think he was the first android given Quaaludes, but it was for a sex addiction."

39

WE RETURN TO PLUTO RELIEVED that we're no poorer and somewhat wiser.

That evening Cortland says that Lois had been after him to audition the drummer she was dating. "I heard him." Cortland sighs. "Filled with sound and fury."

"Did it signify anything?" I ask.

"Nada, nothing. Just a lot of boom-a-lay, boom-a-lay, boom-a-lay, boom. I'll have to break it to her that he doesn't make the cut."

When Cortland tells Lois his decision, Lois's face falls. "You're sure, Dad?" she asks twice.

A few days later, Lois says Shooting Starr broke up with her. I try to comfort her without revealing that I thought he only went out with her to get into one of Cortland's shows. "Dad's auditioning a singer named Zee Pope. He's very nice. He used to work at Molly's Pluto. I understand has a very good voice."

Lois sighs. Shakes her head. "Not interested. Couldn't care less."

"Carmella, the police captain, said he croons like the legendary Frank Sinatra. But she doesn't have your ears and musical discretion. Dad values your opinion. Why don't you go hear him and tell Dad what you think?"

Lois sighs. "If I have nothing better to do."

***

I meet Jersey and Trenton at the lobby cafe. The librarian is having a cup of tea and reading, *The Rise and Fall of the Roman*.

She looks up. "Ever hear of this book?" she asks me.

"Sad ending," I say.

She frowns, lowers her head, and mumbles, "Spoiler."

A waiter takes our order for three coffees. "When is Becky's husband, Burton, coming?" Jersey asks.

My palm signals a call. I look. "It's Becky. Who says there isn't spooky action at a distance?"

"Those who say action has nothing to do with spooks," Trenton says, drumming his fingers on the table.

I take Becky's call and do most of the listening. After I disconnect I say, "Becky told me that she has been sending holos of herself to Burton. He says he's missing so much of her pregnancy that he wants to see what she looks like. I told her she looks beautiful, but she says she doesn't feel beautiful. He should arrive within two weeks."

The waiter brings our coffee. Jersey sips, makes a face. "Well, at least it's hot." She blows on the top of the cup. "What do we know so far?"

Trenton says, "If Lucky was the murderer, his motive might be Herb Tarragon never returning to Molly's Pluto."

"Nebula may have become unhinged when Herb Tarragon broke up with her," I say. "And Dante was upset that Herb Tarragon stopped seeing him. Also, we are not clear how Adam Kools felt when Herb ended that affair. But are these motives enough for murder?"

"Sometimes it takes less," Jersey says. "Tonto and Herb Tarragon could have had disagreements we don't know about even though Tonto was going to invest with him in a new venture, as were Nebula, Zee, and Dante."

I say, "Carmella questioned April May. But I think we should too."

Trenton calls Carmella. "If you weren't with Mars Yard," she huffs, "I wouldn't give you any information. Our forensics are superior to those on other worlds. Question April if you want. She's back in New Darwin."

Trenton disconnects. "I wonder why she has such a low opinion of forensic teams on other worlds?"

***

April sits in a booth in the New Darwin Diner. She waves when we enter. She looks terrible.

Trenton tells her about a silicone wash and blush for androids that hides fatigue and a lubricant drink that boosts energy. She offers us beverages that we decline.

"I don't know what I can tell you that I haven't told the police." She sighs.

"Tell us about your sister, June," I say. "What do you know about her and Sage Tarragon?"

"What does that have to do with anything?" she snaps.

"Just tell us what you know," Jersey says softly.

"We met at a cooking convention in Valentine. At first, Sage was interested in me, but when he realized I was an android, he turned his attention to June. Sage said he was taking a job on Charon. June visits him."

"That much we know. We just came back from Charon."

April says, "Then you know June doesn't like it there and thinks Sage could find work on Pluto if he tried. But Sage loves his job. He told June he would never return unless he was offered the equivalent on Pluto."

"Did you know that the police found a note on Herb's palm from Adam Kools?"

"Yes. I knew about that. Herb told me about his relationship with him and that it was over."

Jersey asks, "Did you believe him?"

April says, "I did. Because he also told me how he wanted to become an android so we would be closer. I'm not sure if he started the process."

We thank April for her time and leave.

"Well, there's motive for June," I say. "June could have thought with Herb Tarragon's death, Sage could step up to the plate. April loved Herb and had no motive that I can see. Now as long as we're here, let's see Zee Pope."

***

Zee meets us at a park a short walk from the Darwin Diner. He smiles when he sees us. I smell freshly mowed grass. Pink and red rosebushes are in bloom to our left. Pale green weeping willow trees on our right grow next to a small pond with aqua and purple swans. A woman walks with a small albino elephant on a leash. I comment on how cute it is. "Albino elephants usually go blind in harsh Earth light," she says. "Here we don't have to worry about that happening."

"I didn't know charming spots like this existed on Pluto," I say to Zee. "Your planet has great natural beauty, but I never saw lovely parks like this one. Valentine is so gray and industrial."

"Valentine was the first city to be built. The budget was tight," Zee says.

There's a bench and table next to a waterfall. We sit. Tiers of blue and pink flowers woven into green ivy grow nearby. A man in a white uniform selling ice cream calls, "Two for one on Pluto Pistachio today."

"My treat," Trenton pipes. "I'll make it four pistachios sundaes."

I see him charge it to Mars Yard.

I savor a melting spoonful then turn to Zee. "Are you going to audition with my husband for a spot in a show? Carmella tells me you have a wonderful voice."

"Don't know if I'm good enough to make the cut." He catches a melting drip with his tongue. "Carmella's a great cop, but I don't know if she knows much beyond do-re-me. I love to sing.

If I could make a living from it, I would do nothing else."

"What do you know about Sage Tarragon?" I ask.

Jersey leans in. "Sage Tarragon, Herb Tarragon's clone. He works on Charon and is dating June May."

Zee looks surprised. "Don't know about that. I once saw April and June arguing. I assumed it was about Herb Tarragon, who was dating April. I thought June might be jealous."

"Did you see Herb Tarragon before he died?" I ask.

"Once. I was going into the Darwin Diner and he was coming out. We didn't greet each other. You waited for him to make the first move. All I saw that day was a stone face. You never knew when you risked getting on his wrong side."

40

ON OUR WAY BACK TO VALENTINE, Carmella calls Trenton. He adjusts the sound on his palm so we can hear what she has to say. "I have important findings that I'm going to share because I like you. I don't have to do this, you know," she says. "Our forensic team just determined that Herb Tarragon, who died while bungee jumping, killed his clone at the wholesale market."

Trenton says, "He said his clone was already dead with a knife in his back when he found him at the wholesale market."

"He lied. We have new security holos from the wholesale market that show Herb Tarragon buying a knife from Zee Pope. It matches the one used to kill his clone. Although knives may look alike, there are always microscopic nicks and striations as unique and distinguishable as fingerprints. Also, the red fabric found on his clone matches that of a jacket we found at his apartment. He must have figured that before the authorities could identify the dead person as his clone, he had time to disappear and start over."

"And he was right," Trenton says.

Jersey says, "Plenty of knives at the restaurant. Why would he buy one from Zee?"

Carmella says, "Probably didn't want it traced to the bistro."

"But it had chocolate on it," I add.

Carmella says, "The day he murdered his clone was most likely not the first time he saw him, but it must have triggered the idea. If he was nervous about his plan and had thought about it a lot, since he already had the knife, he may have used that one in his cooking for a while before hand.

"The exact day may have been selected impulsively while he was working with chocolate. So, being in a hurry before he lost his nerve, wiped the chocolate off rather than taking time to wash it thoroughly."

Trenton says, "But we still don't know who killed the Herb Tarragon who died on the bungee jump in Venture Land."

"We're not finished conducting those tests on his body. Pluto forensics has advanced unique tests."

"What kind of advanced unique tests?" Trenton asks.

Carmella hesitates, then says, "An oxygen timed test, a gold drop blood test, a vitreous aqueous humor test of the eyeball, an X-Ray diffraction test that bombards objects with an X-Ray beam to show the arrangement of molecules resulting in a chemical fingerprint."

Trenton says, "Titan forensics developed the oxygen timed test and the gold drop test thirty years ago. Aqueous humor tests of the eyeball and X-Ray diffraction tests were used on Earth as early as the twenty first century."

"Then our team must have updated and improved them. We also analyzed Herb Tarragon's hair and hair follicle cells. Human hair grows about a half inch a month. Our toxicologists cut his hair to find a time-line of his exposure to the poison."

"Those hair tests were also done on Earth in the twenty-first century," Trenton says.

"No doubt our tests are more thorough. But we did find something unusual."

"Unusual?"

"Herb Tarragon's hair grew slower, like those of an android, and…"

Trenton interrupts. "Saving lots of money on haircuts."

"As I was saying, his autopsy revealed some organs, like his bladder, had been replaced with android counterparts."

Trenton says, "So, Herb Tarragon had begun the process to become an android."

"That's right," Carmella says.

"Thanks for the update, Carmella. Can I get a sample from Herb Tarragon's body so I may send it to Mars Yard?"

Carmella says, "Sure. But I doubt if they will do better than us."

Call ends.

Jersey says, "I thought I told you that I have an android bladder. You tease me because I go to the bathroom so infrequently, Molly."

I say, "But are you considering further transformations?"

"No, I just don't want to get up in the middle of the night to use the bathroom, and I'm tired of waiting on long ladies' room lines while the men pile in and out."

I say, "This case is like Russian Babushka dolls: one doll hiding inside of another and another. I wonder what Mars Yard will find."

Trenton says, "Carmella thinks Pluto forensics are in the forefront of forensic analysis when in fact, they're using lots of old techniques and techniques developed elsewhere."

***

The next day Jersey, Trenton, and I take the tram to Silicone Slings to talk to Avery. It's that quiet time between lunch and dinner. I recognize the sound of a floor polisher coming from the back. We walk to the middle of the room. "Avery," I call. "Avery." The sound stops. Avery comes. He smiles when he sees us. "Any progress on the case?" he asks.

We sit at the bar. I bring him up to date. Trenton orders a Mars Malt and a half order of flat tire crisps that he eats nonstop. Then he orders another half order.

Jersey asks, "Why didn't you just get a whole order?"

"They are crispier and have a stronger burnt rubber flavor

this way."

I ask Avery, "Do you remember anything that would help find Herb's killer?"

"April and Herb were regular visitors to Silicone Slings in New Darwin. They seemed very much in love. In fact, they said that they wanted to get married there."

"April is an amazing new model," Jersey says. "At first I didn't recognize her as an android even when she stood next to her sister."

Avery says, "You can upgrade forever, but at some point, you have to accept that you will age, albeit slower than our carbon-based counterparts, but eventually, we all die. Try to make the most of each day, do the best you can, and be kind to others."

I smile. "Nice advice, but can you think of anything more helpful to this case?"

Avery shakes his head.

"June was dating Sage Tarragon, a clone of Herb Tarragon who was a chef on Charon," I say. "Did you know anything about that?

"No. But once, when Tonto talked about opening more Silicone Slings on Pluto, he said I should consider opening one on Charon. I resisted because I knew that androids become addicted and develop gaming disorders much faster than humans. It happens because counting cards is so easy and tempting for androids. But it makes us overconfident taking risks that lead to big losses. In any event, I didn't want to encourage more androids to go there. Ergo, no Silicone Slings on Charon."

Jersey says, "That happened to you, Trenton, when we went to the Charon Casino."

"Did not," Trenton says.

"We had to give you a Bill Cosby to clear your system," Jersey says.

Trenton frowns. "That didn't happen, or I would have

remembered."

"Knew you would say that. Here, look. I took a holo."

Trenton looks and frowns. "What about that bottle of Merlock on the table? Did I drink that too?"

"Molly and I drank that. It's delicious. Worth the money."

Thinking out loud, I say, "I wonder if April ever went to Charon with June? Or did Herb Tarragon go after he started the process to become an android not realizing it was now easier for him to develop a gaming disorder."

"What would that prove?" Jersey asks.

"Nothing," I say. "But if April went to Charon, she too could count cards and become addicted because she's an android."

Trenton says, "I'm going to see if I can find out about gambling debts on Charon. Charon may be very independent and have their own laws, but when it comes to collecting money, I bet they'll cooperate.

"Money and love are two big motivators," Jersey says. "And money can be the enemy of truth."

Avery says, "I remember a while ago when I was at the Flying Saucer supermarket, I saw Herb Tarragon and Lucky at the check-out. I don't know if it was Herb Tarragon's clone or actually him, but it was Lucky because I spotted the bump he had put on his nose."

We come back to the hotel early in the evening. Valentine's light has dimmed. Sharp unblinking stars shine through the dome that is so clear it looks like it's not there. Charon is a large crescent hanging in the sky. Waiters are cleaning a mess on the floor near the dining room. I ask what happened.

One says, "We installed a tank to hold fish for dinner."

"Nothing like fresh fish for dinner," I say.

"But when we tried to scoop the Jackson Pollack, the tank tipped over and made this mess."

Trenton takes several holos. "Why are you taking holos of that mess?" Jersey asks.

"I can sell it to an art museum for a lot of money as long as I accompany it with a political statement."

Jersey says, "But you don't care about politics, Trenton."

"Yes. But I care about money."

I pop a Chocolate Moon into my mouth and savor its creamy taste. Jersey says, "I saw that. You're addicted to Chocolate Moons!"

"Eating a delicious chocolate candy is not an addiction. Would you like one, Jersey?"

She takes three.

41

"WE SHOULD TALK TO LUCKY," I say.

"Let's go at dinner time," Jersey says. "Even with limited resources, Molly's has the best food in town."

"I'll ask Cortland to join us, but I doubt that he will. It's one thing to put on a show and another to see the construction of a music hall." I palm Cortland. I'm right. He declines.

Before we go to dinner, I call Interplanetary Foods. I want to learn if the delays in the restaurant's opening caused changes to anyone's contract. Or, do they have other plans for my restaurant. They reassure me that they are willing to wait for things to straighten out as long as I am still on board and I assured them I am.

I ask about Tonto's contract. I'm told contracts concerning management are different than contracts for other restaurant employees. Tonto's could be transferred to other restaurants as he was in the past. Herb Tarragon was the only one with a restaurant contract exclusive to Molly's Pluto. Other personnel at the restaurant didn't have contracts and would not be offered one until they worked there a year.

Tonto greets us and leads us to a table. The dining room is ready for business, but we are the only ones there. Feels so strange. Tonto says that the kitchen has the ingredients for atomic shrimp with sautéed microalgae or stem-cell lamb-beef in a Mercurian sunny sauce. On more notice, they could have offered more choices. We tell him its fine considering our other options. Dante takes our orders. Jersey and I have the lamb-beef. Trenton has the shrimp and the lamb-beef. We share profiteroles filled with frozen Grand Canyon ice cream for dessert and have three espressos. We've learned never to say "shots" of espresso because when we did, people tensed and asked if we wanted protection.

Dante brings a few chocolate truffles arranged in a lovely design on a round white plate and hand-dipped candied fruit artistically placed on another. Ah, so beautiful. So civilized.

After dinner, we go in the kitchen and find Lucky, Nebula, and two dishwashers. Dante and Tonto join us.

I look around wistfully. "Such shiny new equipment," I say. "Hope it gets used soon for more than three dinners."

Trenton asks Lucky, "Could we talk to you privately in the bar? It's quiet and the booths are very comfortable."

Lucky looks at the others, who shrug their shoulders or nod.

The four of us slide into a smooth leather booth. Jersey and I face Lucky; Trenton sits next to him. There is a Zen like calm that I find strange; my bar at Molly's Bistro, even at this hour, is usually filled with the sounds of clinking glasses and animated conversation.

Trenton starts. "Someone told us he saw you at a Flying Saucer Supermarket talking to Herb Tarragon. Can you tell us what that was about?"

Lucky clears his throat. "He asked me to meet him there because he wanted to meet in a public place. He thought he was being followed. He told me that he left one of his best carving knives at the restaurant and didn't want to go back to get it. He asked if I could bring it with me. He reassured me that he did not want to return to Molly's Pluto, and as far as he was concerned, the job was mine."

I ask, "How was his demeanor?"

"Strange. Sort of nervous."

I thank him for his input. He leaves and returns to the

kitchen. Trenton calls Carmella. "Lucky met Herb Tarragon at the Flying Saucer supermarket. Herb thought someone was following him. Maybe it will show on a security cam."

"I'll check," Carmella says. "I see you're now at Molly's Pluto."

"How did you know?" I ask.

"Superior technology."

"We just finished a delicious dinner," Jersey says, wiping her mouth with a napkin.

"You had dinner at Molly's Pluto, and you didn't invite me?"

"The restaurant's not open," I say.

"But you had dinner. We don't allow people to eat in closed restaurants. Should I send an inspector from our board of health?"

"Would it help if I asked Tonto to let you have dinner there tomorrow?" I say. "You can bring a friend."

"Yes. But not tomorrow. Tomorrow is Snow Day."

"How can you have snow? You live under a controlled atmospheric dome; a place without seasons."

Carmella says, "So many of our citizens had heard of snow made from water and wanted to experience it. So as a campaign promise, one of Valentine's former mayors hired a team to make it snow for eight hours once a year. I don't want to miss it."

***

The snow day arrives. The hotel concierge lends us warm jackets. One says "The Twilight Zone" in bold green letters on the front and back. The other two say "Property of Venture Land-Winter." Everyone is in a festive mood. Some wear red hats with dangling white pom poms that say "Santa." I hear a child ask who Santa is, and his mother says that he's the man who works the snow machine. People give each other new stockings as gifts.

Everyone waits for the first flakes to fall while singing along to Pluto poet and composer, Carol Christmas, famous for writing jingles for bells, and "The Easter Bunny Parade" a hymn that celebrates reincarnation.

No one is disappointed. The first flakes are larger than what I remember snowflakes to be on Earth. Each sends a sparkle into the air. Faces turn upward, mouths open, tongues outstretched. The sidewalk whitens. Children bend down and make snow balls and throw them at each other. "Must be an instinctive response," I say.

"Or," Jersey says, "they saw it on a holo."

***

Two days later, Carmella calls with results from the Flying Saucer holos. "A preliminary study shows that it was most likely Adam Kools who was following Herb Tarragon," she says. "But it is not clear because he wore a hoodie. We're running it through our infra-pink scanner."

"You mean infra-red?"

"Infra-pink—more refined. Like fingerprints, everyone's measurements are slightly different. If the glove fits, that's it."

Later that day, Carmella calls Trenton and says, "The glove fit. Adam Kools was definitely the man lurking in the shadows."

"Adam Kools has access to all kinds of chemicals and chemical combinations that could be poisonous," I say.

"Everyone knows that," Carmella says. "But that doesn't make him guilty."

Jersey says, "Adam struck me as being very guarded. He seemed to be one of those people who was hard to really see behind his smile."

Tonto calls. "Carmella just made a reservation for dinner for tomorrow night. She said you told her she could bring a friend."

"I did say that."

"She's bringing twenty-three friends. Then she calls again and says if she brings twenty more, she won't send the health inspector to go over the place with a fine tooth."

"Can you handle that many?"

"It's short notice, but I have a network of extra staff delighted to get the work. And the bar is well stocked."

Nebula calls. "Can I ask a favor, Molly?"

"You can try."

"My baby sitter can't come when I must be at the restaurant. Can you come?"

"Of course," I say. "I'll ask Jersey to join me."

***

Nebula opens the door. She hands Andromeda to me. "Thanks for sitting with Andy," she says. "She's stopped being so fussy."

"Don't worry. I brought up twins, remember?"

Nebula leaves.

I say to Jersey, "I haven't been with a baby since Becky and Lois were small. I wonder how being a grandmother will be? I've heard it said that if I knew how much fun grandchildren would be, I would have had them first."

Jersey laughs. Andy coos in my arms. I give her dinner, put her in her crib, and she falls asleep. She has that new baby smell. So, even babies that are hatched have it. Nice.

Jersey says. "Being here gives us a good opportunity to look around. I'm starting with the kitchen." I hear the refrigerator open. "Hey, Molly. Come see this," she calls.

I peer into the refrigerator. "There's two boxes of blue tomatoes."

"So? Lots of people love them."

"There's also lots of food for one person," Jersey says. "And some of it is very expensive like lobster tails and pate, plus a bottle of Venus Sparkling. She must be expecting someone special for dinner."

I check on Andy, who continues to sleep. Jersey looks more but finds nothing of interest.

Hours later, Nebula comes home. "You'll have to restock everything. Pluto police are a tough bunch. Tonto will tell you more." She sighs. "I've never been so exhausted."

42

THE NEXT DAY WE FIND the staff of Molly's Pluto sweeping, vacuuming, polishing, and picking things up from the floor. Tonto rolls his eyes and says, "Those Pluto police can really party."

"Was Interplanetary Foods upset that you charged their meal to them?" I ask.

"On the contrary. They want to open more restaurants in other cities on Pluto, and they need the approval of the Pluto's police. But after last night, we're almost out of everything. We can however make tuna fish or egg salad sandwiches. Any leftovers from last night's meal were taken, including all the flowers."

"They can have the flowers," I say.

"With the vases?"

I have the tuna fish on focaccia bread, Jersey has the egg salad on a whole wheat roll, and Trenton, as usual, has both. It's maddening that he can eat everything, never gain an ounce nor worry about blood sugar levels or cholesterol. It almost, but only almost, makes me rethink becoming an android. But I'll wait until I'm very old or need the procedure for my health.

Nebula comes from the kitchen. She and Tonto give each other long looks. Then they hold hands.

"Am I missing something?" I ask.

"We're dating," Tonto says.

Nebula looks at Tonto. "Tonto is coming for dinner tonight."

"Blue tomatoes make wonderful salads," Jersey says.

"They do,'" Nebula says, "but I'm not making anything with blue tomatoes. Making a salad from hydroponic arugula with candied walnuts, then lobster tails with herb butter. It's all in my refrigerator."

I give Jersey a glare hoping she won't say, "I know." She doesn't.

***

We leave and walk on Carotid Artery, and notice a few new stores. Trenton smiles and makes a thumbs up as he points to one that sells android parts.

Jersey scowls. "You didn't have to give me 'your look' Molly. I wasn't going to say anything to Nebula about the food in her refrigerator."

"Sorry. It was sort of a reflex."

Jersey says, "But I do wonder who those blue tomatoes in her refrigerator could be for? She's not serving them to Tonto. And why would she serve them to Lucky? He's allergic to them."

"Unless she doesn't know he's allergic," Trenton says.

"She must know."

"Not necessarily."

Trenton says, "I want to talk to Adam Kools. Do you think Carmella will be upset if we go to The Hatchery and question him? He's one of the people who have access to a lot of unusual chemicals."

Jersey says, "She's already upset that we're here. Nothing to lose and all to gain."

***

We take the tram to The Hatchery. I peer out the window and see bright lights surrounding the construction of an environmental dome in the distance. Valentine is growing and getting a suburb.

Suddenly everyone lurches forward as the tram brakes abruptly and shudders to a halt. We wait a long time. Finally, we hear an announcement about an earthquake that struck a mile ahead in the direction of the wholesale market and The Hatchery causing extensive damage. There is a flurry of questions. People are bewildered, including us. The tram shakes again. I grab the side of my chair. Two conductors walk through the cars in protective suits pushing a trolley with protective suits. "Put these on!" one snaps.

We each take a puffy drab olive suit. I turn mine every way trying to decide what part are for arms and what part for legs.

"Hurry!" one conductor urges.

I pull the suit on as fast as I can. "The legs are too tight and the sleeves too loose," I say.

Jersey says, "That's because you have it on upside down, Molly."

"These suits are ugly," I say.

The conductor overhears and snaps, "Do you want to live, or you want to be in a fashion show?"

Jersey runs her hand through her hair. "You can be pretty and safe," she says.

"Not here!" he snarls. "Pretty safe is not the same as safe."

The ground shifts more violently. Everyone is thrown to the floor. Then it stops. Jersey says, "My insides feel like a pot after water starts boiling."

I think about how that might feel, and I conclude not good. We continue to wait. Finally, one conductor who is listening on his palm says, "An all-clear signal was just sent. The surface has frozen and stabilized. You can remove your suits."

But as soon as we remove them, there is a stronger rumble.

The other conductor yells, "Put those suits on again." He looks at me. "Unless, of course, you need a different style and color."

Suddenly a wide crack spreads through the floor of the tram

separating the tram into two halves. We are sitting on one end, where the crack is widest, and tumble through and land about twelve feet down. Too far to climb out without help. After a while, a conductor comes and throws down a hammer and chisel.

"Hey," I say. "You could've hit us."

"But I didn't, did I?"

Jersey picks up the hammer. "What should we do with this?"

"Chip the wall and make ladder indents. In the meantime, I'll get a rope to pull you out."

Trenton, being strongest, chisels steps and is hauled out first. Then Jersey struggles to the top and is hauled out. A rope is found. Trenton throws it down to me. I start to climb, but everything is shaking. The crack widens. I stumble backward. My suit rips.

The conductor says, "You'll need a balloon raft to get you out. Just a moment." He turns and walks away. We wait several long minutes until he returns with a bulky item in his arms. He throws it down to me.

"Wrap this around yourself," he says. "Then press the green button. It will inflate and rise."

"I only see a blue button and a yellow button."

"Blue and yellow make green," he shouts. "Press them together."

I hear rumbling as the ground shakes making my fingers fumble the buttons. Finally, I press and rise. As I near the top, Jersey and Trenton grab me and pull me over the edge. I'm helped removing the suit. Trenton scans me for injuries. I'm shaken but fine. The rumbling stops.

There is another announcement that says there will be an announcement.

We check our palms to see if there is information about the quake, but there is no palm service. I wonder if Cortland and the twins were affected by the quake. Finally, we hear, "Attention tram riders. Damage is extensive. There is no tram service. Please exit the tram. Busses will come to take you back to Valentine. There is no service in the direction toward the Hatchery. We hope you have enjoyed your ride with Pluto Transport. Thank you and have a nice day."

"I wonder who thought up 'have a nice day'?" Jersey snarls with a voice that could kill.

43

BY THE TIME WE GET BACK to the Twilight Zone, the lobby is crowded. Everyone is talking about the earthquake. No one wants to be in their room. Stress and nervous tension are passed around like the flu from those who ignored getting a flu shot. We learn that the Hatchery and greenmarket had been destroyed. We spot three empty chairs and grab them.

I palm Cortland, who with Becky and Lois are safe at the Blue Note. They were out of their minds with worry and are relieved to hear from me. They felt a small rumble but nothing else.

A news holo is broadcast in the lobby. The room hushes. It shows the area that used to be the greenmarket. We stand and walk closer to the holo and peer at an enormous crater that has replaced the greenmarket. Jersey tries to lighten the mood by saying, "That's some salad bowl!"

People shake their heads and give her strange looks. They're not wrong.

A reporter says, "We can rebuild a wholesale market, but the Hatchery is a great loss in lives both to those just born and the unborn. Other cities have Hatcheries, but ours was the largest."

The camera shifts to an even larger crater. A different reporter has tears in his eyes and can hardly speak. "This used to be the Valentine Hatchery." He pauses to blow his nose and clear his throat. "Many of you watching, like myself, were born here. Survivors have been taken to a medical facility in Valentine. We are in the process of saving some DNA and some equipment, but most of it is destroyed. We recovered some bodies. Among them is that of its director, Adam Kools."

Everyone gasps. A woman cries, "Five of my clones were there." Others say that they were scheduled for various procedures and now wonder what they are going to do.

Trenton calls Carmella, who doesn't answer.

I say, "I'm calling Avery Spelling. Silicone Slings must have been destroyed also."

With relief, I hear Avery's voice. "I'm in New Darwin. I went this morning to see if I could comfort April about Herb Tarragon. Two of my waiters were recovered from the quake. The rest were buried and their central processing units damaged beyond repair. I'm going to stay here with April for a while."

When I tell Jersey and Trenton what Avery said, Jersey muses, "Comforting April or courting April?"

Cortland and the girls return to the hotel. Cortland reiterates that they only felt a small rumble and reassures me again that all is well.

***

The next morning, I awaken, shower, and dress as the light of the city slowly turns from an orange glow around the horizon to a cerulean blue creating morning. And although other combinations of colors had been tried on other worlds, everyone always voted for colors that resembled a morning on Earth. I wonder if it's a learned or inherent response?

Cortland leaves early because he has an appointment in a new café that just opened near the Blue Note with Oedipus Eisenhauer, a local composer, famous for updating "The Halls of Montezuma" into a love song.

Jersey and Trenton knock on my door and come in. I tell them I'll call Tonto to see if we could have lunch.

Trenton says, "I'm asking Carmella to check insurance

companies and find out if Herb Tarragon had a life insurance policy."

Carmella answers quickly. "Yup, he had a policy with Oort Life and Death. At first, the beneficiary was Adam Kools, but he changed it to Dante Essen."

****

At Molly's Pluto, Tonto asks if we would like roast leg of stem cell lamb or something light like an endive and spacefruit chipotle salad. Jersey and I have salads. Trenton has both.

A busboy clears the table and sets it for dessert. We get up, and tell Tonto want to go in the kitchen to talk to Dante.

We follow him in.

Nebula is in the back. I see her arranging things and taking food from the refrigerator. Dante and Lucky are off to one side. They break from what looks like an embrace when they see us.

Dante says, "You all don't usually come in the kitchen. Lucky and I were just discussing the menu."

Jersey says, "Looks like more than the menu."

Lucky puts his hand on Dante's arm when he says, "Dante and I started seeing each other. We actually have a lot in common."

"Did you know about this, Tonto?" I ask.

"Of course. Relationships in small spaces are hard to hide," he says. "But it has no bearing on their work."

Dante looks nervous. His shoulders hunch.

I turn to Dante. "Did you know that Herb Tarragon had an insurance policy and that he changed the recipient from Adam Kools to you?"

Dante straightens and relaxes. "Insurance policy?" he says, eyebrows rising. "I never knew Herb Tarragon had one. How much is it worth?"

Trenton says, "Carmella has the details. Call her. She'll fill you in."

44

WE GO BACK INTO THE DINING ROOM and wait for dessert.

"Do you think Dante was telling us the truth about not knowing about the insurance policy?" I ask.

"Thinking the same thing, Molly. But no way of knowing at this point," Jersey says.

Trenton checks his palm. Carmella sent a holo from Charon police of Herb Tarragon and Adam Kools talking about Herb owing Adam money.

"With both dead," I say, "we'll never know if that was resolved. Nor can we question Adam to learn if he knew anything about that unusual substance found in Herb's body. Adam was a valuable source of getting and finding out about all kinds of chemicals."

Tonto approaches. "Would you like Chocolate Moon cake for dessert?"

I say, "Chocolate Moon cake? I love Chocolate Moons."

"We know," Tonto says.

"Everyone knows," Jersey adds.

Tonto says, "Lucky realizes that Mars Bistro and Mars Pluto need identical menus to be an Interplanetary Foods franchise. But since we are not yet open, he used his time to experiment and create something new."

"Knife and fork ready," I say.

After a short wait, Lucky, Nebula, and Dante come from the kitchen each holding white plates with large chocolate balls in the center. They put them down in front of us and give us pointed knives. Lucky says, "Pierce the moon, Molly."

I stab the chocolate ball. "I feel like I'm killing a living thing," I say.

Trenton and Jersey do the same. Warm molten chocolate oozes onto the plate making the ball look like a moon floating in chocolate space. I taste it and swoon.

Lucky says, "It's made from chocolate cake infused with chocolate truffles and at the center frozen chocolate custard that melts into the warm molten chocolate."

"This must be added to the menu," I say.

Lucky says, "We can't change the menu without Interplanetary foods approving. I know that Herb Tarragon found standardization of the menu creatively restrictive."

"He did. But I'll insist the Chocolate Moon Cake be added. I'm sorry I never knew how Herb Tarragon felt. Nor did I think about it until much later. I'm going to recommend that chef's contracts be rewritten so new recipes as good as this can be added. Even McBurger varies their foods occasionally."

Lucky smiles.

"Can we talk to you privately?" I ask.

"Of course."

I look at Tonto, Nebula, and Dante and say more strongly, "Privately."

They retreat to the kitchen. Lucky remains.

Trenton says, "Pluto police were following Adam Kools. Did you ever meet him?"

"Once, briefly," Lucky says. "When I went to the Hatchery with Dante."

"Why did you go to the Hatchery with Dante?" I ask.

"Dante has a friend who is a scientist at the Hatchery. He developed a product that caused you to sleep three hours a night and wake up refreshed rather than needing the usual eight. We wanted to get more free time outside of work."

"What's his name?" Trenton asks.

"Taurus Trance. He warned us that the procedure had risks. And when I learned the cost, which was far more than I wanted to pay, I never went back. I think Dante did."

Jersey says, "Can you be more specific. Did he or didn't he go back and get it?"

"I not sure," Lucky says.

I say, "Herb had an insurance policy and made Dante the beneficiary."

"I know nothing about that."

Lucky goes back in the kitchen. Tonto and Nebula come out.

"We have more questions for Dante," I say. "Can he come out of the kitchen?"

Tonto says, "Sorry, he just left."

"Convenient timing," I say.

Trenton says, "Then I want look in his locker."

"Nothing in it but the restaurant clothes he just had on. He took his coat."

"Doesn't matter," Trenton says. "I have infra-red and ultra violet vision plus other abilities. I can detect chemical subtilties people can't see. My scan will take less than a minute and I don't have to touch anything."

When Trenton returns he says, "I'll send my findings to Mars Yard. No need to tell Carmella or she'll just insist that Pluto's forensics are superior and want me to send it there."

Jersey collects her extra meals and we leave.

"I wonder if Dante was telling us the truth when he said he knew nothing about the insurance policy?" I say.

Jersey says, "Getting that insurance money sooner rather than later would be a motive for murder."

***

We walk on the sidewalk of Carotid Artery that is paved in a clean flat gray material. Jersey points to the sidewalk. "They're trying," she says.

"Are they?" I say. "A pretty color costs as much as a dull color. Gray squares are so, so…"

"So…Valentine. So boring," Trenton adds.

The sky has shifted to soft afternoon light. The street fill with people leaving work. Trees glow brighter.

I say, "How about Lucky. Think he told us everything?

Jersey says, "The question is, did we ask the right questions?" Lucky mentioned a sleeping compound that had risks. Could it be more dangerous than first thought?"

Trenton says, "Or dangerous enough kill? Pluto prides itself on being on the cutting edge of research. But it wouldn't be the first time someone in the solar system cut corners with their medical tests or fudged results to gain grant money or prestige. One of the historically famous was of Dr. Scott Reuben, a former member of Pfizer's speakers' bureau who was found guilty to faking dozens of research studies that were published in medical journals back in the twenty-first century. Or the lab on Io that said if you swallowed their gold colored pill you would get rich."

"Oops!" Jersey says looking at the floor.

Carmella calls Trenton. He clicks speaker. Her voice is cheery in a tone that I'm not used to hearing. I wonder what's up. "More from Charon," she chirps.

Trenton says, "Wait a moment. We're walking on Carotid Artery." He motions to a bench next to one of the glowing green trees. We sit. "Yes, Carmella. You were saying."

"There was footage from security cameras about a month before Herb Tarragon died that shows June yanking April from a casino. It would be easier if I sent the holo to your palms rather than try to explain each frame."

A yellow light appears on our palms followed by the holo. The background is noisy, but we can hear June accusing April of becoming addicted to gambling. Then Herb Tarragon approaches. When June sees him, she throws a punch his way, but he catches her hand and stops her. June looks very angry. She says that he shouldn't have taken April to a casino knowing it's easy for androids to become addicted to gambling.

Then the holo is blurry. Next frames show the three in a quiet hallway. Herb Tarragon is saying, "I thought I could recoup April's losses in the Madoff Ponzi scheme."

June says, "You invested April's money in that?"

April lowers her head. "I wasn't going to tell you until we made the money back."

June turns to April and says, "So how much was it?"

April says, "Everything."

June asks, "Even the money we had in a joint account from our parents?"

April cries. The holo ends.

Trenton says, "Thanks for sharing, Carmella. Anything else?"

"As a matter of fact, there is," she says, "I've been offered commissioner of police on Charon."

Trenton says, "Are you going to take it?"

"Yes. After we wrap this case up. It's nice to be a big fish, even if the pond is small."

Jersey mumbles, "Charon is small."

Carmella says, "What did she say?"

"I think that's all," Jersey pipes.

Trenton shakes his head at Jersey. He disconnects.

"June had motives," I say. "Revenge for losing money and trying to get Sage to replace Herb Tarragon at Molly's Pluto."

***

We go back to the hotel and call Zee Pope. He knew April and June for a long time. Maybe he can add something he didn't think of before. We conference call from Jersey and Trenton's room.

Zee says, "After visiting April a few times, she confided that there was lots of rivalry between her and June. June said she also loved Herb Tarragon, and that Sage Tarragon was the closest she could get to having him. April was very upset about this."

I ask, "Did April know Herb Tarragon had an insurance policy and Dante was the beneficiary?"

"I don't know."

"One of us should call April. I don't want to overwhelm her with a conference call." Jersey says, "You call, Molly. You have the friendliest voice."

April answers immediately. She tells me she knew of the insurance policy and Dante was the Recipient, but Herb said he was changing it to her. But he died before he could do it.

"As we speculated earlier, if Dante had any idea that Herb might change his insurance policy, that gave him a motive," Jersey says. "Money and love motivate a lot. Add revenge and Dante has all three," Jersey says.

I call Dante. His pixels form in front of us. He confirms what Lucky said about visiting the Hatchery and learning about a new sleeping process.

"Did you get that new sleeping process?" I ask.

Dante frowns. "I resent your questions. And besides, it doesn't matter now, does it? The Hatchery and its lab are destroyed."

"Was your friend among those who died?" Jersey asks.

"No. He was at Kuiper Belt Academy for his daughter's graduation."

I click my palm off.

Trenton says, "I noticed that Dante avoided answering the question about getting the sleeping compound. He may have gotten it and for some reason not wanted us to know."

***

After all the delays, Molly's Pluto finally opens, Tonto and the staff work out new contracts with Interplanetary Foods that allows greater flexibility with higher pay, so no one is leaving any time soon. The first official dinner is nothing like what I had imagined and a far cry from what the opening of Molly's Bistro in New Chicago on Mars was. Although everyone tries hard to create a festive atmosphere, it is muted because of the earthquake.

Everything is polished and shines. The staff stands at attention in crisp uniforms waiting for orders. Just about every guest wears black including me, albeit with cut-outs exposing my shoulders. The one person who wears navy blue is stared at as though she was wearing a bikini at a Sunday mass. Many, like Adam Kools who were on the list for the first dinner, had died or were hurt badly in the quake and needed to be replaced by lesser celebrities, some of whom I later learned were not very popular. The mayors of New Darwin, New Perth, and New Brisbane were all too upset to come. Other mayors who did attend considered it bad PR to show they were having fun when so many were in mourning. I overhear one guest, as she's led to a table, say that the flowers were like the ones at three of her clones' funerals.

Waiters move through the room and offer Kir Royals on silver trays. "How many of these can I have?" one guest asks.

"As many as you want."

Sprits lift. They rise higher when unlimited smoked salmon and caviar canapes follow.

45

THE EARTHQUAKE TRAGEDY SPURS construction as everyone wants to put the terrible event behind them. Workers descended on Valentine offering services in exchange for free concert tickets. As a result, the Blue Note and adjoining buildings that were added to the project finish ahead of schedule. Everyone is very pleased and amazed because the project far exceeds the original idea, that of simply renovating the Band Box.

The complex is multi-purpose intending to draw performers not only from Pluto but from other worlds for music, ballet, opera, award ceremonies, community events, and charity performances.

There is also a music library, with rare editions of "Music: Expensive Noise", "Tuby Wasn't a Tuba", and "Big Tipper" sung by the Gemini Clones. There are large rehearsal spaces. Pluto University reserves rooms for classes. One class analyzes x-rays of Beethoven's fetus that was shaped like a G Clef. Another explores theories about the mind of emperor Joseph II of Austria when he said that Mozart's Marriage of Figaro had too many notes (the truth) and should be renamed Figaro's Affair (a theory).

***

The Pluto Press, Saturn's Ringling Brothers Media, the Solar Post, and Mars's Carbon Copies Media reserve the best front rows of seats for opening night.

Burton finally arrives. Becky is overjoyed. Burton says that Becky warned him that Valentine was a dreary place and he'll want to leave as soon as possible; but instead, he finds it to be an exciting city.

Cortland is revved up about the talent he has lined up and says it's some of the most unique he has ever heard. He says, "I'm telling you, Molly, these Plutonian musicians make complex layered sounds ranging from Gregorian chanting to symphonic orchestration that's truly amazing. Could the blooming of homegrown creativity be a result of Pluto being relatively isolated and independent of outside influences?"

I tell him that the late Adam Kools, the late Hatchery's director, told me that a gene editing technique that selected and enhanced genetic material was used to create more beautiful and more talented people.

"Whatever," Cortland says. "Nature or nurture. Either way, it's going to be a great show. The Hatchery was destroyed in the earthquake, wasn't it?"

"Yes. But they have smaller Hatcheries in other cities that use the same techniques. Eventually the Valentine Hatchery will be rebuilt."

Cortland says, "I have enough talent for two shows, but I won't plan any more until I see the results from this one."

"Did Zee Pope audition?"

"Who?"

"Carmella says he sings like Frank Sinatra. I promised him you would listen."

Cortland rolls his eyes like a martyr. "I doubt that Carmella is a good judge."

"Have you found a way to include her barbershop quartet?"

"I have. I'll let it be a surprise."

I call Zee. He was unsure if he should audition and hadn't done so. I prod him to make an appointment for tomorrow. I also tell Lois that I would like her opinion about his voice. She moans in protest but reluctantly agrees to hear him.

The next day, we go to one of the rehearsal studios built to the side of the main building to listen to Zee. When Lois sees Zee, she runs her hand through her hair she had mesmerizingly dyed in colors of the rainbow and straightens up because Zee is Pluto handsome. His simple white shirt is tucked into his black pants fastened with a black belt with a silver buckle. He looks at us sitting in the middle of the room and zeros in on Lois in a way that makes her jaw drop. Cortland and I can't help noticing.

The background music Zee brought to accompany him starts. He croons in a smooth voice holding long notes very long. His voice vibrates with depth and a wide range.

When he finishes singing, Cortland jumps up enthusiastically and says, "You're a very strong performer. Everything I heard about you is true."

Zee visibly relaxes, exhales, and smiles.

Cortland says, "I want to consider using a very old piece of music from a show called *Hair* in the concert." It's called 'The Age of Aquarius.' I've updated the arrangement of the music but use the same words. It's a duo. I think you and Lois could swing it."

He points to Lois. "Try this out with Zee. I'll project the words and accompaniment to that corner so you can both study it. When you're ready, Molly and I will listen."

Lois gets up and joins Zee at the side of the room.

A short time later, Lois calls, "Ready." They walk to the front of the room and signal for Cortland to play the accompanying music.

Lois sings: "When the moon is in the Seventh House/ And Jupiter aligns with Mars/ then peace will guide the planets/ and love will steer the stars."

Then the two of them blend harmonies singing the chorus as naturally and easily as if they had sung it together forever.

When they finish, Cortland and I leap from our seats

clapping enthusiastically. Workers who had been quietly putting finishing touches to the back of the room whistle and shout, "More! More!"

"Well, that answers my question if I should use this," Cortland says.

Lois and Zee beam at each other.

***

Later, at the hotel, Cortland says, "That went better than I thought. I want to dig into more music from the past and see if I can incorporate it into the show. I'm calling Trenton because his ability to access the old internet is greater than mine. I also want to find ways to involve the audience so they imagine being transported to another time and place. I feel it's critical to the success of the show."

Jersey is delighted that Cortland reaches out to Trenton and says that they expect free season passes to shows. Cortland complies and mumbles that they are the cheapest people he has ever known, but they are smart and very nice.

"And useful," I add.

A few days later, Trenton calls. "I found something," he says. "But it's better seen in the theater than explained in a hotel room."

The next day we all go to the Blue Note. Cortland whispers to me, "This better be good. Trenton can get caught up in technicalities at the expense of entertainment."

We enter the theater and take seats next to Jersey in the middle of the theater. Trenton goes in the back to set up. I ask Jersey, "What do you know about this?"

"Nothing," she says. "He was very excited but very secretive."

Trenton comes from the back of the stage and sits with us. "I want to see this as the audience would see this. I researched back to the twenty-first century in music history. I think I found something that will work very well."

A few moments later, the lights dim. The stage changes color. An announcer in a twenty-first century costume comes on stage.

Cortland leans over to Trenton and asks, "Is he real or a holograph? He's so clear and with the stage lighting and effects, I honestly can't tell."

Trenton whispers, "I'll tell you after the performance. I don't want to spoil this."

The announcer says, "Ladies and gentlemen, here's Roy Orbison!"

"Roy Orbison" takes center stage stands at a microphone in a gray suit and sunglasses, apparently strumming an electric guitar, nodding and smiling around him and performs in his silky vibrato one of his hits, "Pretty Woman." We all tap our toes and move our heads in rhythm as he sings. When he finishes, we clap. The room lights rise.

Trenton says, "At the Eventim Apollo theater in Hammersmith, London on April 19th 2018, a holo called 'In Dreams' of Roy Orbison, who had died on Earth in 1988, was shown. It was so successful, it went on to tour other cities on Earth. If I can find holos of other performers and groups like The Tenth-Dimension from Venus and The Crater Crackers from Ceres, would you be interested in incorporating some of them into your show? Imagine Lois singing along with Elvis Presley. Wouldn't that be a hoot!"

Cortland says, "Not only a hoot, but I think adding these holographic performers would broaden my audience to attract people of different ages and reach those who shun new music and only want to hear the classics. The Blue Note is vast. We need as many people as possible to fill it. Standing room only is better than empty seats."

Jersey says, "I've never seen holographic concerts. Were they discontinued?"

Trenton says, "Live performers objected. There was just so much space in theaters and time. The music unions lobbied that the holos be taxed at a high rate. Eventually, they were not made. But Pluto has its own laws and I can revive holos cheaply here. After we do the show you can decide if it's worth trying to change laws on other worlds."

46

THE DAY ARRIVES. The Blue Note is sold out, including standing room. Overbooked hotels put people in basements and attics. Airbnb charges quadruple for tiny spaces and throws dogs out of doghouses.

Everyone is a nervous wreck knowing that not only is the concert a big boost for Pluto (with many betting the concert will become a catalyst for reinstating Pluto as a planet), but know they have an opportunity to be part of something that people will talk about for years, like historic Woodstock.

The automated car that we rent pulls into an automated valet slot in front of the theater. When Cortland says that he wonders if we have to leave an automated tip when we retrieve it, an automated sounding voice says, "You do if you want the car back."

Cortland mumbles that artificial intelligence has gone too far.

A voice says, "Not artificial."

The car parks. A generous tip placed. Cortland and Trenton leave us and go backstage.

Music critics who hold front row seats and came early are let in. We wait with the rest of the audience, dressed in finery made for the occasion, and finery that hadn't seen the light of day in years, smile dental-convention smiles while we wait patiently for the doors of the Blue Note to open. When it finally does, we enter through parted velvet ropes in the front of the theater overwhelmed, saying little, voices soft or silent. Nothing as beautiful and luxurious had ever been built on Pluto. It's vaulted interior space is as much cathedral as concert hall.

Melodic and rhythmic music plays. I recognize it as an instrumental mix from the historic jazz fusion band founder Pat Metheny. I know this because Cortland usually puts one of his albums on before he starts to work.

Ushers hand out programs. The welcome on the cover page that Cortland wrote quotes Pat Metheny's *Dialogues between Neuroscience and Society: Music and the brain*: "the goal of maximum consciousness is an essential component of what it takes to be a great musician…" It ends with Cortland thanking Plutonians for the opportunity to work with their musicians whose music he knows will raise the consciousness of all who hear them.

And so, the hall fills. It smells vaguely like a pine forest.

Light passes through diagonal skylights creating patterns on glass curtained walls. The arrangement of the seating, inspired by that in the Grand Ole Opry Ryman Auditorium in Nashville, Tennessee on Earth (that still exists albeit modernized in the twenty second, twenty third, and twenty fourth centuries), are formed in successive arcs radiating from the stage. No one has a bad seat.

An usher in a new blue suit embedded with golden notes escorts Becky, Burton, Jersey, and I to shiny buffed seats. Although the audience sits quietly waiting for the show to begin, there's an edgy anticipation stronger than that of waiting for a new baby's head to crown.

An announcer dressed in a white tuxedo studded with sequins, pearls, and metallic moons that reflect little lights around the theater walks to center stage. Lights blink once to get everyone's attention. He says, "Ladies and gentlemen, for your protection and entertainment, we have a pre-concert treat. Coming straight from being on duty at the police station, please welcome the Cosa Nostra, our very own barbershop quartet, who will sing in four-part harmony their rendition of the Pluto national anthem."

Carman, Aida, Tosca, and Don Giovanni glide to center stage dressed as barbers swinging scissors. People stand and put their right hands over their hearts and listen as they sing; some join in. They are very good. When they finish, they point to their right. Carmella Soprano in her police captain's uniform, comes out. She salutes, waves, and takes a bow. Everyone applauds; a few whistle. An usher comes from the wings and hands her a bouquet. She smiles, waves again with her free hand and exits. Everyone sits.

I whisper to Jersey, "Smart move on Cortland's part to include Carmella."

"Even though she did nothing," Jersey says.

Lights dim. The ceiling grows so dark it looks as though it's not there. A voice booms, "Let the good times roll!"

Points of light like stars appear; some shoot across the space. Glowing treble and base clefs and musical instruments materialize, dance in the air, and fade. Apocalyptic chords alternate with eerie quiet. Becky and Burton grab each other's hand. Jersey and I grab the arms of our chairs as sounds go from seizure to stillness.

Stage lights rise and flutter. I feel a rush anticipating what's to come. Colored lights turn towards the audience and ripple over everyone causing everyone to turn colors. The theater grows brighter and brighter until everyone has to close their eyes. Then I hear, "Ladies and Gentlemen let's welcome direct from the twentieth century, our very own Ziggy Stardust, David Bowie!" I hear the music of David Bowie's "Let's Dance" and open my eyes.

There, next to us in the aisle, is a life-sized holo of David Bowie. Burton reaches toward the image and his hand goes through David's leg. I crane my neck and see other holos of

David in other parts of the room. On the stage, live dancers are stepping to the music with precision and grace. Next, David sings "Loving the Alien." Multiple voices from multiple Davids make a chorus of music that I know Cortland has mixed and remixed.

The music fades. The stage rotates the dancers off-stage while the next act thunders to centerstage.

The announcer says, "And from the Dune Fields of Pluto, Pliny (the Godfather) the Elder, formerly Pliny (the Godfather) the Younger, with the Swinging Mafia performing in Gansta Rap their all-time favorite, 'Cement Shoes' and 'Nothing Personal, It's Just Business.'"

The Mafia raps, "Cement shoes: an offer you can't refuse," while the audience claps and stomps to the beat rising and rising and rising until the hall borders on pandemonium!

I lean toward Jersey and say, "I'm glad Cortland and Trenton were able to work together."

"Trenton never did this before," Jersey says. "But he took to the job as a duck takes to orange sauce."

The Swinging Mafia continues with jittery blots of music sounding like punctuation marks that tremble into high gospel counterpoint filled with post punk rhythms. I know this because I'm reading the program notes.

Pliny and the Mafia move off stage. The theater grows dim and quiet. The scenery changes. A bed with a man sitting on it appears mid-stage. The announcer says, "Let's welcome a surprise guest artist from Europa, and direct descendent of Bruce Springsteen, Bruce Bedspring performing his solar hit, 'Born to Sleep'." His voice rises. "Heeeeeeeere's Bruce!"

Bruce begins, "Born to sleep, counting sheep..."

The audience can't resist singing along almost drowning Bruce out. When he finishes, the applause is muted. Only half of the audience applauds because the other half sleeps in tribute. Bruce, sleeping on the bed, is quietly rolled off stage.

Tigris and Euphrates, a group from Cthulhu Macula along Pluto's equator, replaces Bruce. The announcer says, "Now welcome, singing in Akkadian hip hop, a language of a cult who migrated to Uranus's moon Titania, their history breaking hit, 'The Hammurabi Code.' This will be followed by 'I'm not a Dirty Ice Ball'."

Some in the audience can't resist dancing in the aisles until they hear the announces say, "Now, winner of the Pickled Pepper Award, Peter Piper who will pick a peck of pickled peppers while performing 'Peppers from Heaven'."

Musicians wearing wings play electric harps accompany Peter while green and red holos of peppers fall from the ceiling that the audience tries to catch. It's a vocal spaghetti of cutting-edge new wave that has everyone all grooving together bouncing in their seats throbbing the theater.

And so, the show progresses: non-stop, breathless. It's unadulterated musical genius!

That is, until Lois, hair flowing loosely wearing a sparkling silver sequined gown moves to center stage. And from the other side of the stage a very realistic holo of Elvis Presley walks toward her strumming the opening chords of "Love Me Tender." When they meet, Elvis looks like he's singing directly to Lois. When the music pauses, Lois joins him harmonizing until the song finishes.

At first, the audience doesn't react. They sit in silence as though hypnotized not wanting to break the mood. Then, there's a deafening outpouring of applause and cheers. Many cry. Several faint and must be carried out.

"I think she may have stolen the show," I say to Jersey, who nods in agreement. Becky and Burton signal a thumbs up.

Elvis's pixels dissolve as the lights dim. A brief period of darkness follows. Then lights dance across the stage until they rise. Zee stands next to Lois, her silver dress replaced by one in gold.

Zee looks lovingly at her. The music to the "Age of Aquarius" plays. Lois and Zee sing until they are rotated off the stage and the theater is bathed in a purple light that fragments into droplets of light falling like rain over the audience.

A holo of the singer Prince, with a live chorus from Pandemonium Dorsa behind him, wearing purple robes move to center stage and performs "Purple Rain." Most in the audience raise one arm, rocking and rolling with Prince.

Prince dissolves. Lights brighten. Faster music resumes.

The announcer says, "In homage to Earth's most famous astronaut, Michael Jackson, here's a group from our very own Tartarus Dorsa doing the astronaut's Moon Walk." Jackson's "Billie Jean" plays as the group spins with smooth kinetic energy onstage. Then they back step and side appearing to back float as astronaut Jackson did when he did his Moonwalk on the moon.

Suddenly, the group appears to double in size as a hologram of each performer appears next to each of them doing the Moon Walk. The live performers remain on stage while the holograms Moonwalk over the heads of the audience and spin around the theater until they move back to the stage and merge with their live counterparts.

If the audience was in mania a moment ago, now they are in mania stratosphere.

One act outdoes the next. The audience is transfixed, hypnotized. No one can figure if they're hearing more Aretha Franklin or Maria Callas, more John Lennon or Placido Domingo. More Depeche Mode, The Police, Taylor Swift, Beyoncé, Spice Girls, Mercurian Motown, Grunge, Breakbeat, Jupiter Jump, Saturn Smoothie, Acid, Chill-out, Liquid funk, Groovy Ganymede, Neurochip, and so many others that I can only process it as one explosive sound.

And nobody cares. Nobody cares! Nobody cares! NOBODY CARES! Because they can't catch their breath with all the foot stomping, hand clapping, head nodding, bodies twitching as one act and leaves one and mingles into the next until the show is over.

No one moves from their seat. They can't. They gave all they had processing a magical transformative experience that they didn't want to end and wishes would start all over again. No one moves except Becky who rises, turns to us, and says, "My water just broke!"

"Emergency! Emergency!" Burton shouts as we rush up an aisle to the door.

One woman looks at Becky and says, "Well, if I looked like that, it would be an emergency."

We reach the street. Fortunately, lots of cabs are lined up waiting. We jump into the first one. I give the driver the address to Inside Out.

"Faster!" Burton yells to the driver. "Faster!"

I say, "Becky you're two weeks early. I should never have let you go to the concert."

Becky is trying to breath rhythmically the way she learned in her Lamaze class. "All that music," she says puffing, "all that excitement brought my labor on."

We reach Inside Out and enter. It is exceptionally quiet.

"Where is everyone?" I ask waking up the one person I see napping at the front desk.

She opens her eyes, yawns. "They're at the concert."

Becky cries, "I need to lie down. I need to lie down. NOW!"

The attendant springs to attention. Two others with a wheeled stretcher show up and help Becky onto it. Becky screams and manages to say, "This hurts more than I thought it would." She's wheeled into the delivery room. Burton trails behind.

I palm Lois and Cortland. Jersey palms Trenton. They arrive shortly after.

The bottom line: Becky has healthy twins, a boy and a girl, and is doing fine.

47

THE CONSTRUCTION OF THE NEW music complex spurs a building boom in Valentine that transforms it from a drab town to a city of elegance and success. Overnight wages go up; the economy soars. Prices rise. The renovated Twilight Zone changes its name to The Ritz Carlton. Its restaurant, renamed the Mar-A-Lago Café, serves a tasting menu and Sacher Torts.

Carotid Artery is paved in colorful marble-like patterns. Hundreds of glowing trees are added to the streets.

The hotel moves us into a luxurious new suite. Light bulbs without shades are replaced with gold and crystal sconces. A La-Z-Boy reclining chair in soft beige leather is brought to a corner of the living room. Our king-sized bed is upgraded to emperor size. The mini-bar, replaced by a subzero refrigerator, is filled with Spot of Jupiter champagne and expensive beers. Room service offers beauty and barber services and massages.

Jersey and Trenton are upgraded to a room with picture windows and bathroom that has a bathtub a with a jacuzzi and separate stall shower with large fragrant bars of soap rather than liquid soap in medicinal smelling packets.

Mars Marcus department store opens a branch on Carotid Artery advertising a sale on Savile Row suits in post-modern colors that I recognize as not having sold last year at their main store in New Chicago, Mars, but they look new to Pluto customers who snap them up.

But we are not ready to leave.

Cortland needs to stay longer to decide which acts from the show can travel and make a successful transition to other theaters in the solar system.

Burton has not finished setting up the virtual travel agency in Valentine nor has finished training workers to man it.

Becky is happy nursing the babies and showing them off.

Lois doesn't want to leave at all because she has fallen in love with Zee Pope, who has fallen in love with her.

And Jersey and Trenton take a much-needed vacation to the hotel Jersey saw advertised in the Oort cloud that promised first-class amenities with budget prices.

***

One morning Cortland is awakened from sleep by sounds of banging and drilling. "What's happening?" he asks.

"Workers started construction on a building next to the Twilight Zone."

"Do you know what it will be?"

"Information in the lobby said it's a new art museum. I was going to tell you about a message we got yesterday. The owner of the gallery I bought that painting that I showed you must have told the builders that I like art, and they want us to become patrons."

"They want money," Cortland says.

"Well, we could give something. They'll put our name on the wall."

"Our name is already on the wall of the Blue Note."

I say nothing but continue to look at Cortland.

"Okay, I'll think about it," he says. Time grows short, and it bothers me that I haven't figured out who murdered Herb Tarragon.

Burton and Becky are ready to go home because Burton finished setting up the virtual travel agency and training the staff. The first people who book a trip want to visit the ring built around Earth that has luxury condos and duty-free shops.

Zee Pope wants to join us going back to Mars because Lois has told him so much about her home in New Chicago in the hope that he will move there once he sees it. (Stay tuned.)

***

Finally, at Molly's Pluto during dinner time, I get new information that helps push the case forward.

I notice a man laughing and joking with Dante. They shake hands and smile at each other with the look reserved for old friends. I see Dante tap a code into his palm, and the man nods. Dante walks away and stops at other tables and greets other people.

A Grand Marnier Soufflé is brought to Dante's friend followed by the restaurant's specialty coffee, whose wonderful flavor, in case you want to buy some, comes from beans that are sun roasted in a crater recently renamed "the coffee crater" on Mercury.

I ask him. "How was your meal? I see you know Dante."

"Wonderful," he says. "Dante and I go back a long time. I worked at the Hatchery." He sighs. "Now I'm out of a job until they build the new one. Dante treated me to this meal."

I say, "You're lucky to be alive. Are you, by any chance, Taurus Trance who developed a sleep aid that lets you sleep three hours a night instead of eight and wake up raring to go?"

Taurus says, "How did you know?"

"Dante mentioned your work."

Taurus smiles. "But it was not perfected. I told that to Dante and his friend when they came to the Hatchery. I think his name was Lucky Louie."

"Lucky Luciano. He's our chef."

"I told both of them there were some risks. Far more risks if you were an android. I know Dante isn't an android, and I assume Lucky isn't one either. It used to be easy to tell, but not now, not with today's new procedures. Lucky didn't get it because the price was too high and he was nervous about the risks. But Dante got some. Then, as everyone knows, the Hatchery was destroyed."

"Are you sure Dante got some?"

"Gave it to him myself."

"Do you still have any of the product?"

"Yes. I kept a sample in a safe deposit box. Far away from the Hatchery. All the scientists at the Hatchery kept samples other places in case something happened or they were fired. Adam Kools was charming, especially to visitors, but he was complicated, controversial, not loved by everyone, and difficult to work for. If you didn't produce in the time he thought you should, he would call you incompetent and threaten to fire you. Most of us felt overworked and underpaid."

"You must have had lots clients."

"More than we could handle. There was a long waiting list."

"So, despite the risks, people wanted it," I say.

"Yes. No fatalities. Lots of complaints, some minor, some greater: migraine headaches, temporary blindness and deafness, shaking, low sex drive, not sleeping for almost a month then sleeping for a month as the body adjusted. Things like that. Everyone recovered. It's slow acting. It usually kicks in about two weeks after the product is administered."

"Did you have any clients who were androids?"

"Many came, but we rejected them because every test showed their bodies were incompatible with it, making the risks fatal."

I say, "What if someone was in transition of becoming an android? Had a few procedures, like getting an android bladder, but were still functioning as human."

Taurus says, "As long as that person had the smallest amount of android chemicals in his body, it would put him into the android category. The timing of when the chemicals would activate might be different from humans, but eventually he would die."

"Is there an antidote?"

"Not yet."

"Did Dante know about this?"

"Yes. I think he never got over being in love with Herb Tarragon and thought Herb broke off their relationship because Herb was fascinated by the process of becoming an android and they had less in common. He asked me lots of questions about the process of becoming an android and I think that's when I told him how dangerous the sleeping compound could be to them."

Dante approaches. "I see you've met my friend Taurus. You should think about offering gift certificates, Molly."

"Not a bad idea. I'll suggest it to Tonto. Taurus was telling me about the chemical that causes you to sleep three hours instead of eight. It can kill those who are androids though."

Dante says, "Yes, strange product."

I say nothing hoping he will elaborate more. He doesn't.

48

A FEW DAYS LATER Jersey and Trenton return from their vacation rested and rejuvenated. I bring them up to date on what I learned about androids and the sleeping compound. Trenton says that Mars Yard contacted him while he was on vacation and told him that one of the substances in Dante's locker matched that in the new sleeping compound.

"Well, we know he had some," I say. "His friend Taurus Trance told us.

Trenton palms Carmella. The voice of a politician who just lost an election replaces her former cheery voice. "This had better be good," she snarls. "Because I'm locked, loaded, and ready to go to Charon."

Trenton tells her what Taurus Trance said. We hear Carmella sigh. "And this Taurus Trance kept a sample in a safe?"

Trenton says, "Yes, all the scientists who worked at the Hatchery kept samples of their work elsewhere in case something happened."

Carmella says, "I'll call Taurus and get some and see if it matches what's in Herb Tarragon's body."

And she does, and it's a match!

"Jersey," I say with concern. "Because you have an android bladder you would have the same fate as Herb Tarragon if you took that chemical."

"I know," Jersey says. "But having a few upgraded parts and being Trenton's wife is close enough for now."

I say, "Just because Herb Tarragon had some of the sleeping compound in this system doesn't mean that anyone killed him. He might have killed himself by taking it without realizing the dangers."

Trenton says, "That's possible. But Dante also knew of the dangers and knew Herb was fascinated by becoming an android. He may have correctly guessed that Herb began the transformation process making it lethal if he took any. Also, he may have known more about Herb's insurance policy that he didn't tell us. Not wanting him to change his policy could be a motive for murder."

"This is a long shot," I say, thinking out loud. "Herb Tarragon kept a low profile; especially when he was in Valentine. They both went to the coffee shop where I once met Dante. They might have been there together and a meeting might show up on security holos."

Jersey says, "Good idea. Better than nothing. But a meeting proves nothing."

"Not if something happened at the meeting?" I say.

We go to the coffee shop. The owner doesn't want to show us the security holo but when I tell him I will give him four gift certificates to Molly's Pluto including four double strength Gunslinger cocktails he does.

We leave and go back to the hotel. Trenton scrutinizes the holo. It takes him a long time.

Finally, he says, "I think I found one with Herb Tarragon and Dante Essen at a table drinking coffee. But it is taken from a bad angle. I can't be sure it it's them even after I enlarged it."

"Maybe we can go back and ask the owner if he can do something," Jersey says.

We return to the coffee shop.

"I have several other security holos," the owner says.

"Why didn't you tell us?" I ask.

"You said you wanted to see a security holo. I gave you a

security holo."

"Well, we need to see the others," I say.

"How many gift certificates is it worth to you?"

"How many do you want?"

"Twenty sounds like a nice round number."

"That's too many," I say.

Trenton says, "Mars Yard will reimburse you, Molly."

"Are you sure?"

"We'll see."

"We'll see is not a good answer."

"Got a better one?"

We leave with the three security holos.

***

After viewing the second holo Trenton says, "This is more like it! I can clearly see Herb Tarragon sitting at a table with Dante." Trenton points to two men in the holo.

Jersey and I peer at the holo.

"Watch this part closely," Trenton says. "You can hear Dante asking Herb if someone who looks like Zee entered the shop. Herb looks toward the door then says it's not him. It's a moment long enough for Dante to put something in his coffee. Watch."

Jersey and I see Dante put something in Herb's coffee.

"Doesn't mean it's the sleeping compound," I say. "Could be something else."

"Ah, but as an android and member of Mars' forensic team, I have extraordinary resources and vision and can tell the composition of substances through an ultraviolet color analysis. The colors I saw in what Dante added matched those in the sleeping compound."

"Are you going to tell Carmella?" Jersey asks.

"Of course. I want to tell her what I found but don't want to say what it is. I want to see if her forensic team can also identify what Dante put in Herb's coffee. She's always bragging about how superior her forensic team is compared to Mars Yard. Oh, one more thing: the holo shows Nebula sitting off to one side at another table with a baby in a carrier drinking coffee. She's wearing a hat with a wide brim pulled down over her eyes so it was hard to tell at first if it was her. Then I read the words on the carrier: Andromeda Veil."

Trenton calls Carmella. "Thanks for sharing, Trenton. Sending it to my forensic lab now."

***

Hours later Carmella calls Trenton. "My team can see that Dante put something into Herb's coffee but they couldn't tell what it was. Maybe it was vitamins. Proves nothing. Dead end."

Trenton says, "I also did an analysis that Mars Yard has used for the last five years. It showed positive proof that the chemical that Dante added to Herb's coffee was the sleeping compound. Dante probably guessed correctly that Herb, being fascinated by androids, may has started the transformation process. And he was right."

"Well, I have to admit you seem to have a process that we're not familiar with. I bet my team was on the verge of inventing a superior version."

"But they didn't. Did they, Carmella?"

Carmella says nothing. Then after a long pause: "Well...all that matters is that that's enough to convict him. Will you share that process with Pluto forensics?"

"If it becomes a reciprocal process. We all benefit by becoming more cooperative."

Jersey says, "Herb Tarragon did murder one of his clones and Dante murdered the real Herb Tarragon. Guess both of them got their just desserts."

"Too bad desserts get the rap," I say. "It's my favorite part of a meal."

Trenton says, "Did you realize that the word desserts is the word stressed backwards?

I sigh. "Don't ruin a good thing, Trenton. Quit while you're ahead. Also, I want to show Nebula the holo and ask why she never said anything about seeing Herb and Dante talking together."

Nebula is surprised that she was on the holo. "I did see them, Molly," she says. "But I didn't want to get involved, especially with Herb Tarragon. I had Andy with me and all I wanted to do after I saw them was leave."

***

At last, time to go home. Before we leave, we have a last meal at Molly's Pluto. Zee Pope insists on being a busboy for the evening. He puts two extra cheese twists on Lois's bread plate.

"Did you see that?" Jersey says. "A sign of love."

"Really?" I whisper. "Cheese twists?"

Finally, the staff gathers around our table as we finish a lemon-sun dessert surrounded by dark and white chocolate moons floating in a creamy rum sauce.

"Who knew that space tastes like creamy rum sauce?" I joke. Then my eyes mist. "We've had an interesting time on Pluto. But Pluto could do so much more. It's such a beautiful place."

Tonto looks at Cortland and says, "Thanks to you and the concert, lots of energy is flowing into Valentine."

Cortland says, "These last few weeks I've worked with the Blue Note to establish a music school and a film festival as well as concerts. Your Clone Symphony orchestra is going to tour Mars. That will be good for Pluto that still, unfortunately, has to overcome its reputation as mostly being a penal colony."

Tonto says, "Can any of you get our status changed to a planet rather than a dwarf planet?"

Trenton says, "Maybe in time. But for now, let's start by calling Pluto a little giant."

***

The transport home is slightly better than the one that brought us. Cortland and I go to the observation deck and look in awe at velvet black space and sharp unblinking stars. I think the view so sublime that one can never tire of it, and all the poetry and all the adjectives in every language fall short in their description.

Cortland puts his arm around me. "I'm proud of you, Molly. Case solved. And I needlessly worried about Avery, who turned out to be a good guy." He pulls me closer and looks into my eyes. "But tell me the truth, are we really old enough to be grandparents?"

I smile but say nothing. I think some questions are best left unanswered. Don't you?

Epilogue

Dante is sentenced to Cthulhu Regio prison. Lucky Luciano leaves Molly's Pluto after a year and moves near the prison to be near Dante. Dante says the area should be known for something other than a prison. When he is released he and Lucky build a culinary school manned by former prisoners who want a life of cooking rather than a life of crime.

Tonto promotes Nebula Veil to chef saying that after Carmella and her friends had dinner at the restaurant he could see that Nebula showed grace under pressure and was up to the job. She and Tonto marry and get a son from the newly rebuilt Valentine Hatchery who they name Kale, a name they believe will insure good health.

Carmella doesn't like her life on Charon and returns to Pluto. She reconnects with Carmen, Aida, Don Giovanni, and Tosca, and becomes their manager. She is best known as founder of the Pluto Planet Choir whose robust contrapuntal lines and distinctive harmonies rival Mercury's Monteverdi Choir, Earth's Mormon Tabernacle Choir and The Titan Chorale.

April May marries Avery Spelling and helps manage his chain of Silicone Slings. June May and Sage Tarragon break up because June does not want to live on Charon and Sage says he's married to his job.

Becky and Burton have another child and live in a suburb of New Chicago. Burton continues to work at his parents virtual travel agency, Club Mood, and establishes four Club Moods on the ring around Earth.

Cortland records the Planet Pluto Choir. The album

becomes number one on solar system's hit parade until Zee and Lois' album called *P is for Pluto* knocks it to second place.

I am back at Molly's Bistro. Molly's Pluto thrives. Interplanetary Foods wants to open a Molly's Europa. My chocolate-chip cookie shop becomes a very successful franchise. Every planet and moon including Saturn's smallest moon Aegaeon, only 0.5 kilometer in diameter and classified as a moonlet, wants to have a franchise. I can't decide if I should add oatmeal cookies. Here, try one. Tell me what you think.

Please Leave a Review

Dear Reader,

If you enjoyed this book, please consider leaving a short review somewhere like Amazon, Goodreads, or some other online site. It does not have to be long or detailed. Just a few words expressing your thoughts about the book would be an amazing help. Reviews are of great importance to books from small publishers. They help independent publishers stay in business and able to bring new works to the market. Reviews also help these books get noticed by readers who may enjoy them. A few seconds effort will mean a lot to many people.

We hope you enjoyed reading this book as much as we enjoy writing and bringing it to you.

Thank you,

Jackie Kingon, author
    and
David Stokes, publisher.

About the Author

Jackie Kingon is a teacher, writer, and artist. She has a Bachelor of Arts degree from Lesley University in Cambridge, Massachusetts, a Master of Arts degree from Columbia University Teachers College in New York City and a Bachelor of Fine Arts from the School of Visual Arts in New York City.

She wrote a feature piece for the Education Section of *The New York Times* about her experiences teaching in an inner-city school in the south Bronx, NY called "A Year in the Trenches", and a piece called "Beautiful Music", about her son who has autism and is now a professional pianist with the Alvin Ailey Dance Company in New York City.

Guardbridge Press in St. Andrews, Scotland published her second book, *Sherlock Mars*. It follows with many of the same characters as her first, book, *Chocolate Chocolate Moons*. Each is a stand-alone novel. Readers Favorite said, "Jackie Kingon blends history, science, popular culture, and social issues with imagination and a large dose of humor as she leads her well defined characters through intriguing action throughout the new frontier of space."

Jackie Kingon lives with her husband in New York City. She is always delighted to welcome visitors to her website: www.jackiekingon.net

Here is a sample from Jackie Kingon's previous book,
Sherlock Mars

SUNRISE: BANDS OF PALE PINK LIGHT peek over the horizon of Mars' eastern sky, a remnant of the days before terraforming created another blue marble in the solar system. Communities once under protective domes, looking like giant paperweights surrounded by dry, red earth in an oxygen poor atmosphere, are now thriving without them. Come and see for yourself; my husband and I did over twenty years ago. Come to New Chicago, Mars' capital at the base of Olympus Mons, and enjoy a meal at my restaurant, Molly's Bistro. Mars Media gave it its top rating: four spiral galaxies.

But not today. Definitely not today, even though it's a balmy forty-five degrees Fahrenheit with thin cirrus clouds overhead, almost no chance of a dust storm, and New Chicago Boulevard is filled with strolling shoppers. Don't come today. It's the one day of the week we're closed. Besides, my husband Cortland and I have been invited by Rick Frances, my new neighbor and owner of Virtual Vittles—a virtual restaurant where holographic smoke and mirrors recreate the experience of dining in a fine restaurant—to a virtual meal a week before their grand opening.

When my headwaiter, Frank Carol, hears the news that Virtual Vittles will open next door, he asks, "Is having a virtual restaurant nearby going to be good or bad for good food, Molly?"

I turn the box of Chocolate Moons upside down and shake it. Nothing. Empty.

"We'll soon find out."

When we first got the invitation, Cortland, a successful music producer, protested. Said he didn't want anyone messing with his perceptions and would feel ridiculous thinking he was drinking wine and eating delicious food while swallowing nothing but air. But after weeks of cajoling and saying I wanted to check out the competition and Cortland saying they don't serve real food, ergo no competition, he agreed.

So here we are, standing outside VV's tall wood paneled door second guessing if we should go in. We pause, watching the sky dim, knowing it is eclipse season, a few days each year when the orbit of Mars' moon Phobos is inclined so that it partially covers the sun for about thirty seconds twice a day. It always makes me realize that although I don't miss my earlier life on Earth, I do miss seeing its large moon pass through its phases.

Then, before we can change our minds, Cortland nods, and we go in. A tall man with slicked-back brown hair in a navy blue uniform with gold buttons buttoned to the neck greets us. "Welcome to Virtual Vittles," he says with a slight bow. "I'm Avery Spelling, head waiter. Rick apologizes for not being here. He had to take a call. Please follow me."

We walk through a very quiet white room. I hardly dare breathe. It doesn't help when Cortland says, "This place looks like it was plastered in the stuff used for death masks."

Avery turns and says, "We want no distractions."

"Better to fry our brains," Cortland says.

Avery makes a subtle diplomatic cough that is neither subtle nor diplomatic to show that he heard.

The room is divided into cubicles. Each cubicle has people seated around tables covered with white linen cloths, white china, and crystal glasses. Most are poking at floating colored menu pallets in front of them and talking in hushed voices. Avery stops at an empty cubicle and gestures for us to step inside. He pulls out a white French provincial chair near me. I sit. Then he walks to the other side and does the same for Cortland. A moment later, floating screens appear at eye level in front of us.

"We have over fifty thousand choices on the menu," Avery says. "If you don't find what you want, we can create it."

I ask, "Any recommendations or specials?"

"Everything is special. Study the menu and touch the screen to make your selections. In a moment, someone will come and assist you. Any questions?"

We say nothing.

"Enjoy your meal," Avery says, turning away.

"I wish I had brought crackers or something," I say.

Then after a long delay, Cortland leans forward conspiratorially and says, "Why do I feel like we're in a horror movie?"

"Because maybe we are," I whisper.

Find out what happens next in the Molly Marbles mystery: *Sherlock Mars*.